Praise for COMA JUMP
Sorted by most recent to oldest

MW01171666

"Mitch is 95% full of shit." –Mitch's best friend.

"You're supposed to say something nice about the book, ass-hole." –Mitch

"Fine, Mitch is *90%* full of shit, but his utter disregard for the truth makes for great story telling." –Mitch's *former* best friend

"Time travel [Coma Jumping] by going back in *your own mind* with a machine that greatly enhances *your own memories*? That's brilliant!" –An author, professional speaker and bookseller at the 2019 *When Words Collide* conference.

"I strongly advise you to remove that part. It is for sure funny, and it's still making me laugh, but may not be received well by some readers and literary agents. You should remove it." –Mitch's editor—*who is also a Governor General Award winning poet so I have no idea why he agreed to work with me*—almost every day for 18 months.

"It made me laugh, and then it made me cry. I am not sure there is anything worse than the death of one's child. The writing comes from an author who has lived through this horror. We miss you Mitch." –Mitch's former colleague. Thank you Joan.

"The story is disturbingly original. I have never, ever, seen an ending like that before. The chapters with the *hacking* and *social engineering* are straight-up unethical. I really hope that stuff is not based on something you did in real life. You scare me." –Mitch's former boss.

"Suicide is not explored enough in fiction. Where did you get the idea of someone being offered a year of time travel [in a coma jump] if they agree to an assisted suicide at the end of that year?" –Mitch's aunt.

"It's too messed up, it *has to* be his idea." –Mitch's uncle.

"I am Loving it!!! I am hooked. You should definitely refer to yourself as a writer now. But, umm, make sure not to use your real name when you publish this, *OK?*" –A prominent member of the Calgary business community who is also a life coach. Thank you Nancy.

"Stop whining, get off your ass, and write the book. Time travel through your own mind and memories is a wild idea. Also, stop putting peanut butter in the kid's sandwiches—the school has complained twice already." –Mitch's wife.

"Our children MUST be safe from child predators *aaaaand* peanut butter!" –Mitch re-enacting the historic PTA meeting where this whole *peanut butter is exactly like sarin gas* idea was hatched.

"That's not funny. Do you want a little kid *to die*?" –Mitch's wife, again.

"Look, I know *some* people are actually deathly allergic to peanuts, but even Jimmy Swaggart himself wouldn't be able to convince me that the *smell* of peanuts can kill someone—that, or Al-Qaeda will partner up with the *Planters* snack food company to form its next death squad."
–Mitch, indirectly implying he will use lethal peanut butter force *again*, but was actually just trying to inveigle his wife into making lunches for our boys fulltime.

"But doesn't famished mean *hungry?*" –Mitch's cousin, when she was 12, and Mitch was 15. Thank you Cindy.

"You have a very vivid imagination. Now turn off the Nintendo. Your options are 1. Read a book *or* 2. Go play chess with your Dad." –Mitch's mom—*who was a teacher for over forty years*—when he was little.

Coma Jump

A Novel by Mitch Mohan

Copyright © 2019 by Mitch Mohan
Book Design and Cover Illustration by Ian

ISBN 9781652032120

"He affected to be astonished that I should regret its loss. It was all a true narrative, he exclaimed; if I wished to write a book for the stay-at-homes to read, I could easily invent a thousand lies far more entertaining than any real experiences."

–*Green Mansions,* by W.H. Hudson

For Gerty, Bajo, Ian
&
Elliot

Contents

CHAPTER 1 – A VISIT TO TIME DREAM

I didn't want to go.

It was a bad idea. Dark surrender, with no return. It would kill me...but to see them again.

...

We'd soon be arriving at Time Dream via the speedy sky train, so I gave one last argument against us going. "One hour is 2000 dollars! Do you know what we can get with two grand? A trip to Vegas! Amphetamines! Maybe a nice exotic but curable STD. Probably in that order actually. Not this fake coma jump crap in some kind of mad scientist induced dream from our past."

"We're going! No way you're chickening out this time. I'm not going into this place on my own," my friend Anand said.

He was a senior writer for Rocky Mountain News—aka *RMN*—one of the most visited news sites focused on western United States and Canada. Anand had a huge following and a lot of people knew his name. While I on the other hand was an unknown, low level, cybersecurity analyst for the RCMP—Canada's Federal Police Service.

"You're gonna love it. *Everyone* I've talked to says the experience doesn't just *feel* real, it *is* real. It's like being there all over again. And there are worse ways to spend a Friday night Sean, and besides," he said to me more seriously, "this is research, if this pans out my boss will assign me to cover Time Dream fulltime."

Time Dream had many locations around the world and was the largest and fastest growing company. They also had the most addictive form of entertainment on the planet. It wasn't virtual reality nor was it one of those holodeck knockoffs that never worked. Time Dream was both the name of their company and what they called their magical machine. It allowed you to select an exact date range from your past, and then go back to that time inside your own mind while you're put into an *induced coma jump*, or, *coma jump* for short. Coma jumps could last one hour, one day, one week or even one year—if you're rich enough—and could be from any time in your past.

Everything in the coma jump was supposed to begin exactly as you originally experienced it, but you still had your mind from the present with all memories intact—you controlled the outcome as much as you did when you lived those events for the first time. Some people were paying to relive the same time frame over and over, for as many times as they could afford, until they were broke. Aaaaand, some people were doing *other* things: Want to go to prom again? No problem. Want to ask a different girl or guy to prom? Also no problem. See your Dad, who was already dead, again. See your Mom again. Power? Theft? Sex? Theft with powerful sex! If rumours, Internet blogs, and any gut feeling I had were true, the company name should be changed to Time *Orgy*. You could even revisit a wasted Sunday night fifteen years ago that made you miss the best Stanley Cup Final game seven of all time. The possibilities were endless. Indeed, critics and supporters alike were correct in stating that Time Dream had, in a way, developed the first time machine versus a dream machine—except you were only ever going *back* in time, and *that* was enough to captivate the hearts, minds and wallets of everyone I knew.

Nearing our stop, which was across the street from the Lougheed Time Dream location in Calgary, the train slowed down with its usual vomit inducing deceleration—the price we paid for convenience and German made roller coaster-like transit. It always killed me to hear the rigid yet sexy female computer voice when you stopped: "You have arrived at Lougheed Station." It's the same voice firemen hear in fire halls when the alarm goes off. One day they will admit they got the idea for this voice during some kind of robot porno—Rusty Android Erotica or something like that. Come to think of it, Rusty would be a great character name in a porno. Why aren't there more pornos with a guy named Rusty? "Look wayyyyy up and I'll call Rusty." It was at this moment I realized 1. I was going to have to go into Time Dream with my friend, and 2. With the random shit floating around in *my* head, I hoped to hell they didn't record the coma jumps. Without a doubt, the root of my distrust for this company was what they might be able to see during a coma jump, despite company assurances to the contrary: "Viewing of client coma jumps, by Time Dream personnel, is for safety only, and any distribution or release of coma jump events is against policy and impossible," was played over and over during commercials and endless Internet adds, but I still felt Time Dream could use this information to gain power over people. Power over me and my *robot meets hand puppet* fantasy might not be on their top ten list, but what could they make a nation's president do when they threatened to release *their* fantasies?

We got off the sky train and entered the main entrance of the stadium-sized Time Dream office while a *male* computerized voice welcomed us this time. There wasn't a conventional door to open to get inside. Instead, the building was managed by lasers, sensors, and climate control—all the things I wished my parents' cold basement bathroom had when I was growing up. Also, the whole place smelled like a Porsche dealership: expensive. Goody gumdrops.

We approached the long front counter where a line of customers already waited to check in. The woman behind the counter who greeted people looked like a news anchor and wore jewelry worth more than one of the Porches I'd just imagined.

In sharp contrast to that, the man beside her looked like he ran a pawnshop. Nearly 100 trillion in Time Dream profits and this guy used tape to hold his glasses together. I wondered if their contrasting looks were born out of some kind of statistically backed study saying it would make them more approachable. This thought left me when I realised the rest of the attendants behind the huge counter were lined with men and women pairings from the news anchor lady's gene pool.

"Hello gentlemen," the dishevelled man said. This steered Anand to that check-in booth despite my urging him toward another. "My name is Cordel Brown, and I see this is your first time here, so welcome."

This creeped me out already—apparently the sensors at the entrance were even more invasive than I had thought.

"You must be Anand Dhami," Cordel said, as he lifted his gaze from his console and looked directly at my friend.

"And you must be Sean Riley," the woman said to me. "My name is Janne Lay, and I'm happy to report you both have sufficient funds to experience your first coma jump."

I chuckled to myself because I'd always wanted to meet someone with the last name *Lay* so I could tell them about my idea for a *Lay's* potato chip commercial: The ad would start with a smiling young family of four standing beside each other across the screen. The mom, dad, daughter and son would introduce themselves together: "Hi! We're the Lays!" They could even be eating bags of Lay's potato chips since it's a commercial after all. Then, *Hannibal 'The Cannibal' Lector*, played by Anthony Hopkins of course, would jump up out of nowhere, growling, and sink his teeth into one of the family member's necks from behind—probably the dad, because child eating is not accepted in some cultures. Then, just as the dad keels over from Hannibal's quick two to three second neck and face chewing, the camera would zoom onto Hannibal's face, where he abruptly stops himself from starting in on the next victim, looks up at the audience, and says, "Lays, bet you can't eat just one! ARRGGHHH!" and begins eating the mom. Anyway, I didn't want to piss Anand off too much so I kept this to myself and decided to annoy Janne, and Anand, another way.

"Yes I'm Sean," I said, imitating her voice.

Anand shot me a *don't start* look.

Janne ignored my tone and continued with what sounded like a well-practiced speech, "Just a few more signup questions, and then we'll take you into the back to where the machines are and you can get started."

Her questions were fairly vague and when she was satisfied with my answers, she pressed a button and a sliding door opened up behind her and revealed a poorly lit hallway. She told me to proceed.

Up until now, this place resembled an airline at check-in, minus the feeling of people hating their job. The dark hallway was a twist on this though, since airports usually had lights as bright as Martha Stewart's kitchen across every inch of the building, so everyone showed up nicely on the security cameras. Another woman appeared at the end of the hallway and motioned for me to come to her.

As I walked there, I vacillated between fear and indecision about what my first coma jump should be. How could I pinpoint the most important hour in my life? The high level geniuses at Time Dream had come up with the greatest invention of all time, but most people couldn't easily determine their most significant memories down to the exact hour.

I joined the woman at the end of the dark hallway. Despite an oversized beauty stealing lab coat, her long brown hair and confident look temporarily distracted me from my pre-coma jump jitters. Maybe it was the lab coat and glasses with high-heels combination, I don't know.

"Hello Mr. Riley, my name is Myah."

"Hi," I said, but noted she called me *Mr.* Riley and not Sean. The room was dimly lit and soft jazz played over invisible speakers. So far all of this would probably put most people at ease, but not me. If I wasn't looking over my shoulder in life, I wasn't breathing.

"Please follow me," she said, and directed me to a room behind her.

It had a kitchen table and two chairs and also smelled expensive. I'd paid $1000 instead of the regular $2000 for a one-hour coma jump because Anand's company had given him a *bring a friend* coupon. I pondered if people ever used *Groupons* for joining a new cult, and how I had become as cheap as my father—I was probably about to be lobotomized, for all I knew, yet I was still thinking about the money I just dropped on this fucking science project.

"Please take a seat," she said.

The second I sat down the sliding doors behind me closed and the wall in front of me opened and revealed a glass window with a view of a darker room. It had a reclining chair much like dentists use. I heard a whirling noise above me and a device that looked like four, futuristic, thick electronic guns symmetrically arranged in a circle, slowly lowered from the ceiling. The machine stopped about a foot from my head.

"Mr. Riley, I need you to verbally tell me the exact year, month, day and hour you would like to experience in your coma jump, and then enter it in this tablet," Myah said, and passed me the tablet. It had Time Dream labelled on the top—*were they planning to take over the hand held device market too*? I told her the date and then entered it into the tablet and handed it back to her.

"No time zone?" I asked and flashed a forced grin that I hoped concealed my uneasiness. I was half kidding, but also half wondering what the answer to this would be. I mean seriously, how in the world could they pull this off? I told her the hour from my past I'd chosen to live over was New Year's 1999—January 1st 1999, midnight on the nose to 1am. I remembered that hour clearly because that was the first New Year's after I finished my degree in computer science in the spring of 1998. I was at a party put on by a friend who owned a studio apartment, and the woman I secretly liked for years kissed me at the stroke of midnight. The exact details beyond that were hazy, but because of the timing of that kiss it was one of the few memories I could easily pinpoint.

"Are you nervous?" Myah asked.

"Why are you asking that?" I forced another grin to feign confidence.

Myah grinned back, and answered, "Well, your vitals are elevated like you just went a round with Tyson."

"Yah right, I'd be dead in five seconds, or missing an ear-lobe or two," I joked, but I *was* terrified—I could feel my heart beating in my ears.

Myah laughed and calmly said, "No one is dying here today Mr. Riley."

I laughed with her and then Myah activated more controls. The glass wall of the room with the dentist's chair lifted up, and the lights were increased to reveal the rest of the room. I felt a comforting warmth spread through my body and I was instantly lightheaded—the kind of feeling you get just before passing out. The room was an *exact* replica of my parents' living room while I was growing up, except with a dentist chair smack in the middle of it. The TV was quite old, so this looked to be our living room from when I was ten.

"How is that possible?" I asked, while keeping my gaze on the room. "And I'm pretty sure the house I grew up in didn't have a living room with a fancy hospital chair some doctor might use in Mexico when he's *borrowing* someone's kidneys."

"Sorry Sean, let me introduce myself properly. I'm Doctor Myah Wade, one of five senior coma jump specialists here at the Lougheed Time Dream location. This is possible because the second you crossed the threshold into this room, we started interacting with your brain."

"*Interacting?*"

"Well, to be more precise, we started linking, networking, downloading and mapping your brain.

"What are you seeing on that tablet?" I asked.

"I'm sorry for startling you with this image from your

childhood, but we do this with every client on their first visit. It's part of the presentation and introduction to what we can actually do here at Time Dream."

"I'm not even hooked up to anything yet. You can do all this without hooking me up?" I asked.

"We can, but the actual coma jump will take place with you sitting in that," she motioned towards the reclining chair. "This way we can hold you in place during the coma jump. It is quite impossible to move during a coma jump because of the state we put your brain into, but roughly three percent of the population tend to sleepwalk during their dreams and everyday sleep. So, the straps are there for everyone's protection in case a client decides to go for a wander—impossible as that would be."

"Ohhh, OK, I feel so much better," I said, and stood up to leave, nearly hitting my head on the gun-looking contraption above me.

"Sean just wait." Myah gently put a hand on my wrist. "I can see the New Year's party from 1999 on my screen now too. Here, look at it." She handed me the tablet.

I saw my friend's studio apartment on the screen and it looked exactly like I remembered it from New Year's 1999. But it wasn't a still frame, but a video, and the room was filled with people milling about at a party. It was like watching a TV show someone had recorded, except the point of view was mine from back then. Incredible—I decided in that moment to stay. This was one of the most amazing experiences in my life so far, and it was worth letting Time Dream play with my brain on the offhand chance it could work.

"OK Doc, let's do it."

"I'm glad, and call me Myah. All you have to do is walk into the room and get into the chair, lie back, and I'll give you a countdown. I need you to understand that it won't just *feel* like you're there again, it will *be* like you're there again. It won't be like a dream—it will be like you're living it over again. It can be overwhelming at first, and the coma jump will last for one hour, so if you can see a clock in the room, or a watch, or even if you ask someone for the time, you know your paid for hour will end at 1:00 am. One last thing, and this is a very important detail to remember Sean. If you do get scared, overwhelmed or just want the coma jump to end early, I need you to say the following exit phrase: unrelenting, unrelenting, unrelenting, rescue. Do you understand?"

"Yes."

"Repeat the exit phrase to me Sean."

I did.

Then Myah leaned in and said, "If you use your exit phrase, that's the end of your paid for coma jump. It doesn't matter if it's at the fifty-five minute mark of your hour, or the five minute mark, so consider whether you really want to use it." Myah motioned for me to go into the room and sit in the chair.

I entered the room feeling both excitement and apprehension because this was all so new, so impossible, and yet it was happening. I climbed into the dentist's chair and it immediately reclined to a flat position. Restraints circled my ankles, thighs, waist and chest, but just snug enough to let me know they were there. I heard a mechanical whine above me and a metal helmet-like device lowered over but not onto my head. The glass wall closed to separate Myah's room from mine.

My heart pounded so hard now I could feel the pulse in my fingertips this time. A weird, warm sensation spread throughout my body—like when I had a CT scan at the hospital and they injected some kind of vasodilator iodine in me.

Myah's voice came over the intercom and she told me to relax and close my eyes.

I did, and then she started a count:

"3....2....1....Good luck Sea—"

She was cut off then and there was a brief silence like someone had changed the channel on a TV. I felt for a moment like I was doing somersaults in midair. Then, I heard multiple voices and music playing loudly. The *channel* had been changed

9

to New Year's 1999.

.

CHAPTER 2 – MY FIRST COMA JUMP

"HAPPY NEW YEARRRRRRR!!!!!" at least thirty people yelled at once. My eyes were still clenched shut so I opened them. I was back in 1999 at my friend Mark's New Year's party. I recognized a lot of the people I went to college with. Mark's big screen TV, which was pretty rare to have back then, was turned on to the New Year's celebration at Times Square. *No Doubt* with Gwen Stefani was playing something familiar in the background. I glanced down at my body, my hands, my feet—I was standing. Surreal didn't quite cover how I was feeling, but I was really there! I was jolted out of this temporary acclimatization when a woman stepped close in front of me.

"Do you have a girlfriend?" she asked.

"Wha-what?" I stammered exactly as I had done in 1999.

"Do you have a girlfriend?" she yelled above the music.

This was Heather, the girl I knew from college. She was more gorgeous than I remembered, and her hair looked so thick, her eyes bigger than ever. I also remembered thinking foolishly back in 1999 that I was embarrassed about not having a girl-friend, because I had been single longer than a nun, and considered lying and saying I *did* have a girlfriend, but, I answered the same way I did eighteen years ago.

"No, I don't." I felt a big grin come over my face because I knew what was coming. Heather put her arms around me tightly and kissed me even longer than I remembered. Her lips were so warm and soft I didn't want the kiss to end. I was tingling. I knew at some level I was projected here, but I felt everything as though it were really happening. I had the benefit of knowing what happened next and in the moment that truth frightened me a bit. I knew that after kissing me Heather would return to Paz, her on and off boyfriend for the past three years.

I pondered the prospect of getting my ass kicked by Paz for the last fifty-nine minutes of my first coma jump. I looked around for him and spotted him in a corner surrounded by a small group. He hadn't seen us kiss.

I really liked Heather, but she was so crazy in love with Paz, I didn't think I had any chance with her back then. I didn't have any money or car and shared a small condo with six other guys while I was going to school that year.

So instead I'd been drawn to Roberta. She was supposed to be at this party but never showed up. As my mind raced to re-learn my past, Heather walked away while I remained frozen by the idea that Time Dream had made this possible.

"Seeeeaaaaannnn!!!!!!!" a guy said beside me, in a drunken voice. He sounded like Elaine from *Seinfeld* yelling, "Stellllaaa-aaa!!" a la Brando.

"Duuuuuude, it looked like you were trying to force something out the way you were closing your eyes and clench-ing your fists earlier!" This was Lawrence, my oldest friend. Larry, as everyone called him, had been like my brother, but in present day we'd lost contact. He got married and lived on the other side of Calgary. It was an hour's drive both ways to see each other so our communication was reduced to text messages every couple of months. I had seen him in the flesh twice in the last ten years—the two times I helped him move.

"Don't worry about it man. How are you doing?" I reached out and shook his hand. He was plastered but could still tell something was up.

"You look like a guy who just kissed his Mom's friend in-stead of Heather." Larry smiled, but had one eyebrow up to give me a non-verbal WTF?

"Heather's been in love with Paz for years, and I don't want my face punched in."

"*Paz*?"

"Yes Paz." I pointed to where he was in the most unobvious chicken shit way I could. Larry had known me before I could even read and grew up with me in a small town in the Northwest Territories until I left at age eighteen, so he was safe to talk to about my fear of getting stomped. The rest of the folks at this party were people I met while going to school in Calgary.

"*That guy*?" he said. "You'll be fine. No one in the history of the world has been beaten up by a guy named *Paz*. Molested maybe, but not beaten up." Larry smiled after he said that and then pointed out the fact that Paz was probably big enough to be double my hulking Peter Parker frame. "And if all else fails, you have me for backup."

I knew he meant that in the way only a friend who'd spent thousands of hours growing up with me riding bikes, playing video games at sleepovers, and figuring out how to get out of trouble, had my back. A lot of guys say this, and I'd heard that kind of BS before only to find out someone didn't really have my back after all, but Larry did—always had. It helped that Larry was built like a phone booth. Hell, he'd been nearly that big since he was twelve.

"Thanks man!" I said, "I'm going to the washroom." I started in that direction while taking in the familiar faces as I walked. I didn't really need the washroom, but I was dying to get to a mirror and see what I looked like at this age—I could tell already I was stronger.

After circling for a bit, the washroom's whereabouts still eluded me. The studio apartment was huge because it used to be a bar or business, and its main level backroom storage had tunnels that went right into the sewers of the city. The clock on the wall showed 12:05am—lots of time. Fifty-five minutes to go.

I finally saw the washroom and went in. I closed the door, locked it, and looked in the mirror. I was twenty-one! I took off my oversized glasses and noted my bad haircut. I had no marks on my face—the blemishes and scars I was now used to were gone. The small growth on my cheek was gone. The brown mark on my forehead—gone! My jawline was more prominent too. I was a kid. My elbows didn't hurt. My back didn't hurt. I was wearing a ridiculously thick sweater that had blue stripes and white stripes. I wasn't wearing jeans because Mark had specified a dress code in the email invite for this party. But my shoes were worst of all. They made me grin. I hated wearing dress shoes or formal shoes, so I would always buy running shoes that *looked* like dress shoes. In this instance, I was wearing brown suede hiking boots that were actually Nike cross trainers.

While in the bathroom, I realized some things never change. I still find a corner or a bathroom to hide in at house parties, or *any* public place for that matter. I wasn't comfortable until I had my back to a wall with a view of the door.

Then it hit me—why the fuck was I hiding in the bathroom? How pathetic was I to be sitting in here when Time Dream had granted me a virtual opportunity to rewind? Time to go talk to Heather.

I walked out of the bathroom determined not to repeat how this party, like most I attended at that age, turned out back in 1999, with me sitting there wondering what it would be like to *do* something. I saw Heather on the other side of the room, and was about to cruise over there when a hand grabbed my arm. This guy sitting in a pink leather armchair, a Lazy Boy I think, took hold of me.

"Let me out! Let me outtttt!!!!!!" he shouted. My heart skipped a beat, and he said it again as he let go of my arm. It was like he was pretending or actually believed he was trapped in the chair.

"He just dropped acid man. He's alllll messed up!" the man in the next chair said. It took me a second to recall his name, Chris.

I was about to say something affable or make a smart-ass remark, because this kind of weird shit made me uncomfortable, and seemed to follow me at parties like a cat who always goes to the guy who hates cats, but reminded myself again where I was and just kept on walking until I was in front of Heather. She wasn't with Paz, but was with another girl I remembered, named Carolyn.

"Hey Heather, sorry, um, I don't mean to interrupt, but I have something really important I need to ask you," I said.

"Good, you never talk to me," she said, and then giggled. "Your buddy and I asked you to come over to my girlfriend's house the other day, but you said you were busy *sleeping!*"

It was tough going back two decades in my memory, but I recalled what day she was talking about. Heather had phoned me because she was there with Anand and his girlfriend, and presumably, wanted company. I remembered how much of an idiot I was not to realize what she was asking me back then. I was sleeping in late the way I used to, where I'd get all the shuteye I needed for the week on Saturday, and told her no and went back to bed despite them phoning three times to get me to come over. Fawwwwwk. Not this time.

"So what is this really important thing you need to ask me?" she said with a devilish smile in a sultry voice that even the most seasoned phone sex operator wished they had.

"Wow, nice voice, if you ever become destitute you have a career in telemarketing waiting for you," I said. "That, or your very own 1-900-Heather number. *Psychic* phone line of course, not those dirty phone sex lines that exploit men."

Heather laughed and said, "*Men* eh?" It wasn't a big laugh, and she seemed almost confused and surprised at what I had said, but she did have a big smile. Her friend did *not* laugh and looked like she was somewhere between repulsed and horrified —I was used to that look. I kept talking before Heather could decide to slap me or inform me she was offended as well.

"Yah, anyway, on that note, I've always thought phone sex might be the solution to two of the world's biggest problems," I explained. "I mean, these UNICEF and World Vision commercials always say you can feed, clothe, educate and house starving kids in Africa for only nineteen cents a day. And these phone sex lines charge something like $15.99 a minute, so I hear." I said the last words with a widening sly grin.

"Ok, I'm with you, *and*?!" Heather asked, looking at me in disbelief.

"Well, if we could just get these starving kids in Africa to become phone sex operators, I figure that takes care of everything. First world gratification problem—solved. Third world hunger—also solved.

Heather laughed out loud and playfully put her hand on my chest, but only briefly. I immediately hoped she didn't notice how bony it was. "You're hilarious!"

Her friend Carolyn seemed equally entertained. "You're a sick fuck," she said, as her face turned to a frown. It was a look a husband or wife might have if they walked in on their significant other having sex—*with a chicken*. OK, maybe not so entertained. Carolyn walked away.

Heather laughed some more and said, "I'm sorry, she hasn't ingested nearly enough alcohol for a New Year's Eve party. Anyway, A.D.D. boy, what was this really important thing you needed to ask me?"

"Ahh, it's too serious to bring up," I said.

"*What*? After all that? Just ask me!" she said and giggled again. I loved her laugh.

"What do you think would win in a race: a pig, or a midget?"

Heather laughed louder and put her arms around me, giving me a hug, and kissed me for the second time that night! My mind was racing about what was going to happen next, and at the same time, my head was already swirling with ideas for my next visit to Time Dream, knowing this coma jump thing was for real. It was awesome. Holy shit! Should I kiss her back? I was getting more excited when I felt something—not that kind of something, unfortunately—hit my shoulder heavily, to pry me away from Heather. I turned in pain to see her boyfriend: Paz.

"Get the fuck out of here Riley," Paz said, and because of his usual loud voice and high likelihood he bumped into five people, before bumping me, there was already a crowd looking on. There were no smartphones recording though—another bonus for being back in 1999.

But I wasn't scared for once. I felt more alive if anything. "Get out of here? Why, are you embarrassed to be seen with me?" I asked with my best Bob Hope grin. The crowd laughed. Paz didn't laugh but grabbed my collar and reached back for what I assumed would be lights out for me, if I didn't try and grab a leg, go into the fetal position, or utter my coma jump exit phrase so Myah could get me the fuck outta there. But, as he was about to come around with the biggest right hand I'd seen in quite some time, I felt a violent blur and a bump go between us. The floor practically vibrated as Larry swung at Paz and landed a powerful blow on his chin.

Paz dropped straight down—knocked out cold.

Larry dragged him across the floor.

Mark, the host, yelled to a few of his friends, "Help him get that douchebag outta here!"

Beauty, I hadn't heard the term *douchebag* in over a decade.

I chuckled and turned back to Heather, now that it was safe, and to break the tension I said, "Anyway, on that note, I've always thought douching might be the solution to two of the world's biggest problems." I smiled, and she took my hand and kissed me while pulling me upstairs. For half a second, I wondered why she didn't seem to care that her boyfriend had been laid out, then it hit me: Years later we learned that Paz had been physically abusive to Heather, and a lot of other girls back then. Was she *happy* he was hurt? Was I? Or was this just my brain guessing how she would react? I watched in disbelief as she opened the door to some random room. Then, while still holding my arm, Heather said:

"Sean, I was in a terrible mood, depressed, and wasn't even gonna show up to this party, but you've made me pretty happy young man."

"Well, not yet," I said, with more confidence than I ever displayed before in the real world, during similar moments of my life to that point. "I mean, you can't say happiness without the penis!"

Heather was not laughing but smiled with an impatient look.

I decided to continue, just in case she'd overlooked the fact I was a nerd. "Get it? HA-*PENIS*. Happiness! I invented that."

"Yah I got it Sherlock, now get your ass in here," Heather commanded, as she closed the door and grabbed me.

She didn't have to tell me twice. In the words of any good used car salesmen: "When you hear the answer you want, shut up."

CHAPTER 3 – I WAKE UP…ADDICTED

Afterwards, as I lay there in bed talking with Heather for about thirty minutes, I couldn't remember being so happy.   I lost track of time and forgot about the rest of the world for what I *thought* was only a brief moment. I was chatting away, firing all my thoughts at her, utterly astonished that she remained interested.

I told her I liked her a lot and amazingly, she didn't leave or vomit after I said this. And she was funny—really funny, telling me I could model teenage boys' pajamas if I bulked up. I was about to tell her my less than scientific, bordering deranged, conspiracy theory about bottled water, when I again experienced a short moment of blindness—I felt like I was doing somersaults in midair, flipping over and over. I already knew what was happening before my vision returned, and heard a voice.

"Welcome back Sean," Myah said over the intercom.

I felt like an addict who just came out of a perfect high in a second, with the flick of a switch, instead of the natural come down that was more forgiving to the person a drug had its talons on. No, I *was* an addict now, and the drug was Time Dream, so Myah might as well have been named *Not Heather* as far as I was concerned.

"How are you feeling?"

"I was happy," I said while trying to conceal my frustration as I looked at her through the glass wall. The restraints flew off my chest, waist, thighs and ankles, which drew my attention downwards, instead of sulking over my recently ended and way too short first ever coma jump. I was sweating everywhere and felt particularly wet in my Spider-Man underwear. As a sense of panic came over me, I decided this should've been in some small print or Time Dream disclaimer, since anyone could run into a similar problem.

I looked closer and it was worse than I thought: I had beige kakis on and it looked like someone had poured a bucket of water on my crotch. At first, I thought, no prayed, it was some kind of coma jump induced wet dream that caused this, but when I saw a puddle-sized dampness below my belt, I realized I'd pissed my pants. *WTF?!* I didn't even piss when I was in the washroom during the coma jump. My embarrassment was now overpowering any thought of missing Heather.

"I bet this happens to a lot of folks," I said.

"No," Myah said, and frowned. "Urination during a coma jump is supposed to be impossible based on all our testing and customers around the world."

"Apparently not," I said.

"It's a safety mechanism that goes beyond peeing and is integral to the Time Dream system ensuring your body in the present is not harmed during a coma jump. The fact that this has happened is—"

She didn't say but I knew she meant *a problem.*

I asked her for some fresh underwear and some pants. Or even just pants.

"I'm not sure we have anything like that. But right now, if you can wait, we need to talk about your coma jump, how are you feeli--"

"What?" I cut her off. "You don't have an extra pair of pants? Some shorts? Jogging pants, underwear? Dental floss and some paper towel?"

She typed something on the computer and asked, "What size are you?"

"Gap Kids, boys ages ten to twelve, *Husky Boy's* edition."

She said they would track some clothes down for me, and then started going on and on about research, and did I know how rare it was to have a physical connection to the real world in a coma jump.

"I would like your permission to study your coma jump and submit the data for research. Internal research, by Time Dream only, of course."

"Ahhhh *no*," I said. "There's no way I'll consent to that. Christ sake, what kinda show are you guys running here? You have the most advanced and greatest technology in the world, and you wanna do a pee project on me?" I asked, thinking only I could have this kind of weird luck—karma from my misspent youth, I suppose. I piss all over the high school gym teacher's office just *one* time twenty-three years ago, aaaaand *boom*: my wee-wee becomes a leaky faucet.

"I already sent a note to my boss, the General Manager here at our Lougheed location, and he has approved ten free one-hour coma jumps for you in exchange for your approval, and future cooperation during those coma jumps."

"Make it twenty and I'll shit out a Peanut Buster Parfait for you guys during a coma jump," I said, suddenly feeling a whole lot different about being a guinea pig.

"*Twenty*, and we have a deal?"

"Yes," I said.

She typed some more and then told me the twenty free coma jumps were approved. She picked up the tablet on the desk, and, as she walked towards me, the glass wall opened up. She gave me the tablet, and a stylus, and requested I sign the digital consent form.

I read the form slowly, as I was in no hurry to leave and board the sky train with piss all over my pants. Even though the form was surprisingly easy to follow, and only a page long, I decided I better let Anand have a look, because despite my exhilaration and anxiousness to get back into another coma jump, I didn't trust these guys. A company this big and powerful likely broke a shitload of really good laws to get where they were, so mystifying me with devilish pee contracts was likely not a tall order for them.

After I got cleaned up, Time Dream sprung for some yellow lab overalls and a yellow lab coat in a sealed package, leading me to believe they were unworn, thank God. I followed Myah back out through the dark tunnel into the blinding light of the Time Dream front counter.

Anand was waiting for me there, and after looking me up and down, he laughed. "It's Walter White!" he said loudly and then smiled.

I heard people snicker and felt a lot of eyes on me.

"No wait," Anand continued, propelled by the laughs, "Paddingtonnnnn! You've lost weight!"

"Shut the fuck up man," I whispered curtly.

Anand's expression turned more serious—he must have noticed the panic on my face.

I explained the situation minus a few details, given there were over a hundred people within earshot, and asked him to look over the contract as Myah stood by. Unlike me, who read slowly, Anand was nothing short of a wizard, and could read like the chief editor from Encyclopedia Britannica. He poured through the page in a matter of seconds, then re-read it, and then asked a number of legal questions I didn't understand, and if there were any other accompanying contracts for the on screen approval. Myah, who was now joined by the Lougheed Time Dream location General Manager, Dr. Kozlov, answered everything to Anand's satisfaction, so he nodded to her and then turned to me.

"It looks good. I don't see any problem with it so go ahead and sign it you lucky bastard!" he said, in a quieter voice, so as not to be overheard.

"Good, good, thank you very much to all of you," I said, as I started to calm down. "So, the results of this study aren't gonna end up on CNBC, Twitter or *Gabby's Blog for people with bladder problems*, are they?" I asked, in as friendly a tone as I could manage.

"Not with *your* name attached to it they're not," Anand said, and smiled again. I frowned, so he followed up, "I'm kidding man. The contract says the research will stay internal, and it would be strategically stupid for them to release any kind of proprietary data or science they have cooking to make this place run."

That was good enough for me. I signed the digital form with the stylus on the tablet, and Myah and Dr. Kozlov shook our hands.

Then Dr. Kozlov spoke loudly in his thick Eastern Bloc accent, presumably so all the other giddy Time Dream customers standing in line could hear him: "I very sorry for your trouble Sir. I trust we have compensated you adequately?"

"Absolutely," I said.

Anand and I walked out and then crossed the street, and I was eager to talk about my first coma jump. I think Anand was too. Unfortunately, it was crowded outside Time Dream and the nearby sky train platform was the same. We agreed to wait until we were on the train before talking, but as I stood there, I wished I wasn't with Anand, so I could march back across the street to do another coma jump—*for free!* Hell, I would probably have gone back and paid full price with money I didn't have, but there was no way I was giving Anand the satisfaction of knowing I was addicted already.

After a few minutes we boarded a train and found a seat near the end of the car with a good distance between us and everyone else. Getting to sit down being the only benefit of a late-night train ride, well, that, the smell of urine—which was becoming a theme for me today—and an increased chance of being stabbed. I was excited to tell Anand what happened and was just about to say something when his cell phone went off. His latest ring tone sounded like a Bollywood version of the theme song from Happy Days—I shook my head for the same reason he had, about me, on many occasions in our life.

"This is Anand Dhami's phone."

I shook my head once more. As he chatted away I could

tell it was his boss at Rocky Mountain News.

Anand had hinted at it all week and based on the tone of his conversation, and big smile, it looked like Anand was going to be meeting with the internal bigwigs at Time Dream to write the first ever in-depth article on the company. Anand claimed that every journalist at RMN, and probably the world, wanted this assignment. Not to mention it came with a promotion, expense account and a high probability of free coma jumps. Before today, because I was happily living as one of the last people on earth who hadn't done a coma jump, I really didn't think much about Anand's prospects. But now, sitting across from him on the train, I was completely addicted to the Time Dream experience, and had twenty free coma jumps.

Anand finally hung up the phone and said, "I'm in pal—I'm assigned to Time Dream for the entire year. I meet Dave Sandhu next week!" His jaw dropped and his eyes grew wider than bingo balls.

Dave, or Davey, as he liked to be called, at least publicly and in the media, was the creator of Time Dream—although what *he* originally created, and what it was now, was like comparing apples to space shuttles. Davey was still the heart and soul of the company, but not the one pulling the strings.

"Yah yah, we can talk about that after. Dude, your coma jump, what did you do for yours? This thing is for real man! It actually works! And these fuckers can read minds with that equipment!" I said, revealing a bit too much excitement.

"Oh man, I know, it was amazing! It's real life in there! Anyway, I made out with Heather at Mark's 1999 New Year's Eve party! You do remember *Heather*, don't you?" Anand asked, while looking even more excited than he was a minute earlier, when his boss made his day.

Apparently, coma jumps didn't transcend coincidence—reality bites, even fake reality, but I was more amused than upset. If you can't laugh at that you can't laugh, I thought to myself. What were the odds?

"Yup, I remember her. What about your wife?" I asked.

"It's the same as a dream, right?" he said.

"I suppose. Anyway, I picked that exact date too. Let me guess, you picked that date because you could easily zero in on an exact time you remembered, right? I mean who can remember an exact hour? That should be one of your first questions for Mr. Sandhu," I said.

"I think they make us choose dates and times to free themselves from any *that's not what I wanted refunds*, and to make it less obvious they aren't just reading minds but *downloading* them somehow."

As usual, Anand was a step ahead of me and making me think too hard.

But he then changed gears, "Sooooo, did you have a good time after all?" Anand asked, and smiled with an air of *I told you so* and a dash of something else—a Heather something else, if I had to be more specific.

"Yah, I got in a fight with that Paz guy, and then Larry stepped in and it was lights out for Paz." This wasn't a lie, but a massive omission from my coma jump. Talking to your buddy about the girl you had *both* just slept with was too Jerry Springer for me—coma jump or not.

Anand laughed, because Paz was a dick to him too back in the day. "What was that guy's real name anyway? No way his parents named him Paz!" Anand said, and then chuckled.

I briefly thought of Anand's family: His dad used to work in the Ministry of Defense in India, and his mom was a doctor. His uncle used to be a university math professor in New Delhi for Christ's sake, which was saying something, because grade nine math in India was probably more difficult than fourth year University math in North America—or so Anand always bragged to me. I suspected Paz had a *very* different upbringing.

"So why in the hell did they give *you* all those free coma jumps? What the fuck did ya do *this time*!?" Anand asked, looking both perplexed *and* suspicious, like when he found out I successfully cheated on an exam when we were in college together.

"Nothing," I said, even though I knew that was futile with

Anand. I probably would've got less questions from him if I'd said that I clucked like a chicken when I came out of my coma jump.

"Sean, they put a line in that contract that said, '*physical anomaly research.*'" Anand held his hands up, as if he were lost, and was demanding I fill in the blanks. "I mean Jesus buddy, I'm about to do a lot of inside research on this company, let me know what's up."

"I pissed my pants, okay?" I must have said that too loudly because three teenagers actually stopped texting to look up for two seconds.

"What?" Anand asked, looking both confused and amused.

"Myah said, 'any kind of physical connection to the real world in a coma jump is rare' or impossible, or something like that. She said, 'specifically, it's a safety mechanism that goes beyond peeing and is integral to the Time Dream system ensuring your body in the present is not harmed during a coma jump.'"

Anand sighed briefly then said, "Only you man," and shook his head, and grinned, "Only you." He paused for a while —it wasn't awkward, because we were good friends and had known each other for so long, but something was on his mind.

I had an idea what it might be, but hoped it wasn't.

"Hey, I don't want you to get mad, but—" as Anand hesitated his expression changed to one I hadn't seen for years.

Hundreds of faces flooded into my head, and all of them had that look. A look of pity.

"Now that you know the coma jumps work, will you see them again?"

"Who?" I asked, knowing full well who he meant. I considered pushing the red help button that was on each sky train car, and would usually cause a train stoppage, so I could jump out just to avoid this bullshit. Anand looked mildly frustrated right after my answer, but also more determined.

"Your kids man. For fuck sakes, your kids! I don't give a shit about Time Dream, the article, or any promotion I might get. I was excited today because I knew it meant you could talk to them again. See them again. Man, you deal with grief and crisis situations and the shit life can throw better than anyone I have ever known, but you didn't go to their funeral, you don't talk about them ever. You," Anand paused, "it's like you pretend they never existed." Anand glanced up to observe my expression because he was mostly looking down while saying this.

I was a ball of hate ready to explode.

He couldn't have missed that, but pressed on all the same, "I, I wanted you to see them again. I know you're in pain man. I can't imagi—"

"No, you can't imagine," I interrupted, "so shut up about it!" I said viciously, and horribly.

"Man, I just wanted to—"

"Are you fucking deaf?" I was mad and getting madder, because he didn't look scared or startled, he just looked at me with more and more pity in his eyes.

Neither of us said anything or even looked at each other for the rest of the train ride. The remaining fifteen minute ride felt like it took three hours. When we reached our stop, which was the southernmost destination of the sky train, the doors swung open and we walked out to a reporter from one of the local news stations. There was a camera pointed in our direction.

"Gentlemen, we're live! Who is going to win the next Federal Election?" asked a young reporter with his cameraman already filming us. I had seen the little prick, wannabe, gonzo journalist before—Tim Platt was his name. He shoved a microphone into my face and that was enough.

"Randy Ward could become the first hearing impaired Prime Minister of Canada—your thoughts?"

"*What?*"

"I said Randy Ward could become the first hearing impaired Prime Minister of Canada. What are your thoughts on this?" Platt repeated, like a robot.

"*What?*" I asked again, even though I heard him just fine.

"Randy Ward!" Platt was shouting now, almost like he was talking into a bullhorn, "He could become the first hearing impair—"

"It's *deaf* you stupid fuck, not *hearing impaired. Listening impaired* is what you, my friend here—*I motioned to Anand*—and Randy's colleagues in the House of Commons suffer from, along with a bad dose of effort without the intellect. And *my thoughts*? I think I'm more worried that our next leader could be a guy named *Randy*. Anyone named Randy used to pick up teenage girls from high schools in their *IROC Z28 Camaro* back in the eighties. We elect a Randy as Prime Minister and that's it for Canada. No wait, a guy named *Carl* would be worse—we might as well become the fifty first state of the Union if we have a Carl in charge. It's us, then Puerto Rico."

Platt looked stunned.

Anand still looked like he felt sorry for me.

I pushed the microphone out of the way and bolted to the sky train platform exit feeling bad about saying that, and for leaving Anand on camera with a guy he probably knew as a colleague in the news business, but ultimately, I didn't give a shit. I hurried to my 1970 Buick LeSabre in the sky train parking lot, but as I walked I heard something playing through my head: *Monsters are furry, monsters are fun, but you better watch out, or you'll be done!* I became more sad than mad and stood frozen for a minute while holding the handle on my car door without opening it or letting go of it. I shook my head to snap out of my mini trance. I got in my car, slammed the door shut and drove home with the music playing so loud it drowned out any thoughts I might have.

CHAPTER 4 – DENIED

The next morning, I slept in because it was Saturday. When I woke up, I attempted to recall every good sexual encounter I'd ever had, but sadly, and not surprisingly, this was a short list. Even sadder, remembering the exact date and time down to the hour was bloody difficult, but with a calendar on my computer, some old photos and photo albums, calls and texts to friends *minus Anand*, and some online searches, I put together a pretty decent list of events to head back to Time Dream with—*seven hours later!* The afternoon had flown by while I prepared to go on a coma jump sex spree—which was really just an attempt to squeeze out any sadness, brought on by Anand's questions, with some scientifically engineered worry free humping. I took a shower and then drove to Time Dream—*no sky train bullshit this time.* Before I got there though, I made a little pit stop at Shopper's Drug Mart to buy two boxes of adult diapers. This way there'd be no more *pee in the pants Olympics* during my *next* coma jump.

I ran through the store because I was worried about when Time Dream closed on a Saturday—*maybe they had later hours on the weekend just like Pizza Hut.* Come to think of it, why is Pizza Hut open later on weekends but hospitals have the same visiting hours no matter what day it is? Pizza one, healthcare zero...

When I got to the till, there was a lineup. Several people ahead of me turned back and looked quickly away when they saw my two jumbo packages of *Tranquility* brand adult diapers. It appeared as though they were giggling but I wasn't sure because their backs were to me. The line slowly moved along and whittled itself down to just one more person before me. When I reached the clerk she shoved the diapers into bags large enough to make the contents invisible. I silently thanked her for that.

After my purchase I screamed down the road in my car with lots of confidence, and diapers, on my way to Time Dream. After coming close to breaking the sound barrier I rolled into the parking lot around 7:50 pm.

I was just about to dash in when I remembered I needed to get a pair of my new and pristine adult diapers on. So, rather than doing the sane thing, like going inside to change in one of the fine Time Dream washrooms, I decided to re-enact a bad male stripper routine and attempted to remove my underwear while sitting in the car. Just another one of those surgically stupid things that Homo sapiens do to win a Darwin Award when they are in a hurry and focused on something else.

In the end I had ripped my pants, torn the underwear off and given myself the worst wedgie in the history of any school boys' locker room. At this point, having grown tired of the human pretzel routine, I looked around to make sure no one was watching, and finally opened the door of my car, stood up, and kicked my shoes and pants off—which left me unimpressively naked due to my war-torn underwear coming off seconds earlier. I reached in, grabbed my Tranquility adult diapers, and suited up feeling less than tranquil.

I quickly put my pants and shoes back on and then, just as I was going to close the door and go in, I froze. It was a feeling of terror and surprise like when you realise someone has been watching you pick your nose for God only knows how long.

I didn't even have to turn my head—I could *feel* a bunch of people looking at me. I slowly turned and saw an entire school bus full of elementary students staring at me. And, again, like when you're picking your nose and someone notices, my mind flashed back over everything they might have seen. FUCK!

Their teacher was standing on the last step of the bus in shock. It was a look a mom would have the first time she walked in on her son *exploring himself*. No, that doesn't cover it, it was a look a son would have the first time he walked in on *his mom* exploring herself. I couldn't move. They didn't move. The bus driver didn't even move.

As I stood there terrified, with words like gross misconduct, indecent exposure, felon and pedophile going through my head, the seconds felt like minutes and I briefly recalled NBC's Bob Costas talking about how things slowed down for the greatest athletes during intense or clutch sporting plays. It's possible this wasn't quite the same thing.

Finally, I closed the car door and calmly strolled into the front entrance of Lougheed Time Dream while hopelessly pretending I hadn't noticed the school bus.

I walked in and was greeted by Janne, who was the same lady working the counter from yesterday, and Cordel, the four eyed version of Ron Jeremy.

"I'm sorry Mr. Riley, we are closing in an hour, so no more Time Dream activations are permitted for tonight," Cordel said, with Janne smiling so much it made me wonder what was happening to her lower half underneath the counter.

"But that's a whole hour left yet," I said, "Couldn't I just do a half hour session? I'm here because you guys want to do research on me. Remember?"

"Yes, yes, Mr. Riley, but you can come back on Monday morning and we would be happy to accommodate you," Cordel said.

"Rigggghht, right, closed on Sunday eh? Good thing Time Dream respects the Sabbath." I was pissed off and feeling a bit of coma jump addiction without realizing it, but before I could complain further, I saw a red flash and heard a sound go off at another counter about ten metres to my left.

It was an alarm of some sort. Not as jarring as a fire alarm, but more like a sound on *The Price is Right* after someone guesses how much a his and hers grooming kit is worth, or how much a set of motorhome drapes and an ashtray cost—if you were alive during the 70s.

Several people emerged from the back of the office and

then Dr. Kozlov ran out and joined the others. Although the alarm sounded playful to keep customers at the counter calm, the Time Dream employees looked concerned as they watched the monitor behind the counter.

One of them was on the phone and seemed to be repeating instructions to his colleagues. Then, *they all looked at me.* My immediate instinct was to run and tear ass outta there, but I decided it was futile because this place was wired like a bank, more cameras per square inch than a Vegas casino.

"Mr. Riley!" Dr. Kozlov said as he and a few others came towards me. "Can I please trouble you to come over here Sir?"

"OK." I strolled over and he lifted the tablet monitor off the counter and brought it around to give me.

"Ahhh, take a look at this surveillance video. Is that you standing naked in the parking lot and changing into a diaper?" Doctor Kozlov seemed to ask me this question while hoping the answer was no.

"Of course it is." I said calmly and firmly. Once again, any sane person would follow up with an explanation after quickly admitting to such a thing, but I remained silent. Less is more, I decided.

"Ahhh," Dr. Kozlov paused as his eyes shifted left and right while looking at the ground nervously, "we received a phone call from an elementary school teacher who just visited our Lougheed location here for a field trip. And well—well, do you want to explain this?"

His Russian accent seemed even thicker than usual when he was worried, so he sounded like an overdone lead character in an anti-communist eighties movie. I wondered if I could get him to say, "FOR MOTHER RUSSIA!" if I paid him twenty bucks— probably not a good time for that.

"Not particularly, no." I finally answered. As much as I was amused by seeing their genuine looks of worry, while they considered the possibility I was a weirdo, I realized that unless I got very specific in short order the next red flashing alarm I saw would be on a squad car parked out front.

I swallowed all pride and explained why I had bought the diapers and how I was too embarrassed to walk in with them. Dr. Wade and Dr. Kozlov corroborated my pitiful story and Dr. Kozlov even followed up by saying they had change rooms in addition to the washrooms. I walked out, with a little less pride than I walked in with, wondering if they let me go because they knew I worked for the RCMP, or because no one on earth would be able to make up a story like that.

I spent Sunday sulking about missing out on Time Dream and brainstorming all the ways I could get out of having to go to work the next day. Monday was shit as a general rule for most people, but now I had extra reasons to fabricate an illness or create a story about a long, lost aunt being seriously ill. A chill ran down my spine as I remembered one aggressive aunt who felt it necessary to kiss and borderline grope me as a kid—an eighty-year-old with liver spots trying to make out with me as a teenager, yet the girl I liked in home economics didn't know my name.

I smiled because this made me recall my two sons. When they were alive I used to give them a hard time when older relatives tried to smother them with kisses and their Mom let them run away: "You little buggers are taking those kisses God dammit! I practically had to get licked by my Great Aunt Fay. *Licked boys*! Do you hear me? Licked I say! I could feel her whiskers!" They would laugh because they knew I was trying to make them giggle, and also because their generation never got smacked like mine did, so me getting angry was not a threat.

For the rest of the day I hopelessly focused on this memory. Before Anand had fucked up my system—my coping mechanism, my way to get through the days, my trance...no no, *my coma*—on the train, by bringing them up, I had kept my sons, Alex and Owen, out of my head for so long because of previous experience with days like this. Weeks like this. Months. I wanted to break everything in sight but also felt overwhelming crushing sadness, and guilt, at the same time.

I was paralyzed with grief for the first two years after they died. Even seeing another child that resembled one of them was enough to trigger those emotions. Now, when I saw kids coming, or even a trajectory in life that could end with me around kids, I would go the opposite way and avoid invites to parties —most of my friends had families now. I would do anything to avoid remembering.

As I sat on my bed that night and set the alarm on my thirty-five-year-old General Electric radio clock, I heard the words playing through my head again: *Monsters are furry, monsters are fun, but you better watch out, or you'll be done!* When I closed my eyes and tried to sleep, the words wouldn't go away.

CHAPTER 5 – THE SECOND COMA JUMP...A STABBING AFFAIR

Despite my desire to be at Time Dream, I reported to work the next morning. I entered the RCMP McNeil building about ninety minutes past my start time on Monday morning—consistently late as usual. The main lobby rarely changed, like the rest of the building. The walls were all the same colours, there were swipe card security zones every ten metres, and the broken light for the past five years was still broken. This place, this organization, had been good to me, but it was the world's record holder for exterminating any creativity or sense of humour. When I approached the security guards they were emotionless as usual and seemed to be mere extensions of the lifeless building. I considered it my federal duty, and an attempt to seem alive in this soul stealing fortress, to try and crack them each morning.

"Hey John, what-a-ya got in the bag!?" I asked, as loud as a brigadier general, and flashed a wide grin. This was usually *John's* line right before he put your possessions through the scanner even if you only had a paper bag for lunch with you. John did not like me. For years, I used to fill my pockets and stuff things in my pants just to set his spider-sense off.

"Welllll! Good morning Riley. Hey fellas look, it's the world's skinniest man!" John said, and he and the other security guards—Commissionaires is the official name—laughed at my expense, which ultimately was my goal—to prove these sphinx-like guards had a pulse.

"Say fellas, do you guys have a hundred-foot extension cord I could borrow?"

"No," John said.

"No?" I asked.

"No, and don't start today Riley, I know you don't need an extension cord."

"Yes I do, it's important to me."

"Look, we don't have a hundred-foot extension cord, and if we did, I wouldn't give it to you."

"What about a *five*-foot extension cord?" I asked, while successfully walking through the scanner without setting it off. I could see a few guys exhale in relief.

"Christ, fine." John sighed, looked at one of the guards in the back, and then continued, "Guys, do we have a five-foot extension cord?"

"Sure boss," Derrick said, who tried to hand me a five foot extension cord. *What the hell? I didn't even see him go get it?* I looked away for a second and then he had it. The guy was like Orko, the magician from He-Man, or something.

"Oh, nah, don't worry about it," I said while holding my hands up to overly indicate I was not accepting the cord, "I don't need an extension cord thank you."

John shook his head and without looking at me motioned to his team that I was OK to proceed through the security checkpoint. They obediently buzzed me through. After using my swipe card, I took the elevator to the fourth floor and went to my office. It was tiny, barely the size of an outhouse. There was a sticky note on my door that read, "See Me right away." It wasn't signed because only my boss, the one and only Staff Sergeant Brian Forbes, would leave such a sticky note. He placed notes like this on doors because it was a sure-fire way to find out who arrived late for work. If you *came in on time* you would go to his office around your start time. If you were *ninety minutes late* then you would go ...*ninety minutes late.* It was also a sure-fire way to prove he was an asshole. I didn't bother going into my office or try to login but headed straight to Brian's office, because of his note, and because I could give my reason for leaving work in person—my next coma jump was just a fake sick day and fifteen minutes driving away.

"Morning Brian," I said as I knocked on his open door. I waited outside his office, feigning respect by not walking in.

"You don't need to knock, I can see you," Brian said.

"Right," I said. I wanted to say a lot more but held off.

"Come on in. Shut the door and sit down."

I took a seat in front of his desk and he continued, "Do you know why you're here?"

"A raise?"

"No." He didn't smile or frown.

"You're being transferred?" I asked, sitting up stiffly and purposely showing my excitement.

"Also no." Brian remained expressionless. He had a reputation in the department for being one of the best interviewers —*interrogators*—because of this poker face.

"*I'm* being transferred!" I stated more than asked, looking excited again.

"No. You were on the national news. Pretty good quality on the video too, so I've been getting calls since Saturday by people around here who have identified you." *Now* Brian showed some expression and smiled as he spoke. "Where, in your head, did you think it would be a good idea to go on TV and mock Canada's next Prime Minister, the Deaf, Chevrolet, and all of Puerto Rico in under thirty seconds? I mean Jesus, that has to be some kind of record. Then you swatted the reporter's microphone out of your face!" Brian motioned for me to look at his two over-sized monitors—big monitors have replaced ridiculously big trucks in terms of guys trying to make up for something that's... *smaller*—and while the video from my sky train platform performance played, my heart sank. I looked at the ground. "This will bring disrepute to the RCMP," he said.

"What? No one even knows who I am, let alone that I work here!" I said as I immediately snapped out of pitying myself and countered back. Although Anand and I had been arguing on Friday night, right before the incident, I knew he would've covered for me or pretended he didn't know me, even if Mr. Platt, the try-hard reporter, had pressed him for my identity.

"In this day and age, it will get out. By person, or by social media facial recognition," Brian said. "It's only a matter of time."

"I'm a ghost on the Internet and *any* social media Sir. I'm even Google proof!" I offered the last part in an attempt to make a sound reassurance, but it sounded desperate.

"You better hope. In the meantime, you're suspended with pay for the rest of the week."

Upon hearing this I used every bit of concentration not to smile. I had bragged to colleagues for years that being suspended with pay wouldn't bother me, and that it was almost an unattainable dream of mine. "OK," I said.

"See Linda on the way out to sign a form. I'll see you next Monday. Keep your phone on. I'll contact you if you need to get union representation." His face was expressionless again. I saw his future in my head. He was a mall cop and happily terrifying some teenage girl caught shoplifting.

"Will do on the form, and I'm not in the union," I pointed out. This guy genuinely knew nothing about the people who worked for him—the consistency of it was remarkable. But who cares, I had a week off with pay.

Linda wished me well, and smiled as I started to walk away, then called out, "Try and stay out of trouble!"

"Like telling a dog not to gnaw on a bone!" I said and smiled.

In no time, I was burning down the highway to Time Dream. I put on my Tranquility adult diapers in a Time Dream change room. I checked in at a booth with staff I'd never seen to this point—*must be the day shift*—but within a minute Myah showed up and apologized that Dr. Kozlov was not available. I didn't really understand why he would need to be there and explained that I couldn't care less but was thankful and excited to begin my second coma jump. Two minutes later when Myah sat me down at the kitchen table again, in a spot they called the *screening room,* I had my next date and time ready: The day I lost my virginity at sixteen.

This day would've been my *first* coma jump but I hadn't worked out the exact time it occurred in my life when Anand and I walked in last Friday. I entered in the date and then told Myah, "June 15th 1993, 3:30 pm." I figured this date and time out because I got out of school at 3:15 pm, and this occurred right after I walked home.

"Very Good, and just to remind you, we will be studying you during this and future coma jumps. Nothing will seem different in the coma jump, but I'm required to inform you of the analysis," Myah said and then asked, "Are you ready?"

When I told her I was, she activated the controls to open the glass wall and motioned for me to go in and sit down. The dentist chair looked more inviting than daunting this time.

"Now, I'm *sure* you remember your exit phrase?"

"Yes," I said and sat in the dentist chair. Again it reclined and the restraints immediately circled my ankles, thighs, waist and chest.

"Mr. Riley you kno——"

"I know I know."

"I'm going to count down again," she said and then pressed a button to close the glass wall. Her voice came over the intercom: "Get ready. 3....2....1....Good luck Sea——"

She was cut off from saying my name completely at the exact same time as my first coma jump. Once again, there was a brief silence like someone had changed the channel on a TV, but this time I realized just how quiet this time frame was, and how rare it is to have such complete quiet in your life. Also once again, for a short moment I felt like I was doing somersaults in midair. Then, I heard one of the sweetest voices in the whole world.

"What it mean? *Puberty*?" Cindy Yip asked. She was an exchange student from Hong Kong who had moved in next door when I was sixteen. Our neighbours, the Turgeons, were best friends with my parents, and Cindy had been living at their house with her sister for months before I figured out a reason to go over and visit her. In this moment, which I remembered all too well, we were sitting on the Turgeon's couch near the front door, when Cindy stumbled over the word puberty, and after I failed to give her an adequate definition, she typed the word into her hand held translation device—it was tablet size, long before there were tablets or even laptops anywhere near that small.

"Oh my GOD!" Cindy said after the machine spoke back a definition in Cantonese. I looked at her more closely, and had the same feeling from when this happened to me the first time, more than a couple decades ago: *How did that device explain puberty?* Her face went from shocked—*oh no*, to mad—*uh oh*, to looking like she wanted me to kiss her. Instead, she leaned in and kissed me, and then pulled away. I was lightheaded *and* tingling this time. I really was sixteen!

We were doing homework—I was in grade ten and she was in grade eleven—I failed grade two so that meant I was older than the other students in my grade and in fact had friends in both grade 10 and grade 11. Larry, my best friend growing up, for instance, was a grade ahead.

Cindy moved in to give me another kiss—*a big kiss*. She held the kiss, reached down and rubbed my leg, then started to slide her hand up my thigh...*when the unthinkable happened*...I stopped her reflexively by grabbing her hand. *NOOOOO! What the fuck are you doing?* But it was all too clear: Cindy was a kid in my eyes now, and I was, in reality, more than twice her age. Shit, I wasn't just twice her age I was forty years old! Great, half the world was reportedly living out every deviant, illegal and disgusting sexual fantasy in existence during coma jumps, and I felt guilty about reliving my first blowjob. *FAWWWK!*

"What is your problem?" Cindy asked. "I know you like it." She put her other hand on my belt and I stopped her again. She violently pulled both hands away. "You're being chicken."

"No no, it's not that, I just, I just," I stumbled over my words—this was the worst. What a waste of a coma jump.

"You don't want to with me because I'm Chinese. You're a racist!" she screamed. Her face was red, and if I *was* actually sixteen I'm sure I would've fallen into a debate about that comment, but I wisely stood up instead.

Just then, Mrs. Turgeon—my Mom's best friend—came in, likely hearing Cindy make a commotion. I focused on Cindy and was about to make up some excuse to leave, thinking I could make the most out of this coma jump by going next door to see my Mom and Dad, who were long dead in present day, when I saw Mrs. Turgeon and gasped. She was gorgeous and in 1993 was probably only a couple years older than I am now! Even her glasses looked sexy.

Anand and I were just saying the other day how, as we aged, women our age appealed to us more. Women who, when you were *sixteen*, you wouldn't even think about in *that* way. But I was almost speechless looking at Mrs. Turgeon. All of this was odder than I'd expected, and I felt conflicted.

"What's going on here, Cindy?" Mrs. Turgeon asked, her hands on her hips. She appeared to be annoyed with Cindy and not me. Then I remembered something I learned long after Cindy and her sister had gone back to Hong Kong: Mrs. Turgeon actually thought the two of them were a pain in the ass, and thought Cindy was spoiled. She had relayed as much to my Mom in confidence, but my Mom let little things about it slip out over the years. It was *Mr.* Turgeon that agreed to take them as part of the exchange student program, because he was a Guidance Counsellor at my high school, and because all four of the Turgeon kids had moved out and there was lots of room.

"I was just leaving," I said, trying not to grin as I gazed—*no, gawked*—at her.

"Yes, he was leaving," Cindy said. I was amused at her re-action and behaviour because it was completely foreign for me to turn down a girl in a situation like this...*ever...in my life.*

"That's fine Sean. Cindy, Mr. Turgeon is waiting in the car out front to drive you to volleyball practice. Sean, your Mom said you might be able to help fix our printer."

This sounded so familiar—did this happen for real when I was younger? I was already good with computers by then. Cindy grabbed her bag and hurried out the front door. She didn't look back in my direction once. I looked back at Mrs. Turgeon.

"All right young man, come with me," she said and led me into their computer room and I was immediately filled with memories. It was in this very room that I became captivated with computers and knew, even at age six, that I wanted to work with them for the rest of my life. As a young boy over thirty-five years ago I walked into this room and saw the Tur-geon's oldest son, Stephan, who was nine years older than me, playing the game *One on One: Dr. J vs. Larry Bird* with another teenager on the Apple 2. At the time I thought it was the most amazing thing I'd ever laid eyes on. Boy what I'd give to see my little face at the time, or heck, maybe that was another idea for a future coma jump if I could ever nail the exact date. That aside, I was amazed by something else at the moment: Mrs. Turgeon was bent over and fiddling with the old dot matrix printer and cursing repeatedly. I barely noticed the words—she was spec-tacular! How did I miss this in my teenage years? I kept my gaze on her way too long and her question snapped me out of it.

"Sean. *Sean?* SEAN! For fuck sakes Sean, can you fix this or not?"

I shifted position, so I could better examine the old Epson LQ 2500 printer. It looked like an antique to me but I soon fell back into what to do like it was yesterday. The printer, and then computer, needed to be turned off and on in that order, and then I set the paper, with holes on its horizontal edges, back in the tracks. I also unplugged the serial printer port cable and re-plugged it in. I knew this would work and it did. The old Epson printer groaned to life when the PC booted up, indicating that the printer and computer were talking to each other.

"That sounds better," Mrs. Turgeon said and smiled and winked at me.

The wink made me remember something important I had long forgotten: Some time back then, Mrs. Turgeon had kissed me at a New Year's party hosted by the O'Leary's—a mutual friend of my parents and the Turgeons. When she kissed me, she held the back of my head and ass, and I'd felt shocked and a little scared at the time. But I had been intrigued too. She'd been drinking a lot that night and I smelled gin on her breath.

Just before she kissed me she'd said, "Mmm, Sean, Happy New Year," then kissed me and walked away. Based on that memory and the fact I was in a coma jump and could do what I wanted, I decided to go for it.

"I'm going do a test print to see if it is actually working now," I said. Normally, I just would've typed in the word *TEST*, or something like that, but because this was a coma jump, I wrote: "*Mrs. Turgeon, your eyes are always smiling when you talk, which makes you twice as sexy.*" Then I hit PRINT and the old printer howled and grinded the print job out.

"You did it," Mrs. Turgeon said and reached down to tear off the printed words. It took her longer to read it than I expected, and I saw what I took for concern on her face.

Faaaaccccckkk, that wasn't the expression I was hoping to see.

She stared at the page for what seemed an eternity, and then, started to cry. Slowly for a second, and then with all out gasps and tears for several minutes.

This startled me.

She covered her mouth and turned slightly away from me, but the sobbing didn't stop.

Christ, what have I done?

Then, she turned around again, grabbed me, and pulled me into a hug that wasn't sexual, but forlorn, like someone hanging on tight so they didn't fall over. She cried and sobbed into my shoulder and I hugged her back with the same force she was hugging me. Not sure what else to do.

This continued for another minute and then she pulled away from me but only a few inches. She looked me in the eye and then kissed me and grabbed the back of my head like before, except for longer, and this time I didn't smell any gin on her breath.

My body was instantly ten degrees hotter and the unfathomable scenario had me more aroused than the cast of Glee when someone turns on a jukebox.

I put my hands on her ass while her hands were still around the back of my head. She gasped, this time, and then pulled away from the kiss and lowered her elbows to knock my hands off her bum.

"Sean, you can't do––" I cut her words off by pushing my lips back onto hers, and we both sat down slowly onto the couch, next to the computer, all while being embraced.

No more than three minutes later—a short while later—I lost my virginity, but instead of it being with a seventeen-year-old from Hong Kong, it was with a forty-three-year-old friend of my Mom's.

"I think the printer is working now Mrs. Turgeon," I said and smiled as I searched for my underwear. Finally, I found them half under the couch, and chuckled when I realised they were *He-Man* underwear. Jesus, this coma jump stuff *couldn't* be real if a woman this gorgeous was willing to let a skinny nerd like me make love to her after fixing the family printer. I understood now why the world was addicted to Time Dream's magical machine.

"Ohhh, it's working alright," Mrs. Turgeon said, "And you should call me Susan from now on hun." And then…she just stared at me like she was proud of me, but it wasn't weird, it was the look someone gives you when they…*believe in you.*

I suppose I should've considered the gaze a little bit strange, but happiness is a more powerful emotion than awkwardness. I finished getting dressed but *Susan* didn't attempt to get dressed herself. Not getting dressed right away after sex seemed like her way of telling the world to fuck off. I didn't mind! Once I was fully dressed, I felt paralyzed with lust all over again as I glanced at her still naked on the couch. But I also noticed that the clock behind her read 4pm. I stayed a little while longer and then said I better get home.

I was eager to see my parents for the first time in years. Dad passed away when I was in my late twenties and my Mom had died four years ago.

"Say hi to your mom for me!" Susan said. The joyful expression on her face was such a contrast to earlier. I had the urge to stay longer to find out where that sadness came from, but there wasn't time.

"I will. See you later Susan," I said, and kissed her once more before walking out of the computer room. I felt sad when I left, wondering what was going on in her life at the time, or if it was just something my mind fabricated in the coma jump, but my mood soon changed to excitement as I eagerly bounded across the front lawn on my way to seeing Mom and Dad! I was rounding the corner ready to rush into the house when I heard a familiar voice.

"Hey, what the fuck are you doing?" My Dad asked.

I smiled broadly at the sight of my father for the first time in over ten years.

"What are you grinning about? You ran across the grass again didn't you? Is there something wrong with the goddamn path? Anyway, come here and help me work on this."

I knew he was trying to fix the garage door and already had Ron, my brother-in-law who was dating my ten-years-older sister, Marilee, standing there with his arms in the air to keep the door steady on its rails up above. Ron's arms were shaking like a Mexican space shuttle because Dad no doubt had him stuck like that for close to an hour.

I remembered this event so well because back in 1993 a huge wedge screw driver came uncorked from the precariously balanced garage door above and knocked me out. By some miracle the handle end cracked me instead of the blade end, otherwise it would've been the equivalent of another lawn dart *fatality*. "FLAWLESS VICTORY."

Dad made Ron do this kind of shit all the time. He'd taken pleasure in making Ron's life hell. I didn't understand why then but did later. It was just my father's way of sticking it to the guy who was *sticking it* to his daughter.

Now, I was a pretty good little athlete as a kid and a damn fast runner, which gave Dad plenty of opportunities to be proud, but I don't remember him being prouder than when I pranked Ron, albeit not on purpose.

For years my mom would never let me have sweets, treats or cookies because I was already hyper and that stuff only made me more hyper. So, each day I made it my little James Bond mission to infiltrate the cookie cupboard without being detected.

The better I got at stealing cookies the better my Mom got at discovering the missing cookies, so I came up with a new plan right around the time Marilee started dating Ron. I went into the cupboard, took out the Girl Guide cookies, and carefully opened the box and cellophane with the intention of sealing the box back up afterwards. I peeled apart the cookies and licked out the icing in every single one, before closing each cookie up and putting them back in the tray of the box.

Then, I carefully glued the cellophane up, and glued the box closed too. It was a work of art—only *God* knew the cookie box had been molested. Later that day was the first time Marilee invited Ron for dinner—a big event for her. At the end of the meal my Mom was swooning over Ron being "perfect in every way", while my Dad looked like he was going to bayonet him.

Mom made a comment about being embarrassed she didn't make desert, and quickly grabbed the Girl Guide cookies from the cupboard, before asking Ron to help himself and pass them around. Ron popped a cookie in his mouth, and then another, and another. His eyes lit up while he joyfully exclaimed the cookies *had no icing, the bag was a dud*, and how amazing this was. There was a delay, some stunned looks by my family, and then the three of them all turned towards me. I was grinning and starting to laugh as Marilee and Mom quickly stopped Ron from eating another cookie, and both gave me a look that would scare a Navy Seal.

Ron, realizing what happened, or *was* happening, started to plead *that the box was sealed* and *the cellophane was sealed,* before Marilee shut him down while referring to me with a variety of monikers—all being synonyms for *little fucking bastard* I believe. My Dad, on the other hand, beamed with pride and happiness.

"Ok Dad, I'll help," I said, bringing my mind back to the present, "but ahhh, say Dad, I think that screwdriver is about to shoot loose up there." I kept my distance by not even entering into the garage, knowing a screwdriver to the head would make the last half hour of my coma jump rather painful, *or worse,* if the blade caught me instead of the handle this time.

"What? Just get in here and put your arms up so Ron can get a rest dammit!" Dad said.

"Ahhh, the screwdriver looks pretty unstable," I said.

Then, before I could intervene or explain, Ron reached with one arm—while his other arm stayed vertical holding the garage in place—to grab the screwdriver, and presumably wiggle it to see if it was secure, but as he was reaching the garage door suddenly shifted with a ferocious *BANG*, and Ron went down like a......like a guy who'd just been stabbed in the forehead with a screwdriver!

"FUCK! Fawwwwk!" Dad yelled, a look of raw terror on his face.

When this happened to me for real, Ron claimed for years that if the blade end had hit me I would have died. And now I looked down at Ron lying motionless on the garage floor, proving his own theory.

"God dammit what are you looking at? Go inside and call an ambulance!" Dad said.

I ran into the house while futilely reaching to where my cell phone had been in my pocket for the last fifteen years in the real world, and all but ignored my Mom in the kitchen. I immediately picked up the phone and dialed the local number for an ambulance—in my small home town of Hay River, a sub-arctic community, there is no 9-1-1 service. Twenty rings later, also a by-product of a small town, I talked to a dispatcher who said an ambulance would be there right away. I was sweating all over but calmed down after reminding myself this wasn't real.

Then I heard Marilee's alien-like shrieking in the garage. I ran back outside, and Dad was holding Marilee as she flailed about trying to get to Ron. My mother was outside already and was helping my Dad.

There was a lot of blood around Ron, and he was clearly dead. The blade had gone in through the front of his head and come out the other side. I felt sick to my stomach. *What was the fucking coma jump exit phrase?* Nothing was coming to me. I just sat there unable to move and unable to remember the words. The Ambulance came blaring into the driveway and its siren stirred me out of my mind fuck.

"UNRELENTING, UNRELENTING, UNRELENTING, RESCUE!" I roared.

"What the fuck is wrong with youuuuuu-ahhhhhhhhh!" Marilee screamed, in a harrowing voice. I was about to reply but felt a horrible pain in my head, and then, everything went black and dead silent even though my eyes were open. For a short moment, I felt like I was doing somersaults again in midair. I knew the exit phrase had worked. I awoke to Myah calling me over the intercom.

CHAPTER 6 – THE RIGHT TO DIE

"Are you alright? Do you know where you are?" Myah's voice was very loud yet calm and in control.

"No God dammit, my head hurts like Shaquille O'Neal just sat on it! And not a slim and trim Shaq right out of LSU either, I'm talking a mid-forties, overweight Shaq doing commercials for *Icy Hot* pain relief."

"That's normal, this has happened before—"

"*Someone else* woke up complaining their head was violated by Shaquille O'Neal?" I asked incredulously, hoping to make Myah giggle. She didn't laugh. Nothing. *Probably a Kobe fan.*

"No. But I had to inject you with our wake up serum and this can cause severe pain when you first come out of the coma jump. But, otherwise you're *OK*?"

"As long as you just said *serum* and not another five letter word that starts with *s* and ends in *m*, I'm just fine Doc."

"Well, it didn't affect your sense of humour, that's for sure!" Myah laughed a bit this time before slowly walking me into the screening room to discuss the coma jump. She helped me into a chair at the table and asked two questions: Why I used the exit phrase and whether or not I peed myself again.

"I said the exit phrase because my coma jump turned *Friday the 13th* on me." Then I told her about Ron getting stabbed by the screwdriver. "Yes, I peed again, and maybe more, because

49

I just had the shit scared outta me."

I was thankful that moment for Tranquility Adult Diapers. "Anyway, can you just queue up the same date and time for that coma jump again? It was going perfect and I know how to avoid the bloodshed at the end."

"It really is quite remarkable this keeps happening. Did you go to the washroom in this coma jump?"

"No, I didn't. Can I do that one again right away? Same parameters and all?"

"Unfortunately you—"

"Ah Christ, what's the problem now?" I rudely cut Myah off. My voice was sounding more and more like a junky.

"Unfortunately, you used the exit phrase, which means no more jumps for twenty-four hours. It's standard operating procedure for safety," Myah persisted. She looked me in the eye the whole time without blinking.

"Can't I simply go to another Time Dream location to get around that?" I asked.

"All Time Dream locations are linked worldwide," she said.

Great, I thought, too bad law enforcement couldn't figure this one out. My superiors at the RCMP always gave a number of reasons why universal data sharing was difficult amongst police departments, and I always asked them if they had heard of Blockbuster Video memberships, before Netflix killed them that is.

"Fine, thank you," I said as I quickly left and went down the hallway to get back to the front counter before exiting the building completely.

I heard Myah yell something positive about a "good collection of data and see you tomorrow."

When I got in my car I could tell already I should have taken the adult diapers off in the Time Dream change room, but I didn't want to *look* silly by walking back in, I preferred to *be* silly and sit in my own piss for the drive home. Before I got going, I turned on the radio and started checking messages on my phone. I was flipping through various work emails, and thinking of reaching out to Anand to apologize, when I heard the CBC—Canadian Broadcasting Corporation—Radio announcer break from her consistent five years in a row monotone voice with a little bit of alarm:

"The United States has finally passed the right to die bill for any consenting adult twenty-one years of age or older. The law focuses on assisted suicide specifically, making it legal for others to help in one's suicide if certain conditions, regulations and guidelines are met. Previously, practitioners were only allowed to assist in the suicide of mentally competent adults with enduring and intolerable suffering, in cases where death was reasonably foreseeable. Now, any adult deemed of fit mind by a mental health professional would be eligible to request a medically assisted suicide, even if they were not sick or suffering. All fifty states across the US have formed supporting laws to make this legal. Critics from around the world are debating and attacking the superpower's decision, saying this was simply its latest answer to population control and overcrowding. Canada is expected to be the next nation to follow suit, and pass a similar law, after intense pressure and lobbying—possibly as soon as later this week. Mercedes Smith has more..."

Well, there marks the beginning of the end I figured. I texted Anand to ask if he heard the news. He texted back right away that he had, and he also said he thought I'd be interested in what he'd learned that morning in his first meeting with the Time Dream execs. I texted back that I was suspended from work for a week due to the sky train platform incident, so I had nothing going on.

He insisted we meet for lunch. I agreed and figured this was also a good opportunity to double check Anand hadn't given my name up to Tim Platt—the asshole reporter one must have had in mind when the media slogan, "better first than right" was coined.

We decided to meet at the *Japanese Village* restaurant. I was happy to meet him there, because it had the best food in the city and was reasonably priced at *lunchtime,* versus at *night,* where you had to remortgage your house to afford a suppertime meal. I despised going downtown, but the Japanese Village was the exception. It was at the edge of the core and not in the heart of downtown, at least, so I drove straight there. It felt weird not to be in a rush for the first time in my life.

I had no job to rush back to, no kids, no family, and the closest I had come to a girlfriend recently was the latest video I streamed on PornHub. Perhaps this work suspension would be like a holiday—*just* when you figure out how to unwind and relax, your holiday is over and you have to go back to work. Fuck it, I decided to speed on general principal and not ruin two decades of consistently breaking at least a couple traffic laws every day.

I arrived at the Japanese Village about thirty minutes before Anand and I were supposed to meet. I sat down without having to stand in line at all, because it was a Monday lunch, and because I got there at exactly 11:30am—opening time—for the first time in my life. I loved the restaurant, but even when I was on time for a supper reservation, I usually had to wait outside for a table.

While waiting for Anand, I ordered a couple of drinks I couldn't pronounce, then started up a conversation with a Japanese born waiter I knew well, and a Chinese born waiter who I figured was new.

I was onto my second drink by the time Anand showed up. He smiled at me as soon as he sat down, and I took that to mean he was OK about the sky train incident on Saturday.

"So, who would win in a fight, Jesus, or Bruce Lee?"

Anand chuckled and then said, "That depends, does Bruce have the nunchuks?"

I smiled back and then our server arrived. I ordered my usual steak and shrimp and Anand ordered the same.

"So, I'm sorry about the other night," I said. "I just, I don't ahh," I paused before continuing on, "I can't talk about them or be reminded of them—" I couldn't get any further than that and was annoyed with myself because the words were not coming out right, as usual, when I remembered or spoke of my sons. Extreme sorrow tended to do this to a lot of people. Visceral hatred was the only other thing that could make one mess their words up so quickly, like say two drunk guys about to fight in front of twenty people outside a bar: "*I'm gonna fuckin fuck you in the fucking ass, you, you...you FUCKER!*"

"No worries man. Anyway, forget about me, it sounds like you're in more trouble than even you can talk yourself out of." Anand said, a warm sympathy in his voice.

"*What*? The suspension thing?"

"Ahhhh—yah, the suspension thing for attacking a reporter on national TV," he said, while giving me the *my friend Sean is incapable of changing or avoiding trouble* look.

"*Global News*? Nobody watches that station. Especially any garbage that Platt guy spews out. You didn't give him my name did you?"

"Of course not, and as for nobody watches," Anand shook his head like he was worried, "it got you suspended didn't it?"

"The upside is I just got a week off with pay."

"Only you would be happy about something like that man. You could lose your job," Anand said, continuing the lecture.

"So what, I live alone with no family, no significant other, hell, I don't even have a pet. Not even a goldfish or an ant farm or an imaginary friend. Scratch that, I don't need it to be an imaginary *friend*—I'd take an imaginary *acquaintance*. I'm like a priest, minus the wisdom and proclivity for young boys." I must have said this last sentence too loudly because quite a few people looked at me. I explained it was OK for me to say this since I was raised Catholic, my aunt was a nun, my dad used to be a brother in the Catholic Church, and my mother was once the head of the Northwest Territories Catholic Women's League. This logic was akin to Jack Black, in the movie *Shallow Hal*, saying, "*Oh cool, I used to know a deaf guy*" in response to his date saying she worked with some people at the *Foundation Fighting Blindness*.

"It scares me when you sound like you've got nothing left to live for." Anand wasn't looking only concerned and worried, but for the second time this week it was clear he pitied me.

"Well, they just legalized assisted suicide in the US. And it's only a matter of time before it's legal here. I wish I could be smothered to death by some woman's chest, or even a man's," I said with a poker face, trying not to smile, in a hope of worrying Anand some more.

But he laughed, changing gears back to where I liked all my conversations to be.

"I'll sit on your face right now for free if you give me your *Seinfeld* on Blu-Ray collection!" he said.

"Deal, and I'll throw in the *Curb Your Enthusiasm* DVD set if you take a bath first."

Twenty minutes later, when we were done eating, Anand explained the significance of the assisted suicide law in relation to Time Dream's future business plans. He said they wouldn't reveal what they had coming, but that Time Dream had been counting on the law being passed in well off nations.

After he heard this, Anand told me how he'd dug a little deeper and learned that Time Dream had pushed heavily for the law to be passed, with millions of dollars in silent contributions to the right politicians, researchers, lobbyist groups, and judges. There were even rumours, among lower level Time Dream employees, that the company was originally funded by the US Government to research innovative solutions for population control and global overcrowding—which seemed well outside Time Dream's advertised objective of letting people relive the best moments of their lives in coma jumps.

"I'm confused," I said. "Time Dream already has more money than the next ten richest companies combined. How does assisted suicide help them? If anything, there will be less people for them to bankrupt after they hook them on coma jumps."

"Well, I plan to get to the bottom of this—and if even half of what I learned is true, there's quite a story here."

"Just make sure you don't write yourself out of existence."

"What-a-ya mean?"

"I mean they have more money than most countries. Do
you think they'll let you publish a negative story? They'll burn
your house down and kill your dog," I said, both as a warning
and to make my best friend laugh.

"Yah yah."

"I really am serious," I said. "And they can do worse than
kill you. They'll leak ten stories for every one story you write.
Weird stories, character damaging stories, stories about how
you enjoy watching videos of two dogs making love to a cat,
with a side story on monkey cum."

"Dude! Do you have to say that in here––"

"Stories about how you need to play Star Wars music in
the background during sex, or you can't maintain an erection."

"Fuck sakes Sean," Anand whispered.

"If you publish even a syllable of bad press on Time
Dream, RMN will fire you and you'll be grading papers in a public
school faster than you can say Banzaaaaaaii!!!" I yelled the last
word like I had just won the lottery, or got a job promotion, or
masturbated for the first time.

"Jesus dude, the whole restaurant is looking at us now,"
Anand said with an embarrassed look, or like someone *caught
him* masturbating for the first time.

"I know man, but honestly, I just wanted to yell Ban-
zaaaaiiii in a Japanese restaurant." I had accentuated the word
banzai loudly again, so Anand stood up annoyed, but smiling, as
he shook his head.

"All right all right, I assume this means you want to leave.
Let's go. And you're paying after that bullshit. Jesus Christ."
Anand sighed and we both pushed our chairs in politely before
heading to the counter. "If we could make money off your talent
for antagonizing people we'd both have more cash than Time
Dream."

We walked to the front and I happily paid for our lunch

knowing it was well worth it to get a rise out of him, "Just for shits and giggles"—Austin Powers. I thanked the Japanese Village manager, damned if I could ever get his name, and bombed down the stairs to catch Anand and say goodbye before he headed back to work. However, before he left, he dropped a bomb on me.

"Look buddy, I didn't want to bring this up with all those people around us when we were eating, but has anyone told you about Lawrence?" Anand asked.

My heart sank. Although I hadn't seen Larry face to face in years, my first coma jump made me feel like we'd connected again.

"No," I said.

"He lost his job, his wife and kids have left, and he'll lose his house any day now too," Anand said. He looked at the ground the whole time he was telling me this.

"What the fuck? *How?* He was doing well." As I asked this I felt deeply concerned for my oldest friend Larry, but I felt angry too that Anand knew this before me. I grew up with Larry, and Anand only met him after we were done university and Larry moved south from the Northwest Territories—this juvenile line of thinking always annoyed people because I consistently referred to Larry as *my* friend in front of people who had been his friend for years, if not decades.

"Time Dream brother, *what else?* He became addicted like just about everyone, but I don't mean addicted like he was going in for coma jumps every weekend. I'm talking Robert Downey Jr. before he got clean addicted, or Elvis right before *the end* addicted. Time Dream security actually threw him out at a few locations, because he came in drunk and yelling for the fifth time, with both he *and* Time Dream knowing he couldn't pay. What that company is doing, is—*not cool*," Anand trailed off.

"What?" I snapped, "Not cool? *Not cool* doesn't sum it up my friend. Why the fuck did you keep bugging me to go in with you for a coma jump if you feel this way?" I was worried *and* annoyed at the same time.

"I told you man, I didn't want to go in there on my own for the first visit, and RMN putting me on Time Dream is the gig of a lifetime. Besides, Time Dream's couple billion spent on R and D each year is no match for the legendary Sean Riley A.D.D—you couldn't stay focused long enough to form an addiction to save your life buddy," Anand said.

I knew he meant it as a joke and I took it that way. Normally he'd be right, and I'd appreciate the backhanded compliment, but I'd already concluded that there wasn't anything normal about Time Dream.

Worse yet, I figured *I* was already addicted to it.

"You're too kind. Anyways, fuck Time Dream for the moment. What's Larry going to do?" I asked.

"Why don't you phone him and find out. Ever since your —" Anand paused and looked at the ground, "ever since your life changed you haven't really talked to people much. Some of those *people* might need your help." What a fucker—Anand could lay guilt on better than my mother.

"What is *that* supposed to mean?" I asked.

"I have to get back to work Sean. Give him a call." Anand walked away toward his car. "I'll call you later this week before I do my interview with Dave Sandhu and the other Time Dream executives."

CHAPTER 7 – LARRY

As I drove out of the parking lot after paying the ridiculous parking fee—I was flooded with memories of Larry and me playing together as kids. I remembered the time during summer holidays when his family moved to a new house about a block farther down the street. I was nine that year and went to Larry's *old* house, because I'd forgotten that he moved.

I was expecting Larry, but a girl answered the door instead. I knew her because our parents were friends. Her name was Lisa and she was a couple years younger, and had been begging me to come over for a long time. She became frantic and excited upon seeing me. Before I could make up an excuse to leave, or explain what happened, she called her mom to the door and said how happy she was that I'd come over to play.

Larry was waiting for me at his actual house, and we had our whole day planned out: G.I. Joe, He-Man Masters of the Universe, Atari, Commodore 64, and then later on, maybe hitting pause during a boobs scene from *Police Academy One* on VHS—it was an excitement you felt when you were heading over to play with your best buddy, and didn't know you would *never* feel like that again as an adult, but I also knew with absolute certainty Lisa's little heart would be broken if I left.

So I stayed, and played, *and…*played with her for several hours before I finally took off. Then I ran to Larry's new house. While I ran I felt a wee bit guilty because playing at Lisa's house wasn't as bad as I thought—her mom even let us eat ice cream and cake, which my mom would rarely give me, as it was akin to giving a small rodent the same illegal injection they give a horse trying to win the Belmont Stakes.

When I got settled in at Larry's, and we were well into a battle of Cobra versus G.I. Joe, he asked me what it was like at Lisa's place.

"It sucked," I lied, thinking that was the answer Larry wanted to hear.

Back in the present, I chuckled to myself about this memory, and knowing I couldn't hit Time Dream again until tomorrow, turned my car towards north Calgary where Larry lived.

When I reached his house, the street was so crowded I had to park on the other side of the road. Before knocking on Larry's door, I wondered if I should've phoned first. In the city, people mostly phoned or texted or somehow let people know they were coming over, but back home in the Northwest Territories, where Larry and I had grown up, you usually just went over to someone's house. Fuck it, I thought, if you can't show up unannounced to your oldest friend's house after hearing he was messed up enough to be on an episode of *Intervention*, when can you?

I knocked but nothing happened. Not a sound. No movement. I knocked again, still nothing. I was about to leave when I got an idea: I knocked again, but this time I opened the screen door and used two fists to hammer away, and then gave a loud open palm smack across the door. Something fell inside, and then I heard loud steps come all the way up to the door, but without anyone opening the door—presumably Larry looking through the peephole.

"Girl Guide Cookie for sale," I said in a loud, female voice with a heavy Spanish accent, but I heard nothing inside and no one opened the door. "I know you're there Larry, I can smell you from here," I yelled.

The door opened, and Lawrence "call me *Larry*" Reinhart stood there. He had a beard like he was a defenseman in the 3rd round of the Stanley Cup Playoffs, a sandal on only one foot, his jeans had leaves stuck to them and looked like he had worn them for a month, and he had a white tank top on with more stains than the apron from a line cook in *Hell's Kitchen*. He was also about a hundred pounds overweight, which is a lot when you're already a giant.

I barely recognized him.

"Heyyy-ayyy, John Candy just angry fucked the Trash Heap in *Fraggle Rock*, can he have his body back?" I asked, and then smiled at Larry.

"Heyyy, John Candy just wiped his ass with a muppet, can Kermit have his body back?" Larry shot back. Yup, it really was Larry, as most of his jokes made reference to how scrawny I was, and unlike the rest of the world, when the guy you grew up with said this it didn't bother you, it made you remember a place where *everybody knows your name*. "What are you doing here?" he asked.

"Sure, I would love to come in Larry, how's the wife and kids?" I asked and provoked at the same time—I knew Larry would know I heard about his family leaving.

"Little bastard, come on in man," Larry said as we shook hands. I followed him inside and saw what can only be described as a drug house minus the drugs. Dishes and rotting food everywhere, drapes on the ground, toys all over, and the couch had become Larry's second home inside a home. I wasn't sure what I saw more of, fist size holes in the wall or empty pizza boxes on the sofa. I half expected to see the Jiminy Cricket *Aliens* looking creature from *Spaceballs* come running out of one of the holes to do a dance routine: *Hello My Baby, Hello My Honey...* The finishing touch was his old gaming chair, lying diagonally upside down against the wall, and looking like a gargoyle chewed a chunk out of it. The entire living room looked like a motorcycle gang had attempted to tear it apart.

"I love what you've done with the place," I mocked, "it has a very feng shui meets Chernobyl feel to it." We both sat down on the couch, or rather, on what I *think* was the couch.

"Yah yah," Larry said, "so—you heard she left I presume?"

"By *she*, do you mean the cleaning lady, or your wife?"

"She took the kids man," Larry said, and I could see it was time to quit messing around as his eyebrows wrinkled while he gazed at the floor.

"I did hear that," I said. "I also heard you were going to Time Dream so much they should rename it to *Larry's Dream*."

"More like Larry's nightmare."

"I can think of a worse nightmare pal."

"I know you can," Larry said with a look of, there it was, a look of pity with a defeated smile on my behalf. Here was a guy, who just lost his job and had his whole family leave him, looking at *me* with pity. "Anyway, forget about me for a bit. How are you doing?"

Larry didn't say what I knew he was likely thinking— *Sean, your kids died, your parents died, and your wife left, so you gotta be even more fucked up than I am.*

"I tried Time Dream out myself a couple days ago. Anand and I went."

"*And*?" Larry asked with a look of surprise and concern rolled into one, "What did you come up with for your first Coma Jump?"

"Well, your mother and I had intimate relations with each other," I said.

"*What*? Come on man, I haven't seen you in years, can we have a decent conversation?" Larry said.

"No, she really is quite attractive—I made love to her."

"Dude, what the fuck?! You never had sex with my mom!"

"No, she shut me down back then in real life, but in my coma jump I pulled it off. I was full of confidence. And it wasn't just *sex*—don't cheapen it by calling it that—it was very special to me. I even convinced her to call me Mr. Reinhart."

"Yah you're full of something all right. You got serious problems man!" Larry was yelling *and* glaring at me now.

"I haven't even told you the rest! *You* came in on us and started to have some kind of asthmatic conniption episode be- cause you were upset. Also, I think Duffy,"—Larry's pet dog back then—"may have pissed on one of your mom's plants right

61

before he tried to lick my genitals when you walked in on us. And by *us* I mean your Mom and I—not the dog and I, or your Mom, the dog, and I.....I would put a qualifier on the plant's participation too, but that would be weird." Larry looked at me like he was gonna tear me in half, then shook his head, broke down, and laughed.

"Fuckin guy, where do you get this shit?" Larry scoffed and shook his head some more before continuing, "Anyway, I'm broke man. I bankrupted myself on those coma jumps." I knew these were words he probably couldn't say or admit to anyone else in the world, but he could say them to me because all he saw was the skinny four-year-old kid he grew up with in front of him —not some shithead colleague that would judge him.

"Hey, you and half the world pal," I reminded him, "but hold that thought, I gotta use your washroom to get outta my diaper." I knew these were words I probably couldn't say or admit to anyone else in the world, but I could say them to Larry because all he saw was the skinny four-year-old kid he grew up with in front of him! Nonetheless, I still had the diaper on so I went towards the bathroom. "Any airborne diseases or organisms in here I gotta worry about?" I asked.

"Don't be having any orgasms in my washroom Sean," Larry responded, "and, ahhh, it's probably best if you don't step off the rug in there."

After I was done peeling a used adult diaper off my bony, white ass in the washroom, I walked out and Larry was sitting on the couch with the hockey game on. It was May and the NHL playoffs were in the third round. Not a single Canadian team was left, but we still watch when this happens in Canada because: 1. We are Canadian and 2. All the teams are mostly made up of Canadian players. I sat down immediately, quite thankful that despite claiming to be broke and without a family, Larry had managed to hold on to the essentials in life, like his sixty inch TV, and a full Cable subscription with the NHL hockey package: "From my cold dead hands"—I'm talking about hockey here, not guns like Charlton Heston. I always wished *my* name was Charlton, or maybe Maximus from the movie *Gladiator*. Just think what it would be like when you're eight and get called to the principal's office over the intercom. *"The following two students are to report to the office immediately:"* In a deep voice, *"Maximus Decimus Meridius, and,"* in a little high pitched mouse voice, *"Billy."*

"So, you're still driving the '70 LeSabre I see." Larry gestured to the window, which let you see my car quite easily since his drapes were lying on the floor.

"That's right, it's a classic!" I said with pride.

"Just because something is old it doesn't make it a classic. And it's *beige—a fucking beige car*. What kind of a person drives a car *that* colour? That's Jeffrey Dahmer type shit. Besides, you don't know fuck all about cars. That thing is a rusted steel death trap and a gas guzzler. Give me one good reason why you're still driving it?"

"It's gluten free," I answered.

"Haa, nice—you do realize that car is half the reason the Oil 'n' Gas industry is still alive and well right? What the fuck do you pay in gas every month anyway?" Larry rolled his eyes.

"Haa, you punned yourself!" I said. "You were talking about Oil 'n' Gas and said 'alive and well'. Ha! Get it? *Well*, as in OIL WELL!"

"Yah yah, I fuckin get it man, the *Just for Laughs Comedy Festival* in Montreal is waiting for you. But just in case, don't quit your day job." This made me briefly remember my suspension at work, but then my A.D.D. moved me along.

"Speaking of jobs," I tried to say delicately but probably sounding artificial, "How are you managing with no job?"

"I was almost at full pension when they canned me. I had over twenty years in—so I asked for the money in a lump sum versus any long term defined contribution pension."

"Dude, don't take this the wrong way, but you ain't a guy who should be taking his pension out in a lump sum," I cautioned.

"Oh yah, *why's that*?" Larry asked defensively with one

eyebrow up in the air like he was *The Rock*, back in the day, on *Monday Night Raw*.

"Because you spend money on shitty, unrealistic, get rich quick investments being pandered on infomercials by the same guys who start cults where they mutilate squirrels and put peanut butter on hamburgers! So what is it *this time*?"

"There *is* no *this time*," Larry said grimly, "I was just tapped for funds. No choice really."

"Fine, so instead, you're going to evaporate that pension money by putting your new found funds into Time Dream?"

"No," Larry seemed puzzlingly calm, "I quit going to Time Dream outright. The other parting gift Volker Stevin," the construction company Larry worked at, *err*, used to work at, "gave me, apart from the pink slip, was 100 hours of free counseling with a mental health professional. They helped me kick it. I don't go to Time Dream anymore—nor do I want to."

"A shrink did the trick eh?" I asked.

"That and losing your kids when your wife walks out the door with them!" Larry said, and then looked at me with an awkward and terrified face, similar to Wil Wheaton in the movie *Stand by Me*, when he realizes a leech just got at his nards.

Larry's realization was remembering *I* really had lost my kids forever.

"Ahh, I'm sorry man," Larry looked away at the hockey game briefly, then turned back to look at me, "So, did you see them again with Time Dream?" he asked, his face brightening.

"No."

"Oh...good," he said, "my advice is to never go back there so you don't get hooked on it."

"I was given twenty free coma jumps because of a, well, because of a rare biological uniqueness I showed during the coma jump." After I said this Larry was shaking his head and gritting his teeth like he wanted to fight, or take a gigantic shit —which might have fit right in with his living room at the moment.

"Fuck sakes!" Larry got angrier and looked like he was

coming unglued—his wild and ever changing range of emotions were Dr. Jekyll-like as usual. He continued on angrily while grinding his teeth more. "Those fuckers. Man, they did the exact same thing to me."

"*You got twenty free jumps for pissing your pants too?*" I asked, conceding what happened.

"No, but I got *ten* free jumps because I was their *random one millionth customer* at the Silver City Time Dream location."

"Yah well, my situation was different man. Apparently, an event in a coma jump causing something to happen to your body in the real world is pretty rare," I explained.

"Sean, you're not gettin' it buddy, it's all bullshit. No different than a drug dealer giving you a little taste to get you hooked good and proper. My shrink said he's had quite a few clients talking about free coma jumps when they first showed up at Time Dream. I thought he was a bit of a quack in the beginning, but now that I'm hearing your story I'm *convinced* this is just part of their marketing machine."

My oldest friend made perfect sense, but all I kept thinking about was whether I wanted to see my kids again. Addicted? Who gives a fuck if I become addicted if I can see my kids again in a coma jump! I blocked out thinking of my two boys for so long because there wasn't any chance of seeing them again. Old videos made me sad for weeks, and the shitty, failed virtual reality and holodeck sims just made me miss them more when I tried them. But Time Dream, I thought, Time Dream was another story. Larry somehow had me thinking differently in the last two minutes, albeit not his intention. Coma jumps were real. I could spend a day at the zoo with my kids in one coma jump, and then have sex with their mom, my ex-wife, again for the first time in another coma jump—reliving our fifth date... That's a lie, we had sex on the second date.

"Larry," I said, while looking straight at my friend and ignoring the Predators versus Blackhawks game.

"*Yah?*"

"I gotta see them again."

"I know," Larry paused for a few seconds, "and no matter what *I* say, your kids are your kids. Just be careful—Anand said you got suspended from work for a week." He looked solemn and then smiled, "And I need you to *keep* your job, so I can borrow money when I lose my pension to some *shitty investment!*"

"I know," I said, also smiling, and then standing up, "see ya later buddy. It was fuckin great to see you again."

"You too," he said. "And no more coma jumps involving my mother. Or my childhood pet."

"I won't make any promises," I said with a grin. "Oh yah, one more thing—my suspension wasn't for missing work due to coma jumps. It was for attacking a TV reporter."

"Yah, I know, I was watching Global News when that happened," Larry said.

This surprised me. "*And?*"

"And I know the camera is supposed to add ten pounds, but you still looked like the same scrawny little bastard. And ugly. Really Ugly. Hideous actually."

"Thanks Buddy," I said, grinning some more as I walked to the door.

I headed for home trying not to think about my kids, however, I did feel pretty relieved Larry had a handle on things —I couldn't remember him being that sorted out...*ever*. But while I drove, throughout the remainder of the day, and right up until I went to bed, all I could think about was going to Time Dream on Tuesday morning and seeing my kids again in a coma jump. I felt as if I *had* to see them as soon as possible, for the vice on my heart and soul to be, not released—because that wasn't possible—but loosened. I *needed* to see them. I went to bed feeling quite thankful for my week-long suspension from work, and, once again, I heard a familiar tune playing in my head: *Monsters are furry, monsters are fun, but you better watch out, or you'll be done!*

CHAPTER 8 - ALEX AND OWEN

I walked into the Lougheed Time Dream location around 9:30 am on Tuesday morning. I was so anxious I didn't sleep much the entire night, so Time Dream's *Hercules Moon Belt*-like bright lights felt as if they were burning my corneas. I suddenly sympathized with my drug addict friends from college who used to wear their shades indoors. It made me remember the original BluBlocker sunglasses—a product born out of some of the best nighttime infomercial marketing in history behind Slap Chop and Chuck Norris' Total Gym. I bet even NASA had their astronauts testing BluBlockers at one point.

I went a little farther inside, and in an effort to avoid breaking their creepy tradition, Myah met me before I got to the counter. I chose to ignore this, and pretend it was just good customer service versus their technology detecting me entering the building.

"Do you ever sleep Doc?"

"Good morning Mr. Riley."

"Tell me the truth Doc. You guys have some kind of Google-like living quarters here don't you? Where you hang out all night in expensive evening wear doing equations and mapping the brains of every person who has ever set foot in here."

"No."

"No to the living quarters, or no to the——"

"Why would we waste our time doing that when we could

enjoy a coma jump like everyone else?"

Myah took me down a different hallway than my first two coma jumps. Being paranoid, warped, and usually off on a tangent, I wondered why she was taking the different route, but sure enough, my paranoia was for nothing, because when we arrived at the screening room everything was identical: kitchen table, chairs, weird probe looking stuff in the ceiling, and a glass wall separating us from the dark room with the dentist looking chair for the coma jumps. Everything was the same because companies as big as Time Dream love to replicate what works financially like a rabbit loves to......run, and by run I mean frolic, and by frolic I mean hump, and by hump I mean......I shuddered at the possibility Myah was seeing what I was thinking again: Would my thoughts be regurgitated as an interest in bestiality? She stared at me impatiently, while her hands were in the ready position on the keyboard, like she was awaiting permission to WikiLeak a story onto the Internet about the President of the United States and the Director of the CIA fondling a medium sized animal together—more bestiality...FUCK!...I tried to stop thinking.

"Well, what date and time do you want? Do you still want to do the same coma jump you did yesterday?" Myah asked.

"Ahh—*no*, I'm thinking something a little more...Christmas-ee." I figured a Christmas morning, around nine or ten AM, would be the easiest way to pinpoint a period from the past where I knew for sure my kids would be nearby during a one-hour coma jump. However, one of the things that had kept me up all night was deciding on *which* Christmas morning.

2013 seemed like the best choice: The boys were alive and well—Owen would be five and a half and Alex would be nine—and my wife and I would still be together, plus that Christmas we spent back home in the Northwest Territories at my parent's house—the same house I grew up in. *But*...my Dad wouldn't be alive in 2013, having passed away in 2007. I decided that I could see him in another coma jump one day. Today I wanted to see my sons again. My two sons whose deaths made me as close to becoming an atheist as I could get without starting my own atheist blog and podcast—I still believed in God, or some kind of higher advanced alien race, I just hated him...or her.

I told her the date, *December 25th, 2013, at 9am*, and then settled into the dentist chair.

Again restraints locked me in place, and Myah reminded me of the exit phrase. A few minutes later everything went black and I felt the fake somersaults and spins in midair.

Then...I heard a weird yet familiar sound before my vision came back. I knew this sound: A remote control car whirring "zzzzzzzzzzz" and then "BANG!" as it ran into something hard and unmoveable. My eyesight returned, and what I saw caused three extraordinary emotions in a row: pain, relief and then a happiness I didn't know I could feel.

My oldest son Alex sat on my Mom's kitchen floor and struggled to drive his remote control car, which Santa just delivered, while his little brother Owen furiously grabbed at the remote controls.

"Daaaaad, tell Owen to stop it!" Alex yelled.

"Give it Alexxxx, give it!" Owen yelled back. They wrestled as they often did. In the past that would have gotten on my nerves, but didn't now. Alex was older, but Owen was big for his age.

"One of you is going to get hurrrr-eeerrrt," my mother said, while preparing Christmas morning breakfast. It was amazing to see her alive and well.

I winked at my Mom to let her know I was kidding, and said, "Boys, boys, hold on—the most important thing here is that *I'm* safe. Stop fighting until I leave the room." I walked away while they sat silent, dumbfounded, and rightly suspicious of what I might do next.

I took a few more steps then turned and yelled, "ARRR-RGHHHHHHHHH," like Hulk Hogan when he played Thunderlips in *Rocky 3*, and ran at them like, well, like Hulk Hogan when he played Thunderlips in Rocky 3! They squealed with make-believe fear and very real laughter while pretending to try and get away, but the sounds they made meant they wanted me to grab them. I dove to the ground and tackled them both while rolling with them in my arms.

"Get 'em! Get 'em boys," my wife Angela said as she entered the kitchen. She looked beautiful. I hadn't seen her since shortly after our boys died.

"ARRRRGHHHHHHHHH!" I roared again, "I'm gonna eat ya, don't move," and then put my teeth to Owen's neck.

"AAAAAHHHHHHHH!" Owen screamed, this time not pretending.

"Woh, woh, wohhh, it's OK buddy, I'm not going to eat you," I said to calm him, "I'm just trying to slow you down, so I can sell you to the circus or put you up for adoption."

"That's not true," Owen said.

"Ohhhh yes it is," I said with a semi stern convincing voice, "Mom and I have talked things over and we can't afford to keep both of you, *sooooo*, we have decided to keep *Alex* and put *you* up for adoption Ian." Ian or Eeeeannnaaahhh was my nickname for Owen.

"NO!" Owen protested.

"I'm afraid it's true Owie," Angela said, "and we found a nice young family for you to stay with. It is very nice there but, *wellll*," she trailed off, so I continued.

"*Wellll*, they have a very large snake that lives with them pal, and unfortunately he likes to eat children. This is why they need to adopt a new little boy." I could immediately tell I went too far with this last line, because not only was Owen looking scared and sad, his big brother Alex was looking quite concerned now too.

"Is Daddy teasing you guys?" my Mom asked, and as she said this I gave them both the biggest hug in the world. A hug way longer than even a Christmas morning would warrant. A hug you give your kids after not seeing them or even thinking of them for so long because it was too painful. A hug you give your kids because you were never supposed to see them again—until Time Dream came along. It was in this moment I thought of Larry's words, and knew without question I was wholly and hopelessly addicted—I would spend every penny I had, sell everything I owned, and even consider knocking over a few *7-Elevens* just to keep this feeling going as long as I could. Even with seventeen free coma jumps to go, I was already certain seventeen wouldn't be enough. Worse, the feelings circling inside me weren't possible for a human without Time Dream—I was filled with pure, crushing, unfiltered, heart stopping happiness, but at the same time, I felt a paralyzing sadness too, fueled by the knowledge that my two children in front of me, were already dead...and gone. Forever.

"Daddy is never going to let you guys go! You know that right?" I asked, or maybe, pleaded.

"Yes," Owen said.

"Mm-hmm!" Alex nodded vigorously six times while smiling.

"I love you both very much."

"I love you too Daddy," Alex said.

"Love you Daddy," Owen said.

"All right—now who wants to help me hold down your Mom, so I can tickle her? Get her! Get her!" I yelled. We burned after Angela as she screamed and yelled while running down the hallway out of the kitchen. We all horsed around and ran around for at least another thirty minutes.

My lungs and legs were burning from exertion by the time my Mom called us for Christmas breakfast. I remembered then that I only had about half an hour left in the coma jump. It wasn't enough. I knew when this coma jump ended, something would break inside me.

Seeing them again might have been a mistake, but I ignored that feeling and sat down at the table to eat with my family. What a feast: Mom made the dishes she usually made for Christmas breakfast like scrambled eggs, bacon, sausage, an assortment of fruit, and of course, the crown jewel of the meal—an egg, cheese, and ham casserole with Rice Krispies layered on top.

I was about to start passing things around and helping myself to the food, when I remembered the eighteen years of *bless this meal training* I got from my diehard Catholic mother. So, I offered to say grace. I did the usual sign of the cross and then spoke out loud.

"Bless us oh Lord for these thy gifts, which we are about to receive, from thy bounty, through Christ our Lord. Amen." Then I did the same triple sign of the cross that Sammy Sosa did before each at bat, and then quickly kissed my two fingers on my right hand in one shot, and then pointed up to God with two hands.

"SEAN!" my Mother gasped disapprovingly, like she'd never seen this before, despite having heard and seen me do this since I was about twelve. My kids giggled, which was my goal in this situation, Angela rolled her eyes, and my sister Marilee just looked at me with contempt, as per usual.

"God likes a little bit of flare Mom. He appreciates the effort and an escape from the repetition. When I put some Snap, Crackle, and Pop," as I said this I pointed at the Rice Krispy breakfast dish while maintaining eye contact with my Mom who was sitting diagonally to my left, "into the blessing I can, I can, well, I can feel his pleasure." When I finished this sentence I serenely looked up to the heavens, while tilting my head to the right, and put my hands together in the prayer position. My mom snorted out a laugh upon hearing this, my kids laughed more, *Angela* even chuckled despite looking like she wanted alcohol already, since she was trapped with her in-laws for Christmas in a sub-arctic community, and Marilee...Marilee was less impressed.

"You're a fucking nimrod!" she said. My mom gasped.

"She said *ROD*! She said *rod* Dad! Ha ha haaaaaaa!" Alex cried out with glee and laughed. At age nine, he was already devoted to finding innuendo in every sentence or word he heard.

Owen laughed too, but with no idea *why* he was laughing other than he saw his big brother laughing.

"She also said *fuck*," Owen said in a hushed voice, covering his mouth with his hand.

"Well, Aunty likes to say *fuck* during grace pal," I said, winding Marilee up some more.

"Oh please stop talking like this in front of them," my mom said.

"It wasn't *during* grace it was *after* fucking grace. Can we just eat now?" Marilee said.

"That would be nice," my Mom said.

I saw Angela put Baileys in her Coffee. In-law insanity or not, it was Christmas morning—I couldn't blame her.

"I'm not sure I can eat now. All this talk about fucking has made me lose my appetite. And, also made me..." I purposely did not finish the sentence.

"WHAT? Made you what?!!" Marilee demanded.

"Horny."

"Pig!" Marilee said.

"Did this bacon come from a pig Dad?" Owen asked innocently, and Marilee scoffed some more in annoyance.

"It sure did buddy. Good Job. Let's just eat it OK," I said.

"Thank you," my mom said.

"Idiot," Marilee said.

We ate then, and the peacefulness of Christmas finally set in while we filled our bellies and listened to the Christmas music Mom had playing. Something surprised me though. My sorrow from the real world was indeed drifting away, and my soul was healing every second I looked at my kids in this coma jump, but I also felt love—*or something*—coming from Angela. This feeling was not only foreign because we hadn't spoken or seen each other since the boys died, but also because we were already having problems when we had this Christmas dinner for real.

"Jean, this was an amazing meal," Angela said to my mother, "what do you call this breakfast dish?"

"Well, I'm not sure," my mother answered.

"Oh, well do you think I could have the recipe?"

"I'm not sure I know where it is, hmm," my mother said.

I could tell she was lying, and Angela likely could too, but she didn't say anything.

"Right," Angela said, "well boys, thank Grandma for breakfast and then go get your church clothes on right away. Mom and Dad will help Grandma with the dishes."

"Ahhhhhh," both boys whined, presumably because they had to go to Christmas morning Mass instead of playing with all the presents they just received.

"I'll help them get ready faster," I said, which sounded like an attempt to avoid the dishes, but in reality, I just wanted to spend more time with them. Angela rolled her eyes and scoffed because I was leaving her alone in the kitchen with her crazy sister-in-law, a mother-in-law who never thought she was good enough, and because the boys were old enough to get dressed on their own.

"Sean, just help me do these dishes pleas––" Angela was cut off like someone hit a mute button on life, and everything was black. I was scared, for an instant, the same way you're scared when you accidentally come across a person sleeping in an unusual place—thinking they might be dead—only to find out they're alive, but I soon realized this was nothing more than my coma jump hour ending. I felt the spinning somersault sensation, and then saw rays of light as my vision came back.

"How ya doin' Sean?" Myah asked in a sweet voice, sounding more like a receptionist at a massage parlor than a scientist working for the greatest company in the world.

"FINE," I said impatiently, but I felt even more disorientated than usual, "just put me back in dammit!"

"Excuse me?" Myah asked, although, I'm sure she heard me.

"Just put me back in where I left off."

"What date and time do you want Sean?"

"Jesus, just follow the last one!" I said. "Same date and 9 am."

"You just did 9am. Do you mean *10*, am?"

"Yes, yes, December 25th, 2013, 10am!" I screamed—I wish I could say I yelled, but no, much like the scene in *Deliverance*, minus the raping and Burt Reynolds skewering the rapist with an arrow, I was closer to *squealing* in my desperation to continue and get back to my family.

"Very well, just relax, and don't forget your exit phrase," Myah reminded me again.

I noticed that she didn't release the harnesses on my chair, and none of the apparatus had been recoiled or shutdown in anyway—she *knew* I would want to do another coma jump. Whether this was because she saw the situation I was in as a result of spying on my coma jump, despite company assurances to contrary—"Time Dream does not spy on coma jumps!"—or because I fit the model of addictive behaviour, I didn't know. I decided to relax and be more patient and thennnn, I felt it. FAWWWWWWWK—I had pissed my pants. *Again.* I looked down and, also again, it appeared as if my water had broke before giving birth to the Dionne quintuplets. Fuck it, what's the difference I figured, at least it was the same Time Dream employee seeing this.

"Oooooh, that has to be a record," Myah said overly enthusiastically and joyfully pointed out my mess. "The safety sensor really doesn't block the real world from what's happening in *your* coma jumps does it? No one in Time Dream history has had repeat interactions with the outside world. The only thing that is supposed to be the same is time passing, as you know, where sixty minutes in a coma jump is sixty minutes in the real world."

"Right," I said, "but I didn't even go pee in the coma jump!" I complained. *"Repeat interactions.* Fuck sakes! Is there any way—"

"Just relax Sean," Myah cut me off, and I can't say I blame her, "I'm initiating the coma jump, 3....2....1...."

A few seconds passed, everything went dark, and I felt like I was somersaulting again, and then, just like that, I was back in my Mom's house for Christmas morning of 2013.

And so it went the rest of the day—I kept getting Myah to put me back in at the end of each coma jump. I didn't eat between jumps, I didn't drink. I did go to the washroom, twice apparently to Myah's satisfaction, without getting out of the coma jump chair. The highlight, other than being with my family, was coma jumping directly into the shower, without expecting it, and screaming.

The low point for me was when I realized that the coma jumps never left off from the last coma jump, and hearing Myah explain that I wasn't entitled to free coma jumps beyond one hour, or any twenty-four hour / overnight Time Dream packages, as per the research contract I signed. This meant, for today anyway, each time I started my one-hour coma jump nothing from the previous coma jump had happened, unless it actually happened back in Christmas 2013. Eight coma jumps later I heard Myah's voice, while enduring what felt like the biggest headache of my life, which made her sound like she was on the other end of a manhole.

"Well Sean, that's your ninth coma jump in a row, *and* it's getting close to eight o'clock. I think that's it for today, since we close at nine pm, and you don't have any overnight coma jumps purchased," Myah said.

"NO!" I said reflexively, and then softened my voice, realizing it might get me further to be polite. "I, I ah, I'll purchase one now."

"Mr. Riley it's not a matter of money at this hour. You can't purchase overnight, twenty-four hour or longer coma jumps this late in the day."

"Another standard operating procedure?" I asked sarcastically.

"That, and availability. All coma jumps must be supervised with a doctor present, and only four doctors are available because we only allow four overnight coma jumps at this location. We're booked solid tonight."

"Let me do the last hour then. It was right before bedtimes with my two kids on Christmas Day. My two kids that died a few years ago. I just wanted to tuck them in and do a puppet show for their bedtime story." I had tears in my eyes and recognised that Myah likely saw me as a half-starved man, soaked in his own urine, sobbing in front of her, but I begged her because I had to see them again. "Please Doc, let me go back in for one more. I need the closure." These words could not have been more truthful while still being an absolute lie. I was indeed desperate but had no intention of making this the last coma jump I ever did with my kids. Luckily, Myah was not a parent, so there was a chance my obvious air of desperate deceit fooled her, or more likely, she knew exactly what was going on and felt sorry for me.

"All right," she said simply, and out of character—maybe she was human after all.

"Thank you, Myah," I said with all my strength and focus put into looking her in the eye, to show her how eternally grateful I was.

She blushed, looked down, and even appeared shy and less confident. "I like it when you use my first name. Can we stick with *Sean* and *Myah* from here on in? I mean, generally, seeing a man pee himself twice in one afternoon should mean I'm more acquainted with him than if we were sleeping together!" she said and winked.

"*Sleeping together*? What-a-ya think *tomorrow's* coma jumps will be about Doc?"

"Myah!"

"Yes, Myah it is, sorry!"

"Let's get you back to your kids," she said, and smiled again, this time as big as an upside down rainbow.

"Can we make it 9pm on that same Christmas Day?" I asked, giving an educated guess on when the kids would be going to bed on a holiday.

"Sure."

I felt relieved as Myah started working the controls to start me on one final coma jump for the day. Mostly because I was getting my way, but also because I felt something else too, that I had forgotten, or thought I would never feel again —something I'd buried way deep down. I liked her. I *like liked* her. I laughed to myself, momentarily thinking of Sandra Bullock taunting her co-worker in *Miss Congeniality* by singing, "*You want to kisssss me... You want to huggggg me... You want to lovvvveeee me...*" Then a few more minutes passed, and I heard Myah's familiar encouragement before I coma jumped.

"Good Luck Sean!"

"Thank y––" I was cut off by the darkness, by the spinning, by the pure quiet, and then, I heard a funny sound: A mild gyrating, vibrating, rotating type sound which could only be an electric toothbrush, or, something *very* different I'm quite sure I would've remembered from a Christmas day at my *mother's* house. When I opened my eyes, I was in my mother's green upstairs bathroom, supervising my two sons brushing their teeth.

"Da-*aaaad*, Alex is saying dirty things!" Owen said while struggling to talk with a mouth full of toothpaste.

"*What*?" I asked, trying to catch up.

"Am not!" Alex screamed.

"Yes you are—you're being a pornist!" Owen bellowed.

"A *what*?" I asked.

"A pornist!" Owen repeated, and then both of them forgot their fight and started giggling. I knew, at five, Owen was misusing the word, and was trying to say Alex was being a perve or something to that effect, but, incidentally, pornist *is* actually a word and *Urban Dictionary* defines it as: "A person who is racist about the origin of the man and or woman in a porn video or against a type of porn..."

"Pornist *ehhh*?" I said with a villain type voice—a DC comics villain, I *am* more of a Marvel comics guy, but DC has better villains—while noticing my wife Angela was listening to us, before I continued on. "Pornist makes me think of Ernest, as in the only way *Ernest Saves Christmas* could be funnier is if it was called, *Pornist Saves Christmas*." The boys giggled loudly on purpose, not fully understanding what I'd said, but both wanting to appear grown up, and I thought maybe I heard Angela snicker in the background as well.

"Who's *Ernest* Dad?!" Owen asked loudly.

"Who's *Ernest*?" I asked rhetorically with a loud voice. "Who's ERNEST!? He's one of the greats bud! He had one of the most memorable movie scenes of all time in Ernest Saves Christmas: He's flying Santa's sleigh through the air at about a million miles per hour going straight down, plummeting to-wards earth with no stop in sight, the audience is thinking everyone is going to die, Ernest is thinking he's going to die, and yell's for dear life, 'AHHHHHHHHH', and then you hear *ERR-RRCCCCCHHH*—the sleigh stops right in mid-air! Then Ernest looks left to the audience, while the camera is zoomed in on his face, and says, 'Airrr brakes, *a-he-he-he-he*' in the patented Ernest laugh."

"Why's he driving Santa's sleigh?" Owen asked, lean-ing closer towards me like Johnnie Cochran. Then his eyes squinted, and nose wrinkled, while still smiling and tilting his head slightly, like he did when he was trying to squeeze the truth out of you. I recalled Owen making this same *squeezing* face during potty training.

"Well, he––"

"And where's Santa?" Alex cut me off with another ques-tion.

"Yah, Santa isn't going to let a dumb ass steal his sleigh Dad," Owen counselled, putting me in my place.

"Language!" I scolded. "OK, OK, maybe you guys are right. Time for bed now," I said.

"Sleep with?" Owen asked. To explain, a *sleep with* in our house meant three things: To Owen, it usually meant I laid with him on his bunk bed and did a puppet show where I always used the *Sonic the Hedge Hog* stuffed animal, no matter what, or Owen lost his mind. Owen, on the other hand, used a new stuffed ani-mal for each puppet show.

To Alex, a sleep with meant I laid with him on his bed and made up a bedtime story, or read him a story, despite him easily reading books on his own at this age—*nine*.

For me, a sleep with meant an extra fifteen minutes with each kid before they went to sleep. I never let the boys know it, but sometimes the sleep with used to drive me crazy, but, in reality, now that they're gone from my life in the real world, it's almost impossible for me to go to sleep without the routine of the nightly puppet show and story.

Even when the boys were alive I couldn't function properly if I missed putting them to bed. I worked late too often, and they'd be asleep by the time I got home. I felt so devastated that I didn't get to see them—or tell them that seeing them was the best part of my day. So, after they died, nighttime destroyed me the most. Each day, before I'd go to bed, I'd hear them in my head, running around trying to take as long as possible to get ready, and then begging me for a sleep with. But I wasn't missing one that night—thanks to Time Dream.

"Absolutely buddy!" I happily answered.

"For *both* of us?!" Alex asked.

"Of course," I said.

"Me first!" Owen said.

I went into Owen's bedroom and before I took a second step he commanded me to use Sonic the Hedgehog for his puppet show. I teased him a bit saying Sonic had laryngitis, so he would be more like Charlie Chaplain because he couldn't talk. Owen confidently ignored me, knowing his Dad too well, and then looked at me like he was waiting, which was my queue to ask him how we would proceed.

"OK, do you wanna choose what the puppet show will be about, or do you want Daddy to choose?"

"You choose!" Owen answered quickly—he let me make up the story 99.9% of the time.

"OK, and do you wanna know what it will be about in advance, or do you want Dad to surprise you?"

"Surprise!" Owen yelled out, and for the most part he did always want a surprise, but at the same time, he expected some static reoccurring events to happen in the puppet show that could not be left out. Like some of the prayers my diehard Catholic mother had drilled into my brain, I instantly remembered these reoccurring puppet show events the same way you would a locker combination—as soon as you started to open the lock it all came back.

"Ok pal, you got it. Here we go! Sonic was snoring loudly one morning," as I said this I held the Sonic stuffed animal up in the air horizontally, like he was sleeping, and made an abrasive, loud, startling, grunt-like, rhinoceros meets gargoyle snore as I inhaled, then exhaled in a high, squeaky, Pinocchio breath.

Owen laughed with glee—the best sound in the world, the sound I missed the most—and I heard Alex laugh all the way from the room he was in, across the hall. Owen protested a bit about Alex not being allowed to listen to his puppet show.

But I continued on, "Sonic kept snoring," and I made a few more of the insane snore sounds, and then, "*Grrrr-ahhhhh— ssssppplatttfarrrrt!!*" I imitated the same growly inhaling snore, then the high-pitched exhale, but with the sound of a wet fart at the end. "Sonic woke himself up with a high powered projectile shart that sprayed all over his brother, waking him up! His brother screamed in horror and disgust, 'ahhhhhhh'—which brought Sonic's mother running into the room yelling hysterically, but Sonic was still spraying poo as she came in," and I made more fart sounds for about five seconds before continuing, as Owen started hyperventilating while laughing at his favourite part of any story or puppet show. "Then Sonic's *dad* came in and *he* got hit with Sonic's poo fart like it was coming out of a firehose!" I made a wet fart sound for *ten* seconds this time.

Owen was gasping for air now, as he laughed, and said he was going to pee his pants, so I moved on.

"Anyway, after they cleaned up the mess Sonic and his family went down for breakfast. Sonic's mom looked angry, probably because of all the poo earlier, and asked Sonic what he wanted to eat. Sonic said, 'I want twenty-two pancakes, ten pounds of bacon, five jars of fruit, three glasses of milk and a BIG bowl of Cheerios please'. Sonic's mom said, 'That's ridiculous, you'll never eat all that,' so Sonic said, 'OK, OK, OK, I will have a piece of toast with PLAAAIIIINNNN butter on it'.

'Just toast?' Sonic's mom asked.

'Yes, I'm not hungry Mom,' Sonic said.

'*Whaaaatt*? Why did you ask for all that food then?!' Sonic's mom roared! Sonic jumped up, ran around the kitchen table two times and zoomed out the front door!" I made the zooming sound from the Sonic the Hedgehog video game to accentuate how quickly Sonic ran out of the house.

"Then, Sonic ran at the speed of light all the way to the zoo, where he was meeting his friend Shooter Bear." Owen had picked and was holding—for our puppet show—a white stuffed animal bear, about thirty-five cm in height, with a Star Wars Storm Trooper mask sewn into its head. I always thought this mask made the bear look like some kind of raccoon, but Owen called him Shooter Bear. "'How's it going Shooter?' Sonic asked."

"Aww-wight, how are you?" Owen responded politely in his Shooter Bear voice.

"'Pretty Good. It's prittayyyyy, prittayyyyy, prittayyyyy, pretty good,'" I answered as Sonic in my best Larry David from *Curb Your Enthusiasm* imitation. "Then Sonic reached up and tickled Shooter three times in each armpit and ran into the zoo with Shooter behind him. After they were out of breath, and stopped running, Sonic said, 'Shooter, these animals look very sad, I think we need to free them.'" Then I did Shooter's voice, which Owen was OK with, as long as I let him hold the stuffed animal while it talked, "'Wellll, I dunno if that's a good idea Sonic.' 'What?!' Sonic said, 'Look at them. They look very unhappy, I mean, they just look bored.'" Owen was looking at me with concern now, wondering what was gonna happen next, because he was a kid who thought rules were important, and I, as his father, always felt it was my job to teach him not all rules were important. "'OK OK OK,' Shooter said. 'Good,' Sonic said, 'there's only one way to pull this off: you need to go pull down the pants of that Zoo Keeper, and while the other zoo keeper runs over to help, I'll run right behind him with my super speed and pickpocket the master zoo key. The master zoo key will let us unlock every cage in the entire zoo!'"

"Da-*aaaaad*," Owen complained, "that's dangerous."

"Why?" I asked, then continued before Owen could answer, "'Oh no,' Sonic said after pulling the pants down, 'I think the zoo keeper is one of those guys who doesn't wear any underwear! Ahhhhhhhh!' Sonic and Shooter were so scared at the sight of the naked lower half of the zoo keeper they ran away with no key, a woman fainted, and even the Giraffe in a nearby cage held one of his front legs alllll the way up to cover his eyes in disgust."

"Da-*aadd*!" Owen complained but giggled. "What the!? Dad, can a giraffe do that?"

"Sure," I said with a wink, "and do you remember where the giraffe came from pal?"

"Of course Daddy, the giraffe was invented when Chuck Norris uppercutted a horse!" I heard my Mom snort in the background—evidently Grandma was listening to the puppet show as well.

"That's my boy!" I said, "Anyway, Sonic and Shooter ran around the zoo in horror for another fifteen minutes, stole all the candy from the zoo, fed all that candy to the animals, giving them extraordinary fart capabilities, and then both of them went home. THE END!"

I concluded abruptly—I did have more story to tell in my imagination tickle trunk, and could've gone on longer by involving PETA, and their hatred of zoos, in the puppet show's plot, but started to worry I wouldn't get to Alex before he fell asleep, or worse, my last one hour coma jump of the day might end before I saw him. "Night Night Owen, I love you," I said, and then sang his nickname, "Eeeeannnaaahhh-ooo-ooo-ahhhhh!" in my trademark, ridiculously on purpose, Curious George-like, high voice.

"Night night Daddy! I love you! Can I please have a drink of water?" Owen *always* asked for a drink of water at the last goodnight. I'm quite certain he couldn't go to sleep without the water. I got him some water, gave him the longest hug in the history of our bedtimes, and then went over to the other room to tuck in Alex.

He always pretended to be asleep, and then scared me by yelling loudly in the dark. Here in the coma jump, he did make my heart stop, but not because he scared me, but because I thought he was already asleep and I wouldn't get to talk to him. When I realized he was tricking me, I gave him a big hug and then laid down next to him.

"Dad, can I have a story?" he asked.

"Sure buddy, what kind of story?"

"I don't know, anything. Maybe a real one from when you were younger?"

"How young? You mean like when Grandma used to breastfeed me?"

"Sean!" I heard my mother gasp.

"Whattt!?" Alex half laughed and half shrieked. "Ahh gross Dad, come on."

"Ok buddy, I have one." I thought of about a hundred examples where I got myself into trouble as a kid, but picked a very important moment from my past to tell Alex, partly for him, and partly because I knew my Mother was listening in the hallway.

"Are you ready?"

"Mmm-hmmm," he answered happily.

"Well, when Daddy went into grade twelve in the Northwest Territories, the school hired a new principal. The principal was not from Hay River, he came from southern Alberta. To say he was mean would be like saying Lex Luthor was mean—he wasn't just mean, he seemed to genuinely hate people. I never did find out why he was so angry at the world, but thinking about it now, maybe it was because he moved to a new town and had no family or friends. Anyway, I shouldn't tell you this, but grade twelve is the one year that your grades really count, because they determine what universities you get into.

"So, because grade twelve marks mattered for once, and

because that year I tore my hip flexor in the spring before grade twelve, and couldn't play any sports for two years, I worked really hard and made sure not to get into any trouble at school, which, was unusual for me! The new principal even brought Dad into the office in the first week of grade twelve just to warn me to behave, because I was on the list of mischievous kids, but I explained to the principal that I would be on my best behaviour since it was grade twelve."

"What was the principal's name Dad?" Alex looked worried, already factoring in he could conceivably get the same principal, if we ever moved to Hay River from Calgary, which was an idea I contemplated from time to time.

"Haha, don't worry buddy, he's gone now, but his name was Mr. Whitehand. And things went really well for the first three months of grade twelve for me. I worked really hard and Mr. Whitehand and I never had reason to talk or see each other much. Then, something bad happened in December—kind of bad luck in a way. As Christmas neared, the high school, which is completely purple on the outside by the way, put up about 3000 little mini halogen Christmas lights all around the concourse of the school—including the railings going up the stairs and the railings that were on the second floor overlooking the concourse and lunch area. These lights were very breakable, and a lot of kids thought it was really fun to pick them up, and throw them, or drop them from the second floor to see them burst and splatter across the concourse floor.

"This happened so often that Mr. Whitehand became furious and called an assembly to explain that if ANYONE was caught breaking the Christmas lights again, he would expel them. That means you would be kicked out of the school and not allowed to come back, ever, or at least for a year. Now, this might not seem like the worst thing in a city like Calgary pal, but here in Hay River we only had one high school—so getting kicked out would cause a very serious problem for any student and their family. And any other high schools are in towns a couple hundred kilometres away!

"Mr. Whitehand even sent a note home, with every student in the school, again explaining to parents that any student caught breaking these lights would be expelled. Sure enough, about two weeks later, four kids were kicked out of school for breaking lights on separate occasions. I think a lot of people figured Mr. Whitehand was using the threat of being expelled as a scare tactic, and didn't think he would really kick anyone out of the school—BUT HE DID! And, despite a lot of complaining and threatening from parents, there wasn't anything anyone could do about it.

"Amazingly, a few kids I knew were still throwing the lights, but had evaded being caught by any teacher or Mr. Whitehand. I thought they were nuts. Then one day, after homeroom, I was walking to the gym with my homeroom teacher. We said goodbye to each other, as he was off to teach in a classroom, and I was heading to the gym to shoot some hoops. We were about thirty metres from each other when I looked up, and saw one of my buddy's younger brothers, Tyler, grab three lights off the railing, and then fire them down onto the concourse! They exploded right in front of a girl that a lot of people picked on. By some miracle, the lights didn't hit her or hurt her, but she was so scared that she was shaking afterwards.

"I wasn't thinking too far ahead, about what might happen, and instinctively ran up the stairs—as best I could on my bad hip—and gave Tyler a lecture about *how stupid that was, imagine if you got caught*, and *what were you thinking*? Then I told him to take off as fast as he could, even though there were no teachers around to have seen what happened, just to be safe. I walked back down a different set of stairs, that were closer to the gym, and just as I grabbed the handle of the door to the gym, I felt a strong, powerful, *adult* hand on my shoulder. It was my homeroom teacher, and not far behind him, running towards us, was Principal Whitehand. 'Who did it?' my homeroom teacher asked. I told him I had no idea. He said he saw me run up the stairs and that he was positive I knew who threw the lights and, by now, Mr. Whitehand had joined us and *demanded* I tell him who it was. I claimed there was no one up there, when I ran up the stairs, and was not wearing my glasses so I couldn't see who it was at any point. In reality though, I was wearing my contact lenses, but they didn't know that."

"But Dad, you *did* see who it was. Why didn't you tell them?"

"Well, if it was a different situation, I might have—but they weren't just asking me who had thrown the lights. They were asking me who would be the next student to be expelled! And...Tyler was the younger brother of my friend."

"Did you get in trouble then?"

"Yes, unfortunately both my homeroom teacher and Mr. Whitehand knew I was lying. They knew I could identify who had thrown the lights. Mr. Whitehand said that until I told him who it was he would put me in something called in-school suspension. This meant that I still had to come to school, but I didn't get to go to any of my classes. Instead, I had to sit at a desk near the main office and entrance to the building—so everyone could see that I was in trouble. I had to sit there for six hours each day, with no books, paper, nothing. I was really worried about my marks. It was very easy to fall behind in grade twelve —the only subjects I found easy were Social Studies and Gym. They didn't have a computer class yet otherwise I would've been good at that. By end of day Thursday of that first week I was four whole days behind!"

"What did Grandma and Grandpa do when they found out Daddy?" Alex asked.

This felt surreal—I was telling a life learning lesson type of story to my son who wasn't alive anymore, but in that moment he was. Watching his every expression, his eyes, and holding him next to me, were all things I thought I would never experience again.

"Funny you should ask that! I hadn't told them yet what had happened, which was probably a mistake. But, by the fourth day, I had run out of lies so I confessed to them what was going on at school. You see, whenever I came home from school, your grandpa would ask me about how my day went: What subjects did I have? What was difficult? Who got in a fight? When was my next test? Stuff like that. And, by doing so, Grandpa was able to learn things about what was going on in my life that he wouldn't normally know about. And after four days of me making up what was going on in school, Grandpa figured out what was going on and made me confess."

"Did you get grounded Daddy!?" Alex's keen interest was now rivalling Curious George, and I felt like quitting the story and hugging him for the remainder of my coma jump, but instead, I carried on telling my story like Robert Munsch would to a group of kids hanging on his every word—vigor, expression, wild eyes and all.

"I was sure my mom and dad were going to punish me, and be furious, because this was grade twelve and pretty serious. They didn't punish me. Instead, they said they were disappointed I hadn't told them what happened sooner. Then, to my surprise, my mom went down to the school and lectured Principle Whitehand. She gave him a real earful that would scare the bejesus out of anyone."

My mother taught school for forty years, so she knew a thing or two about teaching!

"She told Mr. Whitehand that she didn't know if it was right or wrong for me to keep quiet and not tell him who the culprit was, but that she was positive it *was* wrong for him to punish me for not ratting out another student, knowing the other student would be expelled for it."

Alex looked satisfied at first, but then a little puzzled. "Well, *should you* have told Mr. Whitehand who broke the glass Daddy?"

"I'm not sure pal. I'm really not. I just know I couldn't say who it was at the time, I, I just couldn't. What would you have done buddy?"

"I guess maybe I wouldn't want my friend to get in trouble, but, if, if he was a jerk maybe I would tell on him!"

We both laughed.

"Well, maybe you're right," I said. "The boy, Tyler, who I didn't rat out, ended up in jail a few years later because he kept getting in more and more trouble. Who knows, maybe if I had told on him his parents would've sent him away to a new school, and he would've got a fresh start. Maybe he would've been better off if I told on him."

"*Dad*?"

"Yah pal?"

"I think you didn't tell on him because you have a good heart. And you said I have a good heart too, because both you and Mommy have a good heart, and because Grandma and Grandpa have a good heart, so, I wouldn't tell on him either."

I felt the tears come to my eyes, and I wanted to say something, but all I could do was hug Alex and hope he didn't see I was crying. My sadness was so intense my whole throat and chest ached with pain, and felt like they would explode, as I started to sob.

"What's wrong Daddy? It's OK, don't cry," Alex consoled me. I wanted to explain I wasn't crying because of what he said, but because he wasn't really there. That he was dead, and I couldn't get him back. That I...I didn't want to live anymore, without him.

"Alex, I love yo––" My voice was cut off. Everything went black. I was spinning again. The coma jump was over, again. My heart sank, and I was lower than I had ever been since Owen and Alex's death. All I felt was a deep sadness. My initial gut feeling to avoid Time Dream, and Larry's advice to never go back, were proving to be heartbreakingly correct.

When I came out of the coma jump and opened my eyes, Myah didn't give me her usual end of coma jump greeting. It was quiet for a moment, and then, I heard it—she was crying. I knew with absolute certainty then that she'd monitored my coma jump on the tablet at the console, behind the glass. I also knew with absolute certainty I didn't care. Nor did I care anymore about the ethical lines Time Dream was crossing to make the coma jump experience happen. I got up quickly when the restraints came off, and attempted to leave while ignoring Myah, and just walk out, but she moved in front of me to block my path, while looking at the ground.

"Sean, I, I think you need to see—"

"I gotta go," I said, realizing that I was crying too.

"Sean, I have a card for you. You can phone him to tal—"

"*Him*...as in a shrink?"

"Yes."

"What is he, on the Time Dream payroll? Do you give these out to all your customers?! You guys gotta make even *more* money?!"

"Sean no, it's my brother, and he has nothing to do with Time Dream. I'll call him, and it would be free."

"Thanks, but I don't need a shrink, I need my kids to be alive." I walked past her and left the room.

I drove home and found a three-quarter full bottle of vodka in the cupboard behind the peanut butter. I drank it all, effectively erasing any thought in my head, including memories of my kids, and passed out on the floor three feet from what was once my son Alex's bed.

CHAPTER 9 – DAVEY SANDHU: THE MAN BEHIND THE MACHINE

I woke up in Alex's bed Wednesday morning—while in the midst of a dream involving whirlpools and strobe lights somewhere in the grotto at the Playboy Mansion—to the theme song of the A-Team, and realized making a ring tone of eighties music and machine guns, for each of Anand's calls, was ill advised when you were hungover. Although, in the sleepy drooling seconds before I answered the phone, it did briefly remind me of a simpler time when I was a kid, where, in each weekly episode, The A-Team are holed up in a barn and manage to create a makeshift tank out of a couple bales of hay and some wood.

I slowly came to and swatted at my ringing phone, knocking it to the floor, so I leaned, reached, and contorted my upper body down to the ground, to grab it, while still keeping my legs balanced in Alex's old bed.

"Hey budddddaaayyyyyy!" Anand shrieked on the other end of the phone.

"What the fuck man? What time is it?" I groggily and grumpily asked.

"It's presently 7:02 in the AM," Anand said, "you at work yet?"

"I'm off this week! Remember?"

"Ohhh yahhhhhhh, I forgot."

"No you didn't. Fuck you."

"You're right, I didn't, but I have a job for you," Anand said, with way too much enthusiasm for 7:02 AM.

"I have a job."

"Not for long, and this pays good money for a half day's work."

"Towel boy at a Turkish bath house?"

"No."

"Towel boy at your house?"

"Also no."

"Well, what am I, a swami—no offense—what is it then?"

"Why would I be offended by you saying *swami*? Cause I'm a brown guy?" Anand was messing with me.

"What's the FUCKING job man?! I'm tired, hungover and doing a one-armed handstand off the side of the bed!"

"Handstand? That's good. You workin' out again?"

"God dammit, ya Russell Peters wannabe, quit fuckin around dude."

"All right, all right, here it is: I'm interviewing Davey Sandhu, founder of Time Dream, and a few other Time Dream execs at their downtown location this morning! All of them are in town. Aaaaand, RMN says I can hire a technical advisor."

"I hope you don't mean me," I complained, but in reality, I was already thinking about doing it.

"Of course I mean you." Anand sounded dejected, and obviously didn't know he'd hooked me already. That, or he was worried about me being depressed again.

"That's amazing—I'd rather be the towel boy...at the bath house, not your house," I said, continuing my act. "What time is the interview at?"

"8am."

"Ahhh for fuck sakes Anand, I'll never make it." Now I actually didn't want to go for real.

"It pays two grand an hour."

"I'll see you at the front entrance at 7:55," I said, then paused for three seconds and hung up the phone.

I jumped out—*err, fell out*—of bed from my handstand, and then showered, shaved and got dressed faster than I could if I had fifteen Oompa Loompas doing it for me. I kept moving fast and was on pace to make it on time, assuming traffic was not too ridiculous, until I caught a glimpse of myself in the mirror and realized the last time I wore a suit was when my sons were buried.

Nobody saw me at the funeral because I stood far away and watched everyone from behind the trees at the graveyard. I stayed long after people left. Long enough to see the patiently waiting City of Calgary workers pour dirt into the hole on top of my sons with a miniature backhoe.

I let out a carnal savage-like roar—which I could do living alone—to snap myself out of this memory, drank a protein shake that tasted like the shoe from one of the City of Calgary employee grave diggers, fixed my tie, and then jumped into my '70 LeSabre and gave an excellent contribution to pollution, global warming, and a few noise bylaws on the way to the sky train station. I caught the downtown train and squeezed myself into the train car like a sardine for the ten-minute ride. I sprinted two blocks to the front entrance of the Time Dream Calgary headquarters, which was *The Bow* building once owned by Cenovus when oil and gas was still thriving.

Anand was pacing nervously out front.

"7:55 on the dot! You made it." Anand laughed and shook his head. "That has to be some kind of record."

"Look man, I was in a rush, so I didn't think about this, but aren't they going to be expecting your technical advisor to be someone—" I paused.

"Someone *what*? We've got to get up there man, we're down to four minutes left," Anand complained, looking more annoyed than nervous.

"Well, like a *real* technical advisor. Some kind of doctor, or scientist, or a guy with a neuroscience degree—someone like that."

"Sean, you *are* a scientist."

"No, I'm a cybersecurity minion for the RCMP," I corrected him.

"OK, you're a *computer* scientist working for the RCMP, and that's all they need to know. Besides, it might be fun to fuck with them by indicating that you're law enforcement."

"But I'm *not* law enforcement, I *work* for law enforcement."

"Semantics! Jesus, you usually love fucking around and giving people false identities buddy. I mean—just—act like you always do."

Anand was my best friend for a reason. His last sentence totally changed the dynamic of the meeting for me and instantly refueled my bullshit tank. "OK," I said and then gave him my best *Crocodile Dundee* smile.

"Let's get in there—and Sean," Anand glared at me as we walked towards the Time Dream Calgary headquarter entrance, "don't be fucking with them too much. I meant *fucking around* as in, you know, to play the part of my technical advisor."

"No worries," I said, "I'll keep the penis jokes to a baker's dozen."

"Great," Anand sighed and rolled his eyes, "OK, let's go in."

When we entered the huge well-lit lobby, I heard the familiar Time Dream male computer voice come over the intercom, *"Anand Dhami and Sean Riley, welcome to Time Dream."*

The voice reminded me I needed to get some fake IDs, so I could hear their intercom and front desk personnel say something other than my name—assuming the sensors were reading the cards in our wallets that is. It occurred to me they could be detecting who we were based on all kinds of facial recognition and other biometrics. Hell, they could probably use their coma jump system to read your mind on the way in.

I stopped day dreaming and moved closer to Anand as we headed for the receptionist, but just as we were about to say hello a man stepped in front of us, extending his arm to shake hands with Anand. He was thin, about 5'8, had greasy dark brown hair and was wearing a fancy light grey suit with a bow tie. If it wasn't for the thick blue rimmed glasses, with what appeared to be diamonds on the arms of the glasses, I would've sworn I was looking Pee-Wee Herman dead in the eye.

I've had a lot of run-ins with folks who look like celebrities. One morning, in my early twenties, while I was walking through the parking lot in front of my office, I saw a child in a full body snowsuit walking in front of me. I paid attention because he seemed awfully small to be on his own. It was that time of year when full on winter hadn't taken over yet, where mud puddles were frozen but *looked* like a thin layer of *unfrozen* water—one of Mother Nature's perfect traps to slip and fall on. Sure enough, the little guy stepped on the ice and fell head over heels, landing on his neck and head. It was a heart stopping fall that, unless you were a complete fucking bastard, instantly removed all social boundaries and had me running over to help. I reached down, while he was very slowly trying to push himself up to his hands and knees, and gripped the shoulder portion of his snowsuit to pull him up. The second I did, he spun around and violently smacked my hand away, growling like a Rottweiler, and before my eyes, I saw no child at all, but a midget that looked exactly like Burt Reynolds—in the face that is, I mean, it was like a cloned smaller identical version of Burt. I said, "Sorry," reflexively, and in fear, and then *Little Burt* ran off like a wild boar.

"Mr. Dhami, my name is Spike Maxwell—it's a pleasure to meet you. I'll take you right up," the Pee-Wee looking guy said and shook Anand's hand.

"Hi Spike, thank you. This is my technical advisor, Sean––"

"Riley," Spike interrupted to finish my name for Anand, "Nice to meet you Sean." We shook hands.

"It's great to meet you Max," I said incorrectly on purpose, and watched Anand shoot me a look of impatience.

"It's Spike, and my last name is Maxwell." Spike looked agitated, almost constipated I would say, which is what I was going for.

"Ahh, right, right—sorry. Great name by the way, almost like the name of a guy who directs pornos for a living."

"*Excuse me?*" Spike looked at me incredulously, and forced a nervous laugh out, while Anand looked like he was regretting his decision to bring me along already.

"Sorry no, well, maybe it's *not* a porn director's name, but Spike Maxwell is at least a name you'd see during the credits of a porno. Maybe listed as a producer or head writer or something," I explained, "Except for, well, who watches all the way to the credits in a porno anyway?! HA HAAAA," I trailed off my sentence with a loud, fake, forced laugh.

"I wouldn't know, I—"

"Just ignore him Max, shall we go up?" Anand interjected, obviously flustered, as he got Spike's name wrong while trying to keep me in check.

"It's Spike, my last name is Maxwell," Spike said again, and now I thought he really did look constipated.

"Yes! Fuck—ah, sorry, excuse my language. Christ sakes, OK, let's go up," Anand said, and as Spike turned towards one of the many elevators, Anand turned to me and whispered, but I'm sure everyone in the lobby could hear him, "Dude, shut...*the fuck*...UP! Stop fuckin around!"

"Hey, you brought *me*," I whispered back.

"God damn it!" Anand said, as we stepped into the elevator.

"Calm down, calm down, I'm just kidding man—I hear ya, don't worry. We're good," I whispered.

"If you say *All Good* I'm gonna pop you—Christ," Anand loosely threatened, starting out with a whisper again, but then almost yelling at the end of his sentence. He sighed and wiped some sweat from his brow with a handkerchief that appeared to be eerily close to the same colour pattern as Spike's bow tie. I took a quick look at Spike, as a health check, to make sure it *wasn't* his bow tie—Anand was pretty cool under pressure, but when he did lose his temper every five years or so, it didn't take long to realize he was an ex power lifter; almost taller sideways than he was standing up.

The elevator doors closed, and we were whisked upwards. As we flew towards the top of the building like a bullet, I ignored the urge to point out elevator music sounded like porno music, because Anand was already upset with my earlier comments, and because Time Dream didn't have the usual elevator porno music—assholes, this was like having no pews in a church—it actually sounded like that radio station where they only played the theme songs from sitcoms. *That,* or the theme song from *Dallas* was popular again.

The doors swung open and another man in a suit with a bow tie was there to greet us. He didn't look like Pee Wee Herman, he looked like a larger, taller and younger version of Pat Sajak.

"Mr. Dhami, I'm Chris Spolanksy, General Manager for Time Dream Canada, we spoke on the phone. It's great to meet you in person. I can take it from here Spike, thanks so much." Spike stayed in the elevator, and the door closed.

"It's great to meet you Chris," Anand said, as they shook hands, speaking more formally than I'd heard him speak before. "This is my technical advisor—Sean Riley."

"Hi therrrreee," I said like a talk show host.

"Hi," Chris said, smirking a bit, before continuing, "OK gents, let me take you into the boardroom where the rest of the team is waiting. Can I get you guys anything to drink?"

"We're fine," Anand answered for both of us—no doubt afraid where I might go with the drink question—as he glanced at the top floor receptionist to the left.

I stayed silent and followed Chris and Anand towards a glass walled boardroom. There was no knob or handle or even a door that I could see, but when Chris got close, the male robot voice broadcasted our three names, then made two repeating high pitched sounds, like you might hear when a large truck is backing up.

Then, the entire glass wall of the boardroom automatically opened, slowly, drawing itself into the ceiling, just like the glass wall between where you did coma jumps and the coma jump screening room. We walked in.

It wasn't world record big, but it was easily the coolest looking boardroom I had ever seen—especially when compared with the boring, mind numbing, militarily never changing RCMP boardrooms I was used to. There were usb ports and power outlets at every seating spot of the massive, plastic, translucent table, and a huge TV screen high up on the wall that went around the entire border of the room—above the windows and spot where we walked in—it even curved around the four corners. The ceiling had to be sixteen feet high, and when I looked up there I saw why, as a hologram materialized to show a live feed from outside the front entrance of the building. As for the people in the room—there were six, so with the three of us entering that made nine—I could see two things for sure: They wore suits worth more than a car, and none of them were Davey Sandhu, the *actual* founder of Time Dream.

"Mr. Dhami, it's great to finally meet you, I'm a huge fan of your writing," a tall man who looked like Don Draper said. He had risen from the head of the table and came around to shake our hands, so I figured he was in charge.

"Mr. Byrne, thank you for agreeing to do this," Anand said, "Time Dream has been nothing but supportive of RMN's series on your company."

"We're glad to help the Rocky Mountain News—and call me Eric, Anand, Mr. Byrne is my father's name!" I heard a few forced laughs from the other men around the table, who likely had the pleasure of kissing up to this guy for a living.

"And who might you be?" Eric asked, looking at me, which I found strange since the intercom said my name forty seconds ago. I was about to answer with a, "Pleased to meet you Eric Anand," to put a play on his words, but Anand answered before I could utter a syllable.

"This is Sean Riley, my technical advisor."

"Ahh, nice to meet you Sean," Eric said. No *mister* for me.

"Likewise, and please, call me Sean." Anand gave me another look of death, about the third one today already, and Eric Byrne did a double take at me while looking confused, then started to sit down with the rest of us and began talking again.

"Ahh well, it's great to see you face to face," Eric paused, and then looked a little frustrated and confused, again, "ahh—sorry, ahh—*Sean?*—*what* do you do exactly at Rocky Mountain News?"

"Sean doesn't work for RMN Eric, he's a technical consultant hired by us to—"

"I work for the RCMP," I said, cutting Anand off, and purposely leaving out any more details or background on myself, knowing it would make everyone in the room nervous—biggest company in the world or not. Heck, this was even suggested by Anand downstairs, so he couldn't get angry at me for this one. And, sure enough, I did see some worried looks—apparently these guys spent too much time doing equations to learn any IBM boardroom tactics or read any of Doyle Brunson's books on controlling your poker face.

"Sean," Anand said loudly, while looking at me, and then back at Eric, "is a cybersecurity analyst with the RCMP, and has over twenty years of experience working as a computer scientist."

Haa, computer scientist—I remembered when I met a girl at a party and she told me her father was a computer scientist. I was really impressed, thinking *wow*, that's a cool job, before I realized her dad just worked in I.T. like me and everyone else I knew in I.T. It was like a janitor saying he's a *custodial engineer*, or Vin Diesel saying he's an actor.

Eric introduced the rest of the suits, who, with the exception of Time Dream Canada GM Chris Spolanksy, were all vice presidents or directors flown in from the USA, including Eric, who I found out was the president of Time Dream—not just Time Dream Canada, but Time Dream worldwide—something anyone else in the universe besides me would know, and that I probably should've googled in advance of the meeting. There was a bit more chitchat, and then as we were about to get started, a late straggler came in who turned out to be the head of Legal for Time Dream Canada. All in all, a lot of fire power was brought in for just the two of us—I started humming the song *Just the two of us* nervously to myself....

"Well, I'd like to start the interview now," Anand said, and took out his cassette recorder, which caused eyebrows to go up in the room. This is why I loved my buddy—these guys had more money, power and technology than Darth Vader and Microsoft combined, and Anand pulls out some equipment most kids had lying under their bed in 1985.

"Sure, please just fire away Anand, and anything we don't know, we'll get back to you on," Eric said, "and, by the way, that's a great piece of tech you got there!"

I didn't like them teasing my friend, but decided they might have a point, so I quietly pressed record on my smartphone just in case.

Anand did the same on his cassette recorder, and then said, "First question: Where is Davey Sandhu? Why isn't the *founder* of Time Dream at an interview where you're finally gonna tell the world what Time Dream is all about? I mean, all due respect, Time Dream has been resistant to any media or questions since the beginning. Some would say aggressive, even."

Good, it looked like Anand was gonna quit kissing ass and bareknuckle these guys in the actual interview.

"Ahh, we'll get back to you on that," Eric said, he then did a deep belly laugh and so did the rest of the execs.

"Classic," one of the laughing execs said. His nametag read, 'Carl Evans', which made sense, because that was the kind of shit a guy named *Carl* would say.

"No seriously, why isn't he here?" Anand repeated, and didn't smile.

"Well, I'm sure you must know—from some of the media we *have* done recently—that Davey isn't involved with running the company anymore. He's a scientist and an inventor, but he lacked the sort of panache and vision Time Dream needed from its leadership to move us to the next level. His focus is on R & D and engineering, which is where Davey wanted to be, and where he belongs," Eric said, his voice staying flat the whole time.

This sounded like horseshit to me, because Eric's description of what Davey was lacking were the two most visible qualities Davey possessed, but I knew when to shut up and stay quiet —this was why RMN paid Anand the big bucks.

"Really, OK, well, what *I've* heard indicates that Davey was forced out of the boardroom, executive team, and any organizational decision making. Is that true?" Anand asked.

"That's completely false." Eric answered, "Also, I don't know why--"

"Next question," interrupted the head of legal for Time Dream Canada: Lucius Green.

"Fair enough, moving on," Anand said, "OK, so, *why* are you doing this interview? Time Dream is already the biggest and most profitable company on earth. Your competitor's efforts to replicate what Time Dream is doing have failed, and your customer can't stop coming back. Why have you agreed to tell the world more about Time Dream today?" Anand was an artist at this racket, and often came across as a mind reader when he did these sorts of interviews. He always asked the question the public wanted to hear an answer to.

"Ahh—you're too kind Sir," Eric said.

What an asshole, he perceived Anand's question and body language as if this was a compliment, or perhaps this president of the *company of all companies* was sneakier and more seasoned than anything I could comprehend. Keep in mind I worked with cops for a living where the most consistent, yet conflicting, qualities at large were loyalty and honesty, making most folks pretty transparent—my gut told me Eric Byrne was anything but.

"Anyway," Eric went on, "We are about to unveil some new services, here at Time Dream, that will change the world. Some will criticize these changes, like they did when we first opened, but we want to make a change for the better where

101

Time Dream is a transparent *partner* to all of humanity, and not just a company providing the greatest product of all time."

He was definitely smooth, and actually used the word *transparency*! And the statement about product couldn't have been a more obvious synonym for *addictive service* if he had said *addictive service*.

"Aaaaand, *this* is why you have agreed to tell the world more about Time Dream?" Anand asked semi sarcastically, yet thoughtfully, guiding Eric back to answering the question.

"Exactly," Eric said.

I scoffed quietly to myself, again, as this guy wasn't exactly Winston Churchill. That or the legal team advised him to use one-word answers wherever possible, which was another thing I knew well from working with police and spending more time in the principal's office as a kid than......the principal.

"Very good," Anand said, "By the way, I'm happy to hear from anyone else in the room on these questions guys. If you're *allowed* to answer, that is."

I recognized that he was hoping to provoke someone to speak out of turn. Clearly, he was fucking with these guys a bit to make them squirm. I knew more was coming and loved it. I would've done this for free no questions asked, yet I was not only getting paid $2000 an hour for sitting there, but was also getting my *suspended with pay* monies from the RCMP at the same time—shrewd. Perhaps I would be able to pay for more of the *greatest product of all time* after all.

"Everyone in here is free to speak on behalf of the company," Eric said and then glanced around the room as though to prove his point.

"OK, in that case Eric, *and* gentlemen who are allowed to speak freely, feel free to answer this: You mentioned the greatest product of all time, but some also believe it is the most *addictive* product of all time. People have stopped working, sold everything they have, and turned to crime so they can keep going to their nearest Time Dream location for another coma jump. I have a number of friends whose lives have been destroyed by your company."

"FYI," I cut in before Anand went further, "Anand is not my friend, I only came in today because I was told you guys would have donuts. But you don't," I paused, looking left and then right, "have donuts. Nothing actually. Not even a muffin or a croissant or some mints. 100 Trillion in profits and you guys can't have a dish of *Tic Tacs* on the table? Maybe you can put up a *picture* of a delicious continental breakfast on the hologram above us. I'm getting tired of looking at the sidewalk out front anyway."

Anand ignored this, and a few execs looked at me for less than a second before turning their gaze back to Anand, obviously feeling the effects of what Anand was saying to them. I felt stupid for interrupting, well, in this room, I was stupid. What's the rule in Poker? If you can't spot the sucker at the table in the first thirty minutes, then you *are* the sucker.

Anand continued, "One friend just lost his job and saw his wife and kids leave recently, and this is *mild* compared to the horrible stories we are hearing about all the time. And Time Dream, you keep turning in profitable record-breaking quarters, while the rest of the world deteriorates around you. You—"

"Is there a question coming?" Lucius cut in. *Lawyers...*

"Yes," Anand said, "is coma jumping dangerously addictive?"

"What is dangerous?" Eric shot back.

"OK, the president of the biggest company in the world doesn't know what dangerous is. Fine. IS IT ADDICTIVE?" Anand asked as loudly as one could get before it would be considered yelling.

Eric leaned in to listen to Lucius—who had wheeled his chair closer to Eric like some kind of attorney ninja—whisper in his ear. Nobody was smiling anymore.

"I don't think I can answer that," Eric responded, his voice flat again.

"Why not?" Anand asked.

"Because no one in here is qualified to speak to addiction

or what constitutes an addiction," Eric said with a face of confidence and feigned confusion.

"Rigggghtttt," Anand mocked like Dr. Evil, "OK, do you think Time Dream has reacted responsibly to the fallout from people doing anything to keep coming back to your locations—to do more coma jumps? Do you even care?"

"Stop recording, NOW," Lucius said.

I was taken aback by his abruptness and felt nervous. Not nervous like you have to give your first speech, but more like the barrel of a gun was pointing at you and there was no way to know if it was loaded.

Anand nodded and pressed stop on his tape recorder.

I left my phone recording, even though I was frightened.

"Erase that last question from your interview and move on to your next question." Lucius commanded again. He certainly wasn't asking—that's for sure.

"What about me, should I stop recording too?" I asked, holding up my phone. "Hmm, maybe I'll just upload this to Dropbox, OneDrive, Google Drive, ElephantDrive, Ashley Madison, Tinder, Grindr, Chatelaine—hell—maybe even AOL. Did you guys know over two million Americans still use AOL's *dial-up* service to get on the Internet? Dial-up! Coincidently, these are probably the same two million people who've never even been in a Time Dream location because they were poor to begin with. You do know what *poor* means, right?" As I said this I saw Eric smile, and before he said anything I knew why, right away. I looked down to see there was absolutely no signal in this room on my phone. It had less connectivity to the Internet than Anand's tape recorder.

"As a technical advisor, I'm surprised you didn't realize there's no connectivity in here," Eric taunted.

"Soooo—*what*? You're planning on illegally seizing my phone before we leave too? Along with Anand's companion to the Lite-Brite." I motioned towards Anand's tape recorder.

"Look, we don't need to seize anything," Lucius stepped in, "the contract RMN signed with us says we have final say, review, and veto authority before ANYTHING is published."

"It's fine Sean," Anand counseled me, while holding two hands up indicating I should stand down, but just before he turned his gaze away, he winked at me. "There's no issue gentlemen. Can we move on to the next question?"

"Absolutely," Eric said.

Anand hit record on his tape recorder again. "You mentioned some new services. What are they?" Anand asked. This less aggressive question seemed to put everyone at ease and calm things down, but I knew my friend, this was simply him throwing a few jabs before he wound up for another haymaker.

"We're not prepared to discuss these new services yet. However, as I mentioned, they're going to change the world and will be announced very soon." Eric said evenly, but not calmly anymore—the hull remained but Anand was chipping away.

"Hmm, interesting, interesting," Anand paused, and then launched a scud, outlining what he had told me on Monday, "I don't know if this ties into the new *service plan*, but I've heard rumours from lower level Time Dream employees, *your* employees, claiming that the company was originally funded by the US Government to research innovative solutions for population control and global over-crowding—which seems a far cry outside Time Dream's advertised scope of letting people relive the best moments of their lives in coma jumps. And—"

"And, once again, is there a question coming?" Lucius interrupted, looking more and more incensed. No one was at ease anymore.

"And, would you like to comment on these rumours?"

"I don't comment on rumours," Eric shot back.

"Well, I find rumours turn out to be true, sometimes, when they're as specific as this. So, let me ask you: Did you ever receive funding from the US Government? At any point?" Anand leaned in as he asked this.

Lucius whispered into Eric's ear again and both looked at the tablet in Eric's hand.

I was pretty sure it wasn't the latest Beyoncé video.

"Yes," Eric answered, with one word again.

"And what was the funding for?" Anand asked, not letting up.

"We're not required to answer, nor are we allowed to, as per the non-disclosure agreement we signed with them." Lucius said smugly.

"OK, who is *them*? Can you say which agency or part of the US Government it was?" Anand asked.

"We can't reveal that either," Lucius answered, like a broken record.

I'd had enough, and I figured Anand had too much to lose so he would likely comply with this censorship bullshit, but I had nothing to lose, and decided to piss on their rug a bit. "Chicken shits." I said loudly, without any anger, in a pretend high voice like Nelson from *The Simpsons*.

"Excuse me?" Eric said, exasperated.

"No, I don't think I will." I said quickly.

"Sean, don't––"

"What the fuck are you guys doing here?" I asked, ignoring Anand's attempt to interject. "It's like my friend is interviewing *The Borg*. From Star Trek that is, unfortunately. If Bjorn Borg was here maybe we could actually hear some good McEnroe stories. And if Johnny Mac was here he'd say you're a bunch of elitist, information withholding, jackasses, who aren't fit to carry Davey Sandhu's jockstrap, or his electron microscope, as it were. He's the guy who built this compa––"

"That's it," Eric cut in. "I'm sorry Anand, but if this interview is going to continue, Mr. Riley will have to wait outside." Then, the glass boardroom walls went up into the ceiling ten times faster than when we first arrived. "Also, I'll expect you to stay on this floor, seated right outside these walls in that chair," Eric said, looking back at me, and pointed at the chair closest to the elevator, "until security escorts you down later on, or with Anand when the interview is completed."

Eric looked annoyed, Lucius looked pissed, the other VPs looked way too much like sheep to be the brightest minds on earth, and, surprisingly, Anand didn't look angry at all, but had the same look he did when I got kicked out of the room in a university class we were in together a long time ago. At the time, Anand said he'd never heard of someone getting punted out of a college auditorium—high school yes, but not a poli-sci course. To the point, as I have mentioned Anand doing before, he just shook his head the way you shake your head and smile after someone close to you does something to show they aren't ever going to change, and you have to respect and love that kind of friend.

I left the boardroom, sat down in my special chair outside the room, and as soon as my ass had been in the seat mere seconds, the glass boardroom walls closed and became tinted so I couldn't see inside. I immediately regretted my wit-lacking comments, because Anand was on his own now. He would be fine in terms of the interview—it was Time Dream that should be worried there, not him—but I remembered my warning to Anand about how dangerous it would be to challenge this country-like organization, or write anything damaging about them.

Five minutes passed with me sitting there, then ten, then I read a *Chatelaine* magazine they had lying around on a table, and then......the impossible happened: A door opened on the other side of reception and in walked Davey Sandhu—inventor, mechanical engineer, psychologist, cognitive neuroscientist, possibly the wealthiest and smartest person in the world, and the founder and creator of Time Dream! I was stunned. I didn't know what was cooler, the fact I was seeing him in person or his *not of this universe* outfit: He had a white, yellow and black ship captain hat on with obviously still wet black hair; goggles, and not the small speedo goggles, but more like something a photographer from National Geographic would wear when he plunged underwater inside a shark cage—*which is also an accepted definition of marriage*; a white t-shirt with a picture of his face and three successively larger giant mosquitos, in sequence, diagonally to the right of his head, with the first one having its stinger in his temple, showing itself growing at an alarming rate from sucking Davey's infinite brain—I suppose; white rubber gloves; baggy banana-yellow snow pants with suspenders; and a pair of bright red ski boots—all in all it was like looking at some kind of Nordic-Sikh-mad scientist-Ronald McDonald-scuba diver.

I couldn't help but wonder if this was what a male stripper would wear at the beginning of a clown bachelor party. I watched him lean in close to the receptionist, smile, and whisper something that caused her to giggle hysterically, although I'm sure his appearance alone could've brought a smile to anyone's face. Davey ran his hands through his wet hair on the sides of his head, like he did on TV a million times before—when he was about to answer a tough question—and then walked over to me.

"Hi there, my name's Davey. Who are you?"

I was still in disbelief, wondering whether Davey was another hologram, or if Time Dream slipped a hallucinogen into me, but managed to spit out, "Sean. Sean Riley."

"Sean Riley?"

"Yes."

"Haaa, you should have said Riley, Sean Riley—like Bond, James Bond," Davey joked, doing a perfectly accurate Sean Connery voice.

"Thanks, I'll remember that," I said, chuckling. "Nice shirt, you should make that the Time Dream company logo."

Davey laughed.

So I went on, "How do you keep those goggles from fogging?"

"I wash 'em with toothpaste."

"Seriously?"

"Yup."

"So could I put toothpaste on my goldfish tank or the windshield of my car?" I asked, pondering whether this was the best question for one of the smartest humans in history.

"Theoretically."

"Huh, well," I looked at the ground and smirked and tried

not to laugh. I collected myself and went on, "I don't actually have any goldfish, I'm ahh, more of a *Swank Adult Magazine* kind of guy, so——"

"Swank Magazine!" Davey said, and laughed again, increasing my confidence, and then blew me and my nonexistent goldfish out of the water with, "Did you know Swank was actually founded by Victor Fox, of *Fox Comics*? And then later relaunched by Martin Goodman—the founder of *Marvel Comics*."

"No Sir, but that explains the spandex and unnaturally large bulge in the pants of all the Marvel superheroes."

He smiled, glanced at me sideways like he was sizing me up, peeled off the rubber glove of his right hand, and then shook my hand before asking, "Right, OK *Sean*, what are you doing here?"

"I got kicked out of the boardroom," I said, motioning towards it with my head, a little embarrassed.

"Ha, me too kid—a few years ago. That's too bad."

"You're telling me," I said, feeling more and more comfortable as Davey put me at ease, "I haven't been this sad since *Dog the Bounty Hunter* was cancelled."

Davey laughed out loud. He laughed!

"That's pretty clever." I was on top of the world. The smartest person to ever live, short of the guy who invented sippy cups, just told me I was clever.

"Clever? Jesus Davey, coming from you that's like hearing Einstein tell someone they're smart, or Gretzky saying you're good at hockey, or the Pope telling a pedophile he's good at molesting kids."

Davey laughed even louder this time and then said, "Alright alright," laughed some more, and then said, "I'm starting to see why you got kicked out of that boardroom." Davey smiled and went on, "So seriously, what were you doing in there before you got kicked out?"

"Well, my friend Anand Dhami and I were in there——"

"The writer? For Rocky Mountain News?"

"The one and only."

"No kidding? I like what he writes. He always has something to say. He's worth reading."

"Anand is writing a series of articles on Time Dream and this," I pointed at the boardroom, "is the first big interview, or maybe the only interview the way things are going. Anand brought me along as a technical consultant, but then Eric Byrne kicked me out."

"Eric Byrne is in *there*?" Davey motioned towards the boardroom while looking surprised and confused, then went on, "Actually, I do remember *why* they're doing the interview, even though I didn't know about it. It's because of the new services we are about to unveil."

Davey looked extraordinarily sad after he said this, but snapped out of it quickly, so I continued.

"Yah, also Chris Spolanksy, a lawyer named Lucius, and some other important vice-president looking dudes. You're saying you didn't know about this interview?"

"Nope," Davey said and flashed a wide smile, "like I said, I got kicked out of the boardroom years ago. So, you were brought along as a *technical consultant*?" Davey continued smiling like he saw right through me, or into my head, and with the technology in this place that was a possibility. "What do you do for a living?"

"I'm a clothing designer."

"I *almost* believe that one."

"No really, I'm working on a new line of corduroy evening wear," I said, hoping to keep Davey entertained. He smiled again, but a little impatiently this time, so I came clean. "I'm a cybersecurity analyst for the RCMP."

"Really?" Davey asked, not in a disappointed way, but with more of a shocked even mildly impressed look on his face. "Hey, come to think of it, didn't I see you on the news the other night?"

I was dumbfounded. This guy's brain and memory were truly android like. I was so impressed I didn't even try to deny it. "Yah, that was me," I said, feeling embarrassed and borderline idiotic, "but it did get me suspended with pay for a week, so I'm pretty happy about that. Anyway Davey, if you didn't know about this interview, what are you doing in Calgary?" I looked towards his feet, in the bright red ski boots, as I said this.

"Well, I was going to go skiing, but they tell me all the hills are pretty much closed this time of year."

"Good," I said, purposely looking Davey up and down, "I just wanted to make sure you weren't shooting an underwater adult film, or a remake of *Hot Dog... The Movie.*"

"Haa," Davey chuckled again before continuing, "Well, it sounds like you got some free time between being kicked out of boardrooms and suspended with pay. Do you want to grab some breakfast?"

I couldn't believe it, and I'm not sure who was more shocked, me, or the receptionist listening to our conversation.

"Jesus Davey, I mean, that sounds good, but I didn't bring any condoms, so—"

"AHHH," the receptionist gasped, but then giggled.

"Nice, OK seriously, I'm hungry, and I'm leaving now. Are you in Sean—of the Riley clan?"

"Well, my frien—"

"Well, I don't know if we're friends yet, but we just met," Davey interjected, before I could say *my* friend, as in Anand, would probably like to come along. "Come on, let's go. I've got a chopper waiting on the roof that was going to take me skiing, but now we'll just get 'em to fly us somewhere good to eat. You grew up around here right?"

"Actually, no, I was born and raised in the Northwest Territories, but I've been here long enough that I can think of somewhere to eat. How much gas you got in *Airwolf* upstairs?"

"Completely solar powered," Davey bragged.

"Great," I said nervously, trying to remember if the forecast called for sun, and hoping the chopper had solar battery cells in reserve. Fucking Time Dream...I wondered how long it would be before they started to sell—err, *cell*—helicopters.

"OK, so let's get going."

"Right, but Anand's going to be looking for me soon—he would probably love to come with us—and Eric Byrne told me to sit in that seat and not move," I said, pointing at the chair.

"Fuck Eric Byrne, and as for your friend Anand and the chair problem, I'm pretty sure Eric likes meetings more than having sex, so they could very well still be in there by the time we get back. I'll tell you what, you can ask me anything you want about Time Dream in the chopper ride—maybe get some real answers for Anand's story."

"Sold," I said, even though I was pretty sure Anand might get "ejected" from the meeting not long after me. Then I looked at the receptionist: "Can I take this copy of *Chatelaine*?" Only Canada would have a magazine talking about BeaverTails—the pastry chain, not the animal—and the Queen in the same article. If I had a nickel for every...

Ten minutes later, I was aboard Davey's helicopter and flying above the city, only, it wasn't like any helicopter I'd ever seen. On top of the solar power bullshit, the engine was nearly silent when it flew, the craft was almost all windows—*translucent solar panels* according to Davey—and it had an artificial intelligence pilot that interacted with Davey through voice commands. It had the same creepy robotic man voice used at all the Time Dream locations. Christ, with all their money you'd think they'd get a real person like Shatner to do the voice. Davey called him, and by *him* I mean the A.I., the helicopter, etc: 'ALICE'—which was some kind of acronym. Fucking *Alice*?? What kind of eccentric prick invents something amazing like this and names it Alice? Personally, I would've gone with TILF: The Intelligent Lightweight Flyer, which has the added benefit of making people think of TILF: Transvestite I'd Like to......

Anyway, after I finally became comfortable we weren't going to fall out of the sky, and we told Alice to fly to *Eggs & More* restaurant—mostly because they served the best all day breakfast in Calgary, and because there was an open field nearby where we could land—I decided to ask Davey a few questions I thought Anand would like me to get answered...and maybe a few questions of my own...OK maybe *just* my own.

"So Davey, I have a question. Also, can I record the Q & A with my phone? Only to stop Anand from murdering me, and instead, only maiming me."

"Go for it. Fire away."

"OK, well, what's to stop me from doing a coma jump tomorrow and walking up to a political figure, a movie star, one of you guys, etc, and asking for your email password, online banking password, underwear size, nuclear launch codes, or whatever, during the coma jump?"

Davey smiled, and I felt stupid for about the fourth time in the twenty minutes since I'd met him.

"Nothing, you're in control of the coma jump just like you always are, but the password would only be what it *really is* if you heard or learned it at some point in the past, from your real life, so your brain would actually be storing it to be relived in your coma jump. We *do* download content from each customer's brain, to help with their next coma jump, but we haven't linked everyone's brains together—*yet!*" Davey winked at me before continuing, "You could however, and many business executives and heads of state already do this, enter a coma jump to *recall* passwords, key conversations, etc to get an edge. I know a few world leaders who have told me they do role playing in coma jumps for international summits, negotiations and G7 meetings."

"Yah, I *bet* they role play," I said.

Davey snickered and went on, "Hey, it's no secret the whole world uses coma jumps for sex and a lot of seriously dark shit, but at least the dark shit is happening in a coma jump and not in the real world. That's the *good* the coma jumps bring that everyone forgets about. It's one of the reasons why I built the Time Dream system."

I couldn't help but wonder if Davey meant *everyone* as in the current people running the ship at Time Dream. Or maybe I felt this way because I figured Davey should still be the head of Time Dream. His answers to the media were always raw, but not damaging or too revealing, in my opinion. The public used to love watching him on TV. *I* used to love watching him on TV.

"OK, this one has been drivin' me crazy since I did my first coma jump. What is with picking an exact date and time for each coma jump? Do you know how much easier it would be if someone could just describe an event in their life and you guys zeroed in on it?"

Davey grinned again, and although I felt like a bug asking how a watch worked, his facial expression was not condescending at all, but the conscientious look you would get from only the best teachers, coaches, or *leaders*—in his case.

"Well, we *could* do that actually, but some of the lawyers and financial people figured it would save time, eliminate disputes on what was wanted, and shield us from privacy and legal complaints."

"Got it." I took a deep breath before asking my next question, mostly because I wasn't even remotely qualified to ask it. "So how do you guys do it? How do you do coma jumps? I know you can't get too technical, and I wouldn't understand it if you did, but do you want to take a shot at explaining it? I'm sure every journalist, researcher and scientist in the world—hell, *anyone*—would love to hear some kind of answer to this."

Davey smiled even more this time. Now I *was* like a bug asking God—Allah, Buddha, Iron Man—the meaning of life.

"Sure thing Sean. Do you know what a flashback is?"

"Yah, I mean, pretty much. It's when you remember something from your past."

"Yes, and to elaborate on that, flashbacks are involuntary —*and often recurring*—memories, in which an individual has a sudden powerful re-experiencing of a past memory, sometimes so intense that the person *re-lives* the experience, unable to fully recognize it as a memory and not something that is really happening. Such involuntary memories are often of traumatic events or highly-charged emotional happenings, and often occur at times of high stress or food deprivation, although the exact causes and mechanisms were not clear to scientists and researchers for years. At Time Dream, we found a way to zero in on the exact cause, extract it, greatly enhance it, and induce it, creating the completely real to the mind flashback that the world knows as a coma jump."

I was following, and nodded that I understood, but must have looked partially confused, because Davey went on.

"Have you noticed how you remember bad, extremely sad, or dangerous events from your life in more accurate detail than the good events from your life?"

"Yah, for the most part—for sure. The example I can think of is how poker players have trouble remembering the exact details of their greatest wins or hands, but they can recall their worst hands and losses with remarkable accuracy."

"Exactly, and that's not an accident, it's an evolutionary adaptation, given that it's better to err on the side of caution and ignore a few pleasant experiences than to overlook a negative, and possibly dangerous, event. The brain in general, and memory in particular, has a distinct negativity bias. It pays more attention to, and highlights, unpleasant experiences to help prevent us from repeating them. The brain typically detects negative information faster than positive information, and the hippocampus specifically flags negative events to ensure such events are stored in memory. Negative experiences leave an indelible trace in the memory, even when efforts are made to unlearn them. However, the second breakthrough we made at Time Dream was to recognize that memory was a moving collage of interconnections—versus, say, like a traditional computer storage system—and although negative experiences are more easily found in the collage, *all* memories are available."

"Can you explain *collage* more? Bear with me, anything beyond two syllables makes my...*hippocampus* hurt! I'm not even gonna touch that one, I mean, come on, you made that word up just now to mess with me, right?"

"No, pay attention," Davey said with a consoling smile, "I can tell you almost have this." I was not so sure, but he went on anyway. "Each element of a memory (sights, sounds, words, emotions) is encoded in the same part of the brain that originally created that fragment (visual cortex, motor cortex, language area, etc), and at Time Dream, we've learned how to pinpoint, store, recall, and more importantly, reproduce a memory by effectively reactivating the neural patterns generated during the original encoding—just like our brains do naturally every day, but with a bit of a kick; it's enhanced. Thus, a better analogy might be that of a complex web, in which the threads symbolize the various elements of a memory, that join at nodes or intersection points to form a whole rounded memory of a person, object or event. This kind of distributed memory ensures that even if part of the brain is damaged, some parts of an experience may still remain."

"Damaged brains eh? Is this why Time Dream is boasting they have the cure for Alzheimer's and a plethora of other things."

"Sean, listen to what I just told you, and this part *is* off the record only because it hasn't been achieved yet, but we could very well have the cure for everything—indirectly—or, at least every brain disease. Right now, coma jumps still ultimately occur inside each person's brain, but when the time comes where we figure out how to have multiple people enjoying a coma jump together, the possibilities are endless. What that achievement could mean for medicine, healing the brain, the body, and even psychoanalysis—where a counselor could walk through your memories with you—is beyond what any of us can even fathom at this point. We don't know where it could go."

"Is this part of the new services that Eric Byrne alluded to?" This wasn't what I wanted to ask next, with my mind spinning out of control with curiosity and wonder, but I could see we were close to *Eggs & More*, and tried to ask what Anand would finish with, since Davey said I could ask anything I wanted about Time Dream *during* the helicopter ride. "You mentioned you were aware of these new services, earlier."

"No," Davey answered, looking at the ground, "that's something different. I have nothing to do with those new services." Davey's face was somewhere between deep rooted rage and sadness.

I knew the look because I saw it in my own eyes every morning when I looked in the mirror and thought of my sons, and dearly missed their screams and laughs to start each day. Something about these new services bothered Davey in a way that frightened me—a person of his stature looking worried was analogous to a president ignoring his or her media relations people by showing uncertainty to the public.

"ALICE, land in that open field down below!" Davey said, snapping out of whatever was on his mind.

"*Yes Sir, I already identified the field as the optimum location for landing,*" Alice said.

"So, when Eric said 'announced very soon', *when* did he mean exactly?" I asked, to squeeze in one last question.

"That's off the record too, but it will likely be all over the news tomorrow."

"Thanks Davey, that was incredible. It was like listening to Einstein or something, or Aristotle, or The Fonz."

"You're welcome kid, let's go get some food."

When we landed there was no noticeable impact or sound on the landing whatsoever. We simply touched down and then the helicopter went quiet. We strolled across the field, stepped over the fence into the parking lot, and walked into *Eggs & More* at exactly 9 am.

Julie, the waitress who was there nearly every time I set foot in the place, smiled and greeted us at the door. There were days when Julie worked every table in the restaurant on her own —no wonder she had forearms like Mark McGuire, despite her petite build.

"Hi Sean, seat by the window as usual, so you can keep an eye on your car?" Julie asked, and tilted her head slightly to the right and smiled with her mouth closed and eyes squinted, just like your Grandmother would when inquiring if you ate some of her favourite pistachios.

"No car today Julie," I said.

"Why, was it stolen—or *towed* finally? I didn't notice any cranes out front!" Julie teased, in reference to my *heavier than a tank* '70 LeSabre.

Nope, I thought to myself, no cranes, just a helicopter worth more than Fort Knox.

"Ahhh," I stuttered, "I––"

"Oh my GOD! He's always saying he's gonna get stabbed in the parking lot because this area is unsafe," Julie teased some more, leaving me a little embarrassed, not because she was making fun of me, but because it was obvious I came to *Eggs & More* as often as the cook. Then Julie straightened and put her hands on her hips while looking at Davey, "Hey, umm, are you? Ahhh," now Julie stuttered, "are you...do you know you look just like *Davey Sandhu*!?"

"That idiot? The last I heard of him was some news report saying he was at a mud wrestling event in Tijuana." Davey said, grinning.

I decided to change the subject because Julie was nobody's fool, and clearly believed the founder of Time Dream, and one of the most recognizable people on earth, was in front of her. "That window seat would be great Julie," I said.

"Sure," Julie said, and led us to a table by the window, looking back suspiciously at Davey, head to toe, much like I had done earlier. Perhaps Davey's outfit was the one thing casting doubt into her mind on whether it was really him—he still had the red ski boots on for crying out loud.

We sat down, bullshitted a bit about how great the all-day breakfast menu looked, and then Julie took our orders.

Not long after that, we both sat up straighter in our seats when we heard the CBC announcer come over the radio in a formal voice—*Eggs & More* always played CBC on the intercom—indicating a special announcement from Ottawa:

"*Bill C-14 has just been amended in Canada to match the USA's recent 'right to die' bill on suicides. With this change, both countries have made it legal for others to help in one's suicide if certain conditions, regulations and guidelines are met. Previously, practitioners were only allowed to assist in the suicide of mentally competent adults with enduring and intolerable suffering, in cases where death was reasonably foreseeable. Now, any adult deemed of fit mind by a mental health professional would be eligible to request a medically assisted suicide, even if they were not sick or suffering. Once again, critics from around the world are debating and attacking this decision, saying this was simply the United States' latest answer to population control and overcrowding—and Canada following its big brother superpower's lead without enough research of its own. The one noticeable difference between the two countries, in regards to their new law, is the consenting age: In the USA, across every state, you must be twenty-one years of age or older to legally request an assisted suicide. In Canada, you only need to be eighteen. Mercedes Smith has more..."*

The room was quiet, and Davey broke the silence at our table.

"Well?" he asked, and I couldn't help but notice Davey didn't look the least bit surprised when the announcer spoke, but he did look even more troubled than he had earlier.

"Well, I guess I'm disappointed," I said. "Despite CBC predicting Canada would follow the USA's lead on the law, my false sense of Canadian nationalistic pride had me believing we would be better, or at least different from the US on suicides—I was wrong."

"DEAD WRONG," Davey quipped, forcing a slight smile, and then following up after seeing me shake my head, "Too soon?"

I laughed, "Maybe."

CHAPTER 10 – DEATH

The elevator doors opened to let me out on the bottom floor of Time Dream's Calgary headquarters, and I saw Anand pacing in the lobby. As soon as he saw me, he stopped pacing and hurried towards me. Spike, the Pee-Wee Herman look alike, was escorting me out—with ten security guards alongside him. The guards were so close to Spike that he looked like Michael Jackson with the dancing zombies in Thriller—synchronized flailing arms and all. Anand completed the scene with dead man, wide-open, angry eyes looking directly at me as he charged forward like a bull. I tried to calm him down.

"It's OK man! It's OK, don't worry I—"

"HAVE A GREAT DAY MR. RILEY!" Spike said, distracting me.

I turned to thank him, but the former child entertainer look alike was already back in the elevator with the doors halfway closed.

I turned back around to see Anand stop about ten feet away and point at me like a dictator identifying someone guilty of treason.

"LET'S GO," he said, gritting his teeth, and looking like he wanted to murder someone. "I have a cab waiting for us out front."

His face was so angry it reminded me of two opposing NHL hockey coaches yelling at each other during a game: With the team benches separated by Plexiglas, coaches get even angrier than two players fighting each other because there's no release that comes with physical contact. I chuckled, thinking *release* and *physical contact* sounded more like something from an erotic novel you bought at the checkout counter of the grocery store, than an anecdote about aggression. So, in light of Anand's Incredible Hulk impersonation, versus imitating one of Danielle Steel's studs, I decided to say nothing, keep my head down, and walked out the front entrance with him. As soon as we were on the street, Anand started into me.

"What the fuck? Were you--"

"Not yet," I cut him off, "wait until we get in the cab—they can probably still hear us."

We got in the cab, told the driver to head south, and remained silent for a few blocks. Rain was gently coming down as we drove, the sky was grey, and there was no music in the car, so the muffled sounds of the wet city streets soothed my nerves.

A few more minutes passed, and Anand seemed to calm down as well. He sighed, took a deep breath, and turned to me.

"Japanese Village?" he asked, smiling like the old friend I knew, and ignoring what was on both our minds for the moment.

"Sure," I said, and smiled back, and decided now wasn't a good time to say I was already full from eating the *Southern Gents* breakfast special at Eggs & More—you could feed half of Bangladesh with that meal.

Fifteen minutes later we were seated at the Japanese Village eating our lunch. Anand spoke first.

"I'm sorry, Sean, I apologize," he said wearily. "I was up late and I'm tired. It's been a really long day and it's only noon!"

I nodded sympathetically and chuckled, but said nothing, and felt guilty about leaving my friend alone in the boardroom for a couple hours.

"Anyway," Anand continued, "you're obviously all right, so can you tell me what happened?"

Now I felt even guiltier. I was so self-absorbed and starstruck, I hadn't grasped that his anger was born out of fear and concern for me. It is a rare thing indeed to find a friend who is protective of you like a parent.

"For sure, and don't be sorry man. *I'm* sorry for leaving you alone in there. You didn't phone me up on short notice just to see me get kicked out."

"Or did I?" Anand said, with a sly grin, making me wonder. "Anyway, fuck that, the Time Dream staff said you went offsite with Davey Sandhu in his chopper? Are you kidding me? You were with him all that time? *Davey Sandhu*!??" Anand's eyes were filled with excitement now.

"Yes Sir. It wasn't the visit with Magnum P.I. and a ride in TC's chopper I've always dreamed of, but it was a close second!

"I got fuck all out of them during that interview after you left. I confirmed a few suspicions and rumours at best."

I smiled at Anand because I knew what I was about to tell him would make up for any disappointment he had. I told him how Davey and I met, and about Alice—the sentient, silent running, solar powered, spaceship-like helicopter—in detail, and then pressed play on my smartphone to let Anand hear the interview I recorded.

He listened all the way through and then asked me to play it again—pausing and replaying certain parts several times.

When I looked at the time it was almost 3pm, well past lunchtime closing, and the Japanese Village staff were circling our table to suggest it was time to leave.

"I can't believe it," Anand said.

"I know, pretty amazing stuff *eh*?" I said, like a little kid seeking approval.

"No," Anand said, "I meant I can't believe you didn't ask him my question: What happens if you do a coma jump *within* a coma jump?" Anand kept a straight face, saw me frown, then laughed out loud. "OK OK, what-a-ya want? A hero cookie? A pat on the back?"

"So—it *is* good stuff I got for ya?" I asked wishfully, hoping for some kind of concrete affirmation that I'd *dun good*, as my Mom used to say.

"It's only one of the most important interviews of the century."

"Really?"

"Yah really," Anand shook his head, "This is a little cliché to say, but that is more than *good stuff*. It's groundbreaking. So much so I'm already having serious doubts about whether Time Dream will let me print any of it."

"What?!" I asked, feeling deflated after my momentary high from the interview and Anand's praise.

"I'm serious. I'm not sure they'll allow even one word, and I'm wondering if Davey was even allowed to talk to you after having his wings clipped a few years ago. *You* being media, in this case."

"He built that place man!" I said.

"Being the richest guy in a company doesn't mean you're the head of the company. Especially in this case, I mean, they found a way to kick him off the board a couple years ago—based on trumped up mental health problems they claimed he was experiencing."

"I never heard that," I said and stood up and followed Anand to the front.

"There were articles about it everywhere, Jesus, I even wrote a few. Do you read anything outside the sports section?"

"Playmate hobbies. I also really liked to read Allan Fotheringham at the back of *Mclean's* magazine for years—but now Dr. Foth is retired and *Playboy* has committed the cardinal sin of removing nudity from their publication. Do you hear me? No nudity in *Playboy*! It's like the sky without the sun God dammit!"

"Why did I even ask you? You're paying, by the way," Anand said, and then smiled. "When *I* get to ride in Davey Sandhu's chopper, then I'll pay for lunch. But yah, the mental health stuff about Davey is how they punted him."

"Well, it's total bullshit," I said, "that guy's brain is switched on in a way only aliens from an advanced planet could understand." Upon saying this I realized it made Davey sound crazy but didn't think I needed to convince Anand of Davey's sanity.

I paid the bill, and when we were out the front door and on the familiar sidewalk outside Japanese Village I said, "The only time he seemed upset was when I asked him about these new services Time Dream is gonna unveil."

"Really?" Anand asked, "I couldn't tell that from the audio —did he look worried?"

"I would go so far as to say he looked sad," I said, "really sad and he appeared even more defeated when CBC announced the changes to Bill C-14."

"Like they're connected?" Anand speculated.

"Maybe, well, I'm not sure, but I have a theory."

"A theory eh?" Anand looked at me and lifted one eyebrow.

"Yah, and I don't mean a theory on what the new services *are*, or even *how* they're connected to the new suicide laws. My theory is that Davey being at Time Dream was no accident—and feeding me all that information was no accident. Is it possible he was trying to tell us something? I mean you do remember the part where he said 'you were a good writer' and 'worth reading' and all that, right?"

"Go on," Anand said.

"Well, what if he heard about your interview and arranged to be there."

"That's one hell of a theory." Anand squinted and looked at the ground, thinking deeply, just like he did when he solved things in university I am *still* trying to figure out. "And you said Davey specifically told you to be listening to the news tomorrow? I *think* that was on the last part of the recording?"

"I remember that well enough I don't even need to play it back."

"Alrighty, I gotta get back to the office to start talking with the lawyers and my editor about what I can use from your Davey interview. Then we'll get on the horn with Time Dream. Can you send me that recording."

"Already done—I sent it using Signal Private Messenger. The one I got you to install last year."

"Yah, I use it a lot actually. You were right, it *can* do everything WhatsApp can."

"And Signal isn't owned by fucking Facebook, like WhatsApp is, so you can be assured Zuckerberg isn't reading all your texts while he's jerking off to some penguin videos."

"Good. I'll see you later," Anand said and flagged down a cab. Before he got in, he turned back to me and said, "I almost forgot, you just made eight thousand dollars. RMN will deposit that in your account before day's end."

He disappeared into the cab and then stuck his head out the window and gave me the finger before it drove off.

I, on the other hand, was still suspended with pay from work, and had half a day to kill before Time Dream's big announcement. So, I decided to do the only sane thing any man would do with free coma jumps, an extra eight grand, and a longing to forget about the kids that were taken from him: Get drunk, head over to the Lougheed Time Dream location, then go back to 1993 and see Mrs. Turgeon for the second, third and fourth time in one week.

Five hours, five coma jumps, and a shitload of different *extracurricular activities* with Mrs. Turgeon later, it was already Wednesday evening. So make that six visits in one week with Mrs. Turgeon—well, that's a lie, in the interest of full transparency I feel compelled to point out I went back a little further than 1993 in one coma jump, and tried to claim the right of Prima Nocta with Mrs. Turgeon's much younger sister on her wedding night, to no avail, because for some reason she wasn't interested in me at age twelve. I would've kept going, but I was down to only three more free coma jumps left—apparently time flies when you're getting more acquainted with your mom's best friend.

When I finished my last coma jump I avoided talking to Myah because I knew she'd bring up her brother the shrink, but she stopped me just before I got to the door.

"Did you give Casey a call?" she asked, looking like my mom when she asked if I'd finished my homework, knowing the answer was no.

"*Casey?*"

"Yes, my brother, *the shrink*," Myah said, doing the quote symbols with her hands as she said this.

"No, but hearing that name I'm not only gonna see 'em, I'm gonna pick up a Finnegan—from *Mr. Dressup*—hand puppet before our first session and answer everything with puppet nods and puppet body language."

"It doesn't have to be a full session or anything formal Sean."

"I'm serious, I'm gonna be Finnegan even when I'm waiting in reception at your brother's office. Some woman will be sitting there and Finnegan will turn his head," I used my bare hand to simulate Finnegan's head turning towards Myah, "to stare—while I'm looking innocently ahead of course—look her up and down, slowly, then make a sort of low humming, shifting to high pitched, pervert-like eureka sound. Then his mouth will go wide open while he starts bouncing up and down like a happy puppy dog. I would immediately scold Finnegan under my breath like a parent, like he's a real person, and I'm embarrassed, telling him not to stare and swearing under my breath again. Then I would look over at the woman myself, to see if she is creeped out or amused, and apologize for Finnegan's behaviour. Finnegan would turn around because I betrayed him with this public ridicule, and aggressively latch onto my neck like a King-Cobra," I grabbed my own neck as I did this, "which would really just be me strangling myself with a sock over my hand, while my other hand tries to pry me, err, Finnegan, off."

"Does that ever work?" Myah asked.

I could see she was holding back a laugh—trying to hide the fact that she, a brilliant doctor, was entertained by my sock innuendo. Orrrr, more likely, she thought I was crazy—like I regularly talk to imaginary gerbils *crazy*, not Evel Knievel *crazy* —she *was* trying to steer me towards her psychiatrist brother after all.

"Does what work?" I asked.

"Have you ever done that to any women without getting arrested?"

"Well, I've only ever done the puppet routine twice," I lied.

"What happened the first time?"

"I met my wife."

"Bullshit," Myah said, and then laughed. "And the second time?"

"I don't know, I'll tell you tomorrow, but it's looking good so far!" I said, smiling ear to ear.

"Oh my God," Myah said, rolling her eyes, "OK Maverick, time to go home." Myah smiled, and overtly checked me out, just like Finnegan—aka my hand—looked at her earlier, and went back to her tablet and turned away, still grinning.

"Good night Doc," I said, and walked down the hallway towards the front desks, but turned my head to look back at her as I walked.

"It's *Myah*, and make sure to phone Casey," she said, and then spun around and ran towards me. I turned to face her. Myah took out the business card she mentioned yesterday, looked at it, looked at me, then reached over and slowly shoved it in my pocket while keeping her eyes locked on mine. My *front* jeans pocket. She winked, smiled, and ran back down the hall-way—in heels—to get on her tablet again.

My heart had tripled its beat and I felt my head go warm and flush with blood—both *heads* actually. I also realized right then that I hadn't peed my pants in the last coma jump, which was good, because it would have made her hand going in my front pocket a slightly different experience.

When I sat down in my car I didn't drive right away. I pulled out the card and phoned Dr. Casey Wade. He was expecting my call, which weirded me out a little bit because it meant Myah had me pegged for phoning all along. Casey sounded like a decent guy on the phone, so I made an appointment for 11am the next morning.

I drove home feeling like I had a good day—the first one in

ages, almost happy—but when I entered the dark empty house that used to be filled with screams of joy and laughter from my children, another type of darkness took over.

When they were alive, and I came home, Alex and Owen used to come running at me like uncaged animals, screaming with glee the whole way from the living room. They would tackle me, and their squeezes were the instant antidote to anything bad in my day. The smell of my wife Angela's cooking would be in the air, and she'd call out I was home just in time for supper. Whether I arrived home from work at five o'clock or nine pm, somehow, supper had always *just* been cooked when I walked in.

Today however, I nuked a frozen pizza in the microwave, watched a rerun of *Rocky IV* while I consumed more vodka than all the Russians in Rocky IV, and then collapsed in Owen's room. I made it to the bed this time, instead of falling asleep on the floor for the first half of the night, like in Alex's room the night before.

One of the last arguments I had with Angela, before she left a few weeks after our boys died, was about my refusal to wash the sheets on Owen and Alex's beds, or their dirty clothes in the laundry baskets. I would lie down in one of their beds, with one of their shirts, and smell them, as I did tonight, only the smell was fading now, just like my will to continue without them. When I closed my eyes the haunting and familiar words played in my head again as I fell asleep: *Monsters are furry, monsters are fun, but you better watch out, or you'll be done!*

I woke up in the morning feeling energized. Normally, I can barely scrape myself off the bed, and only a shower, caffeine or some high powered amphetamines can get me going—nothing like an unscheduled week off work with pay to let an unworthy soul get some extra rest by sleeping in. I had time before my 11am appointment with Casey Wade, so I made a short pit stop—in an area of Calgary called *Forest Lawn*—to get some *materials* for a little prank I had brewing in my head.

Forest Lawn sounds nice, but it's nice like *Queens* sounded nice to Eddie Murphy and Arsenio Hall before they actually got to New York in the movie *Coming to America*. They arrived and found out there weren't many queens—and Forest Lawn is no different. Forest Lawn does, however, have a lot of pawnshops —the most in Calgary. Despite bad press and a lot of crime in Forest Lawn, I loved going in and out of these pawnshops when I arrived in the city at age eighteen. I was a student, had no car, and my transit route would often take me through the neighborhood, and have me waiting long periods of time for the next bus.

At first, I wandered through the pawnshops to stay warm in the winter, or to stay off the street where I felt unsafe at the bus stop, but after a while I discovered all kinds of cool items at cheap prices. Some of it worked when you got home, and some of it didn't, but what I enjoyed the most was walking through the whole store and memorizing each item.

Sometimes, I would have to catch the next bus coming because I dicked around for too long and missed the bus I was waiting for. After a couple years, I even started to become quite friendly with the pawnshop owners and workers, much the same way I did with bus drivers because I took the exact same transit route for three years in a row. The bus driver I knew best was John—this guy was weird, straight up, but he was very kind to me and even let me drive the bus once, which none of my friends believe to this day. The pawnshop owner I knew best was Quan, of *Rick's Pawn Shop*. Quan bought the place and was too cheap to change the sign, company business cards, etc, baring Rick's name, but honestly, knowing Quan, I think he would've done the same thing if he had a billion dollars in the bank.

So, you go with what you know, and I pulled into the parking lot beside Rick's Pawn Shop. Years had passed since I was there, but I remembered Quan was pretty good at creating fake IDs—*deadly good*. My friends and I needed IDs back then for a variety of reasons, and Quan always delivered for rock bottom price. I got out of my '70 LeSabre, which fit into the scene of Forest Lawn like a glove, and strolled through the front entrance. The first thing I noticed was a young Chinese woman, about eighteen or nineteen, who noticed me and walked over.

"Hi, may I help you find anything?"

"Does Quan still work here?" I asked.

"Yes."

I was taken aback: I realised this was Quan's daughter Joanna who used to run around the store all the time as a little girl!

"I'll go get him from the back." She paused then added, "But no one has asked for him by name in years. Do you know him?"

"I sure do Joanna," I said, and watched Joanna's eyes go big with surprise, "tell him the skinny kid from the north wants his money back for the broken DVD player he sold me."

"Will do," she said and walked away. A few minutes later an old man who looked like Quan came out.

"Hey Sean, you skinny fuck!" It was Quan, with his Chinese accent just as thick as ever. "Aww sales aww final! And you pay me in fake dollahs once anyway," he said with a big smile, jogging my memory, and I immediately felt bad.

"Oh yah, I forgot about that. Did you get in any trouble?" I asked, with genuine concern. We both reached out to shake hands at the same time.

"You-no-dam-right," he said, which made me smirk, and think *Uno Damright* would be a good name for a character in *The Hunger Games*. "Anyway, what can I do ya for Sean?"

"Well, in a nutshell, I need some fake driver's licenses and credit cards. For myself—I'm not distributing or anything like that, and they don't even need to have my picture or work properly. I just want the barcode and chip info on each card to contain the names I give you. Do you still do that kind of work?"

"Of course, just give me names."

I gave Quan ten of the most ridiculous, dirty, and inappropriate names I could think of. We chatted for a bit, I paid two dollars for a Finnegan hand puppet, and Quan said I could pick up the fake IDs tomorrow morning, which was still way faster than any one of the million or so fake id websites on the Inter-net—I typed *fake id* into Google to get over 450 million results. Then again, I got just under a million and a half results when I searched up *goat fucker*, so I wasn't surprised. I shook hands with Quan and left.

Thankfully, I still had tires on my car when I went out. There was only about twenty minutes until my appointment at Casey's office, so I gunned it the whole way there. I left a trail of dirty toxic smoke so long that my car lowered the life ex-pectancy in Forest Lawn faster than the train that *accidentally* dropped Schindler's Jews off at Auschwitz.

I got to Casey's office five minutes early, but came in a minute late because it was one of those businesses that looked like a regular house, and was located in a residential area among actual houses. I hated that—it was a needle in a haystack, and my little brain preferred things that stuck out like a Wookiee at an Ewok concert. Then again, maybe it wasn't the best thing in the world to have a psychiatry and psychology clinic adjacent to a strip mall with a popular guns and hobby shop.

I walked inside, signed in, and sat down in the waiting area of reception. Unfortunately, I was the only one there, so I was disappointed I couldn't try out any puppet show *Finnegan shenanigans*—which would be the greatest name ever for an Irish race horse—on an unsuspecting mentally unstable patient. So, not to be discouraged, or to be bored in the waiting room, I took out the Finnegan hand puppet provided by Quan, put it on my right hand, and walked up to the receptionist—I think her name was Tammy.

It was gold, not only did I nail the routine I practiced on Myah earlier, but while doing the puppet show it dawned on me that some people in here were probably bat shit crazy for real—so Tammy had to act accordingly. I even threw in a new part at the end where I whipped off the Finnegan puppet from my right hand and started frantically yelling, "AHHHHHHHHHHH!!!" with my mouth positioned behind my right hand, like Finnegan was talking, and yelled, "I'm naked! I'M NAKEDDDDDDDDD!" Of course, at the height of this yelling, Dr. Casey Wade opened the door to bring me in. But, like Tammy the receptionist, he was pretty much required to take this in stride. Casey smiled and came over to shake my hand.

"Hi Sean, it's nice to meet you, I'm glad you came by. Come on in."

"Hi," was all I could spit out in return, suddenly feeling uncomfortable, so I just followed Casey into the back, and by *into the back* I mean down the hallway of the house, which was unlike any normal office, and up the stairs. The house was creaky and smelled old, but pleasant, reminding me of the way my grandmother's house used to smell. There were plants and paintings everywhere, including along the wall of the stairs. One of the paintings looked like the famous Bluenose racing schooner out at sea, with sails blazing and a little rusting brown buoy, closer up in perspective, for the viewer. The grey sky in the background around the Bluenose, and the endless blue of the ocean, were the perfect mental health, mood setting, mind fuck—I was starting to feel depressed already. We walked a little farther upstairs until Casey stopped and opened a bright *red as Heinz Ketchup* door, motioning for me to go inside.

"Have a seat Sean," he said, and smiled, but still appeared respectful and serious.

"Thanks," I said and chose an old, varnished, wooden rocking chair. It was quite comfortable and seemed like an unusual piece of furniture for a shrink to have. Unusual as in kind of cool, not unusual as in my Aunt Mildred walking naked into the kitchen wearing only a red hat from the *Red Hat Society*, with an ash leaking cigarette in her mouth, and smelling of formaldehyde.

"So, how are you doing today?"

"Good good, I've been washing with Zest, no more of that white milky film." I answered.

"My sister Myah––"

"You mean *Gertrude*?" I interrupted, on purpose.

"No, I mea––"

"*Lou-Ann?*"

"No, my sister *Myah*, from Time Dream," Casey said, looking less professional and more confused now.

"Ahh, I don't know anyone named *Myah*," I said, smiling mischievously.

"Ohhh—K OK" Casey chuckled, shaking his head, "Myah warned me about you. Look, I know the stigma around—"

"No worries Doc, I was ordered to see RCMP Psych services for months upon months not too long ago. I'm almost wondering if the RCMP invented this racket versus anything Freud came up with. You were gonna say something like, 'I know the stigma around psychoanalysis, but in reality, all I'm here to do is help you solve problems', right?"

"More or less, yes." Casey paused for a moment. "Fair enough, this isn't how I like to do things usually, but after hearing that, let's get to it then. What is your biggest problem?"

"My two sons are dead."

"Oh," Casey said, sympathetically nodding his head.

"Yyyyy-*uuuup*, that's what the last guy said. You got any more pearls of wisdom in the tickle trunk?"

"I'm sorry to hear that, but with all due respect..."

I loved the line *with all due respect*—this was a staple in military and para-military policing organizations. With the RCMP where I worked, for example, it had become so overused and infused with immunity granting status you could say just about anything if you led with that line: "*Superintendent, all due respect, I had brutal anal sex with your wife, your brother, and that good looking Arabian Stallion at your horse acreage outside of town. I also burned down your house and killed your dog.*" In short, when someone led with *all due respect*, you could bet money they were about to be the exact opposite of respectful.

"...*why* is it a problem that they're dead?" There was a challenging look in Casey's eyes.

Christ, I'd like to recant what I said earlier and start over —if someone leads with *all due respect* they are indeed about to say something disrespectful but could also say something exceedingly stupid.

"Why do you think it's a problem?" I asked sarcastically with an edge of hostility in my voice.

"I think your children being dead is incredibly sad, and not something I can ever comprehend, who could? But is *that* your problem?"

I stared at Casey. I wasn't mad, I was just trying to decide if he might be the world's worst shrink. In a profession where establishing trust, listening, saying less, and saying the right thing seemed to be key, this guy was batting zero so far. I wasn't instantly bored like I was with the RCMP appointed shrinks though, so I gave him points for that.

"Are you unhappy?" Casey asked and then paused, and before I could answer—well, I didn't have an answer truth be told —he continued, "When was the last time you *were* happy?"

"It was earlier today. Your sister stuffed your business card in my *front* pocket," I said, pulling the business card out of my pocket and then winking repeatedly four or five times, almost like a girl in a porno right before a guy *ends the scene*. Then, the unexpected happened. Nothing to do with ejaculation—I was at a shrink's office, not a rectory.

"Go fuck yourself. Get the fuck out of my office," Casey said seriously but impressively devoid of any anger. Then he turned the other direction, opened a drawer, pulled out a newspaper, shook it aggressively to straighten it, then reclined back in his chair and started reading.

I was thrown by this for sure, but Casey reading the paper also gave me a flashback—hmm, Davey Sandhu said he'd basically hacked the brain's flashback to invent coma jumping—to grade seven where a substitute teacher named Mario pulled the same stunt: We had chewed up ten substitute teachers in a row with bad behaviour, and started in on Mario like we had the others, only he didn't care, he just sat there reading the paper. We knew what he was doing of course, but after almost four days we started to wonder if Mario was using a tactic, or just going to sit there the whole semester. It got quiet, we stopped messing around, and Mario put down the paper and started to teach—hand on The Bible, The Quran, The Torah, The Book of Mormon, and the 1st edition of Maxim magazine, that's how it happened. But I'd never heard of a psychologist or psychiatrist doing this. I looked at Casey some more. I think he might have been reading the sports section.

"No, you go fuck yourself," I volleyed back, somewhat baffled as to where this was going.

"Faccckkkkk yoooouuu, ya runty little bastard," he said quickly, not looking up from what appeared to be an article about the Edmonton Oilers. Calgary's NHL hockey team was the Flames, but I was an Oilers fan, so this caught my eye.

"Nice," I said, and then chuckled. "What the hell kind of shrink are you? You look like a cross between Mr. Rogers and a guy taking a break from working the ticket booth at Northlands Coliseum," the arena for the Oilers in the eighties, "even though 17,000 people are lined up, and his colleagues' booths are so busy the whole place looks like the next *Running of the Bulls*."

"Daaaaaa—Bulls," he said, looking away from the paper and at me again. "And I ain't your shrink, my sister asked me to talk to you. And I'm pretty sure no one up front asked you for your insurance or health care card." No one had. "You an Oilers fan?"

"Yup."

"Me too, what's your excuse?"

"I was born and raised in the Northwest Territories. Up north, we didn't even have TFC, we had OFC—one fucking channel—for a lot of the time. And, that one TV channel was ITV—who carried the Oilers in the eighties, as you probably know," I explained.

"Yah! Do you remember Tim Spelliscy?"

"Of course! What about Bill Matheson, the ITV weatherman? I got so used to his routine I would start thinking about high-pressure low-pressure areas when I was bored in school. If I didn't hear his broadcast before an Oilers game as a kid, I felt like it would jinx them."

"High-pressure low-pressure areas!" Casey laughed, and then said, "I know, and I swear to God he made up half the stuff he was saying in relation to the weather, but no one cared 'cause he was five times more entertaining than anything else on the news. Actually, other than the Oilers in the eighties, he *was* the most entertaining thing on ITV! I remember the map of Canada looked like a game of Snakes & Ladders by the time he was done scribbling and darting around. He was all over the place!"

"He was a swashbuckler with that marker! I once saw him go through four markers in one segment! He'd just chuck the thing across the room—live on camera—and pull out another one from his suit pocket," I described, pointing to the left side of my chest where Bill's corduroy suit pocket full of pens and markers used to be.

We both laughed.

"So, did you grow up in Edmonton?" I asked. This was awesome, I felt like I was talking to one of my buddies back home.

"Born and raised," Casey said.

"How did you end up here in Calgary?" I asked.

"Came for university. I applied to U of A too but only the University of Calgary accepted me. How did you end up here— all the way from the Northwest Territories?"

"Pretty much the same reason, except there was no post-secondary school to go to back home, so I *had* to come south. I wanted to go to Edmonton to see the Oilers of course, but I didn't know anyone in Edmonton, and my uncle and cousins lived here in Calgary. So U of C it was. My uncle let me stay at his place for a while when I first came here practically right out of high-school. He got me a job too, so I worked full time while going to school. All in all, I was better off, because I didn't have any money or time to go to an Oilers game back then anyway."

"I was the same," Casey said, "I would get through week-days on less than four hours sleep a night between school, study-ing, beer, getting rejected by girls, and work. Not always in that order. Then, I would sleep fourteen hours a night on Saturday and Sunday."

"Really?" I asked, with a shit eating grin, "I always wondered what it would be like to get a psychology or psychiatry degree. Everyone I knew always slept in or skipped their psych classes all year long, and then crammed for the midterm and final. Does that mean you guys showed up for like eleven classes in four years to get your degree?"

We both laughed again.

"OK OK, what the fuck did you take then? Fifty to one it was computer science," Casey guessed correctly, pegging me.

"Yes, but I should've been a Phys Ed. Teacher, or a farmer."

"I'd have walked away from baseball and I'd have bought a farm!" Casey said, quoting Wilford Brimley from the movie *The Natural* perfectly. The Natural was in my top three movies list, easy. It was also amusing to hear a guy named Casey—as in *Casey at the Bat*—talk about baseball.

"Nothing like a farm," I said, quoting Robert Redford from The Natural. "Nothing like being around animals, fixing things. There's nothing like being in the field with the corn and the winter wheat. The greenest stuff you ever saw."

"You know, my mother told me I ought to be a farmer." Casey said.

"My dad wanted me to be a baseball player." We both laughed as I finished off doing Redford. "That last part's actually true in my own life," I said.

"Really?"

"Yes, well, I mean, school came first, but baseball was his favourite sport, so he wanted me to play that." In my head I could see my father in his Lazy Boy armchair as I spoke.

"But you didn't?" Casey asked.

"No, I loved baseball, loved it, but the track & field coach, from grade seven to grade twelve, was one of those old school guys who said, 'When you're on my team you do track and nothing else, or you're off the team.' Kind of like one of the coaches you see in a football movie, set in Texas, where the guy would toss his baby into the Gulf of Mexico to make the next first down."

"Are your folks here in Calgary these days?" Casey asked.

"Nah, they both died years ago," I said.

"What about that uncle you lived with?"

"Also dead," I smiled, slightly.

"Any siblings?"

"One—a drug addict sister locked up in the funny farm."

"You're serious?"

"No, I said *funny* farm, not the *serious* farm. Yes, I'm serious. She's been in there for a while."

"Well God damn," Casey said, "the only thing worse would be for you to say your kids are dead." He wasn't smiling. He wasn't frowning. He looked at me thoughtfully. My best description would be to say I felt like a chess master was looking back at me across the board—*desk* in this case—his gaze pervading into my head. It wasn't impressive he could see how I was feeling *now*, but that like a chess master, he'd brought us to this point in the conversation by seeing a few moves ahead, and apparently, knew how I would react to his words. I laughed affably, but also in a way you would after someone beats you so handily you wanted to tip your hat to them, or clap—like when a centre fielder catches a ball no one had any business catching. You respected them. I looked at the ground with no response. Casey, however, was fixated on me. "What happened to them Sean?"

"They died in a car crash."

Casey frowned. "How? Can you tell me what happened?"

I changed, in an instant, surrounded by sadness, yes, but more so with the vivid memory of the events leading up to their death. I felt like I was right there again, before it happened—everything clear in my head, everything else in my mind cocooned off.

I started to talk: "It was late on a Saturday night in January, and very snowy and cold outside—minus thirty-five below. Grandma and Grandpa were over—my wife's parents.

They're good people. Great people. The kind of in-laws that make you marry someone sooner rather than later. My kids loved them and begged us to see their Grandparents all the time. My parents were already dead at this point.

"Anyway, we had eaten dinner, and just finished playing a game called *Ticket to Ride*. We usually played cards. Ticket to Ride though, was a two to four-hour game most of the time, and one of those addictive games where you become more focused on finishing than trying to win, so it was almost midnight when we were done playing. Doug and Bonnie, my in-laws, got up to leave, but we did the usual twenty-minute talk at the door before anyone left. This always annoyed me because we could be sitting down for those twenty minutes. It was worse when we did this same unending goodbye bullshit out in the cold."

Casey smirked and nodded a few times knowingly because most Canadians have frozen themselves at least once doing the same thing. I went on, "During those twenty minutes it was decided Alex and Owen would leave with Grandma and Grandpa for a sleepover at their house. The boys, already up later than they should've been, started screaming with glee. During the commotion of their yells and happy cries, including them running upstairs to get some pajamas and a change of clothes for the next morning, I whispered to my wife, Angela, that I didn't feel good about them going out in that weather, and that her parents looked tired. I suggested we ask them to stay at our house for the night, which would be safer, and would also modulate Alex and Owen's disappointment.

"This pissed Angela off. Maybe because our relationship wasn't doing very well, maybe because she was tired, maybe because she needed a break from the kids—heck, we both did. Angela felt like I was always denying them fun because I was so paranoid about every little thing—which was probably true. So, after a few vitriolic curses fired my way, under her breath, I relented.

"Like most kids, smarter than their parents give them credit for, the boys cheered because they had picked up on our conversation, and knew they were going with their grandparents for sure. In losing this argument, I'd already moved to my next secret conversation, which was to whisper into each boy's ear that they should get into Grandpa's truck and drive with him, and not with Grandma, who had come in her own car.

"My father in law, Doug, was a farm boy, and had been driving since he was about seven. Bonnie grew up in Chicago and didn't learn to drive until she was about thirty-five, after she had no choice, when she and Doug moved out of the city to the farm. Anyway, the boys nodded yes to my plan, and were about to go out the door with their Grandpa, when Owen said he couldn't leave until he got his book: *Monster Fun*. Doug, already frustrated at the delay in leaving—understandably—said he was going outside to start the cars, and they had five minutes before he was leaving. 'After that, you're riding with Grandma if you wanna come to the farm'.

"I told Owen to forget about the book, but it was like asking someone to jump out of a plane without a parachute—not going to happen—he needed that book. We ran upstairs into Owen's room, and dug through piles of Lego, toys, other books and clothes. Finally, we found *Monster Fun*, and I quickly glanced out Owen's window to see Grandpa hadn't left yet. I grabbed Owen by the arm and started guiding him quickly across the upstairs hallway towards the stairs, but he yanked his arm back, planted his feet, and said, 'Daddy can you read it to me real quick?' I said no, even though it was short, so he asked again —with tears in his eyes, and they weren't fake tears—'Please Daddy, can you just read a little bit to me.' I felt bad, because even though Owen was excited to go to his Grandparent's house, he still wanted to get a story in with me, so I read it to him at the top of the stairs while he hugged me.

"The mall is big, and tiring too – lots of things to see and do. Monsters are furry, monsters are fun, but you better watch out, or you'll be done!" I paused, because just like Davey Sandhu explained the day before, my hippocampus had done a great job storing the words from this story, and the immortal sorrow they caused me, in my brain. And also like Davey explained, this *negative experience* was impossible to erase from my memory.

I went through the rest of the story with Casey, almost like I was reading the book to Owen again, with all the monsters saying "you better watch out, or you'll be done" until I got to the end.

"When I finished, I gave Owen a kiss on the head and took him down the stairs. His brother Alex had been listening at the bottom of the stairs. I quickly moved to look out the front door and saw Doug driving away. 'Looks like you're coming with me,' said their Grandma. Bonnie looked dreadfully tired. I almost insisted again that the kids stay, or for Bonnie to stay with us, but I said nothing. The boys hugged Angela and me one more time, then left in the car with their Grandma."

I looked up at Casey, and he was looking at the floor, so I looked back at the floor before going on.

"The RCMP rang our doorbell about two hours later, around 2am. They said that Bonnie, Alex, and Owen, were killed outside of Calgary when their car was hit by a garbage truck that ran a red light. A *garbage truck*...on the road at *midnight*? They said the car was destroyed and everyone was killed instantly.

"This was not completely true. Later that week, I abused my computer access rights—being a cybersecurity analyst for the RCMP—and read the reports from a few of the first responders: EMS, FIRE and RCMP. Each responder wrote that when they arrived on scene the car was upside down, damaged, and on fire, and," I paused, "and they heard screaming coming from the car. The Fire department was the last to arrive, and by the time they turned on the water to put out the flaming car, the screams had already stopped. I hoped maybe the screams were something else, or maybe the reports were wrong, so I abused my computer access further, and confirmed what I'd read by watching RCMP body worn camera footage of the fire.

"The screams were real. I recognized the screams were coming from my sons. You understand what I'm saying here right?" I looked at Casey. He nodded but again didn't speak.

"They were trapped like that for fifteen minutes before the responders even got there to record that body worn camera footage. Months later, I legally obtained all of the same reports and video through a freedom of information and protection of privacy request. I watched the video every day for over a year. Do you know *why*? I watched it over and over again because I was hopelessly praying I would discover it wasn't them screaming in agony in the video. That maybe I imagined it. I didn't imagine it—it was all real."

I looked up at Casey, waiting for him to meet my gaze.

When he did, I said, "So, to answer your question, maybe it isn't just that they are dead, but *how* they died *is* my problem. A problem half of psych services at the RCMP could not help me solve—so I stopped going. A problem I'm tired of living with."

CHAPTER 11 – THE ANNOUNCEMENT

Casey and I stood outside the entrance of his house-like building and shook hands. He'd walked me to the door, and we were
bullshitting about sports and anything besides what I just un-
leashed on him, when he became more serious again.

"Come back any time. Free of charge,"

"Doc, I have great mental health coverage on my plan. If I
ever come back, I can claim it. I told ya, I work for the Mounties
—between the PTSD and sleep disorders we probably have more
shrinks than guns at this point."

"OK, fuck that then, I need the money! If you come back,
you're paying!" Casey said, before smiling briefly, and then continuing, "But seriously, please come back."

"Thanks," I said, and headed down the front steps and towards the curb. Half way down, I turned back, "Hey Casey, can I
ask you something?"

"No, fuck off."

"Fuck you."

"Sure," he said, and smiled again.

"Why do you think your sister sent me your way?"

"Ahh," he paused, then answered, "I think Myah is worried
about you. She's always getting worried about pathetic fucks."

"Christ, what are you? Like the worst shrink in the
world?" I asked rhetorically, and then shook my head and
smiled, but wanted to say something more to convey my

thanks. Not because Casey solved anything, but because he was the best mental health professional for someone like *me*, with the way I was, right then. He was a like a friend, like someone I'd known for a long time.

"Do you mind if I ask *you* a question?"

"Fire away," I said.

"Your wife—you guys aren't together anymore are you?"

"No," I said, "I reminded her too much of the boys. Alex looked a lot like me, Owen looked more like Angela, but a lot of what they would say came from me. So she didn't want to be around someone that made her remember them all the time. I suppose I felt the same way about her. Anyway, she left two weeks after they died."

Casey didn't say anything.

I paused for a bit, we said our goodbyes, and then I walked to my car and got in. I didn't start driving—I just sat there for a while. Was I any better off after talking to Casey? He was a good guy, and I'm sure many *experts* would say it was good for me to talk about Alex and Owen's death—don't bottle things up and all that bullshit—but the truth is, Casey only moved the dial a little on how I felt. I felt less *anger* than when I walked in earlier, but also more *sadness*, and for me, there is more strength and resolve in rage and denial, than in sorrow. You'll often hear people—intelligent people who have studied what I was going through, religious people, healers, whatever—say the opposite: Communication, exploration, and understanding are the paths to healing. But I knew *my* survival so far, if not healing, was dependent upon blocking out the past in my head. Where were the Men in Black when you needed them? They could "neuralyze" your brain with a flash of light.

This is the big question: Would I erase the memory of my children if it meant the pain of their death would go away? I don't think I could, which probably means what I said earlier about denial is fundamentally incorrect, but like the best coaches will tell you, that extra inch for the win between elite athletes often comes from heart, not fundamentals. So it is for life sometimes—you keep going even when you don't know why, or in my case, even when you don't want to.

"*Good afternoon!*" the car radio crackled, CBC's announcer bellowing with frenzy in her voice again, bringing me out of my daydream.

I swear radio stations find a way to increase the volume just like television stations do for commercials—somehow tripling the volume without you ever touching the dial. "*We now take you live to Time Dream world headquarters in California, for an announcement being broadcast all over the world. The next voice you hear will be that of Eric Byrne, the president and head of Time Dream.*"

Hmm, Davey was right in predicting the announcement —I guess he wasn't as far removed from the Time Dream board-room as Eric Byrne thought. That said, even though Eric was a dick, it was kind of cool knowing I talked to him in person the day before.

"*Good morning, good afternoon, and good evening, my name is Eric Byrne. Thank you all for coming, and for watching or listen-ing from wherever you are in the world. Time Dream is a lot of things to people. The new service we are about to unveil is going to change the world. Many will criticize us, like they did when we first opened, like they did when demand for coma jumps caused us to increase pri-cing, but we want to make a change for the better, where Time Dream is a transparent partner to all of humanity, and not just a company providing the greatest product of all time. Here in the United States, and in Canada, you may have heard about recent changes in the law regarding assisted suicides and the right to die. Demand is rising for people to end their life, in a dignified way, without pain and suffer-ing. Pain and suffering that is felt by families and friends. Pain and suffering, whether physical or mental, that can go on for years, decades sometimes, tearing lives and families apart. The law was changed to end this suffering. Time Dream wants to be a part of this, and we believe in the new law. Starting tomorrow, all Time Dream locations in the United States and Canada will be offering FREE as-sisted suicides.*"

I heard the people at Time Dream headquarters gasp in the background. Eric continued: *"We have the resources, and the space, to welcome people no matter what their economic situation is. Furthermore, any person who comes to Time Dream, for a free and painless assisted suicide, will be given a one-year coma jump for free, before they die."*

I could hear even more commotion in the background after that last statement, and, ignoring my own shock, decided I better pay attention, because there was no way this guy had the balls to take follow up questions after an announcement like this.

"After so much pain, people will be able to choose a time from their life when they were happy, and that will be the last year they have before dying. A year of happiness or adventure or love. Or all three! A life with dignity for some, when they thought that would never be possible again. Not a year in a hospital room, or a hospice, or in pain, or without loved ones—a year where they live out the greatest time in their life. As I said earlier, Time Dream has been criticized over the cost of its services, but as many of you know, a one-year coma jump has a value of ten million dollars. We are pleased to announce the only cost for this free assisted suicide, preceded by a free one-year coma jump, is that one agrees to be an organ donor—lives will be saved, with lives being ended. We have already been working with healthcare professionals, hospital administrators, and end of life caregivers.

All of them expect Time Dream's entrance into this market will free up thousands upon thousands of hospital beds, and reduce the load on healthcare more than anything in the history of the world. Time Dream has the full support of both the United States government, and the Canadian government, including support from state and provincial governments. We are actively working with other nations around the world to effect the same change in their countries. We will not be taking questions today, but will be holding press conferences tomorrow, and in the near future, to make sure everyone has the information they need. In the meantime, please go to the Time Dream website, or download the Time Dream app, for more information. Thank you."

I tried to wrap my head around what I just heard. Thankfully, I didn't have to struggle long, because less than a minute after Eric was done casting a spell on the entire planet, Anand was phoning me.

"Holy shit you answered the phone quickly," Anand said, "I didn't even hear your phone ring! *Please* tell me you heard the announcement."

"I did."

"How quickly can you get to my office?"

"That's thirty minutes away, I'll be there in ten," I said, doing my best Harvey Keitel voice.

"OK Mr. Wolf, see you in ten."

Nine minutes and thirty-seven seconds later, I pulled into the parking lot of Rocky Mountain News. Well, it was more like twenty-five minutes because I hit some traffic, and then Cher came on the radio, so I didn't get out of the car right away after parking. The only thing that ever got me more pumped up than a good Cher song like *Believe*—Cher's robotic yet melodious voice singing, *"Do you believe in life after love?"*—was when Patrick Duffy came out topless in the opening credits of *DALLAS*, with the theme music blasting in the background; it's like listening to the American national anthem before a Blackhawks game at the United Center.

I walked through the front entrance of RMN and headed straight for the elevators. Given that I'd worked with the RCMP for nearly fifteen years, it was refreshing to walk past dozing security guards that wouldn't notice Andre the Giant in the lobby if he was on fire. Sometimes you get tired of all the security and long for places like the airport back home—still without any formal security, yet more secure than any airport in the world because everybody knew everybody. When I got to Anand's office, there were two other people in with him, and they were yelling more than talking.

"Hey buddy," Anand said, then sighed before going on, "Come on in. This is Paul Lambert and Wanda Poole. Paul is with legal, and Wanda is a senior editor here at RMN."

"Hi, nice to meet y––"

"For fuck sakes, what are we gonna do about this Anand?" Wanda asked, ignoring the introduction.

"We can't do anything about it," Paul said. He had a thick French Canadian accent.

"Oh, you guys heard the announcement too, eh?" I asked. "Is that what you're worried about? The end of the wor––"

"We're a fucking international newspaper Sherlock— what do *you* think?" Wanda turned her gaze toward Anand, "They're saying you can't use *any* of the interview Anand."

"You mean the part Sean did with Davey Sandhu, right? Shit, no one even knew Davey was in the country. They took umbrage with that because it was unscheduled—I presume?" Anand asked, calmly, trying to bring the tension in the room down a notch.

"No, not just Sean's piece," Paul said, "All of it. Their legal team says we have to drop the whole thing."

"What?" I said, disappointed that my try at reporting may never see the light of day.

"Ohh, look who finally caught up! Dumbass," Wanda said —I could tell she really liked me. "We have *nothing* to publish Anand! Nothing! And that interview, coupled with the announcement Time Dream just made, would've had everyone in the world reading your article. We *needed* that boost to avoid the impending layoffs—you know this. And nowwww— nothing. Three days in a row and all I hear out of you is 'amazing, groundbreaking, and they're cooperating more than I expected'. What the hell happened?"

"It's all Sean's fault," Anand said, which made me laugh, but Anand's colleagues didn't even smirk.

"Maybe *before* inviting your *buddy*—who doesn't even work in this industry—you could consult with us next time after you get invited to talk with the most powerful man in the world!" Wanda was vibrating, and I'm pretty sure she hadn't blinked yet either.

"You got to talk with *Hulk Hogan*, man?" I mocked, with seriously overstated enthusiasm—like a sheriff's sidekick in a low budget movie based out of Texas, usually being half the size of the sheriff himself, excitedly stating, "*Come on Bubba! Come on! We gonna get 'em! We gonna get 'em Bubba!*"—while I looked at Anand, just to wind Paul and Wanda up some more.

"What the fuck?!" Wanda yelled. She swore more than my old hockey coach when I was nine—I kind of liked it.

Anand jumped right in, with a Hulk Hogan voice, "What you gonna do Time Dream, when the real truth, the twenty-four-inch pythons and Hulkamania, runs wild on youuu!!" Then he did a couple bicep poses.

"Hey, come on guys," Paul pleaded, "dis is serious ah? I'm really starting—"

"*I am a real Ah-merican,*" Anand was singing now, "*fight for the rights of every man!*"

I liked this, so I started singing too, finishing off the first bit of Hulkster's theme song. "*I am a real Ah-merican, fight for what's right, fight for your LIFE!*" Then *I* did a couple bicep poses, which was more amusing than when Anand did it, because I have twelve inch arms, not twenty-four inch pythons.

"Shut the fuck up, ya little prick! Can we get serious? What are we gonna do?" Wanda asked again.

"Well, I could always leak it online by accident," Anand said, which made me become serious as well, because that sounded dangerous.

"That's not a good idea," I said.

"It's a stupid idea," Wanda said.

"It's also an illegal idea," Paul chimed in, making it three of us piling on my friend. "Anand, they had us sign an information sharing agreement before you said a single word to anyone at Time Dream. As amazing and unlikely as Sean's interview was, Davey said things that even *we* would consider proprietary information."

"Well, we're not gonna solve it in the next five minutes are we?" Anand said. "Can I eat my lunch now?"

"Fine," Wanda said, and walked out.

"Oh, sorry Anand," Paul said, a tad more politely than Wanda, and then left Anand's office as well.

"You didn't eat yet, man?" I asked, taking the now vacant seat in front of Anand's desk.

"Of course I did," Anand said, and then smiled. "I just wanted to get them outta here. Shut the door, will ya?" I shut the door. "So, did you catch *all* of Eric's broadcast?"

"Yah, there's just one thing I can't figure out. How the hell do they make money out of this?" I asked, looking to my smarter friend for answers.

"That's where your mind is at? After *that* announcement?" Anand asked, looking at me in disbelief. "According to the World Health Organization, approximately 1.2 million people commit suicide each year worldwide—that we know about. There are probably many millions more who wake up every day struggling to find a reason not to end their life. Thankfully, the majority of them are OK, but Time Dream just gave every person who wakes up feeling that way a ten million dollar joyride incentive to end their life. And there's more, did you know if two doctors sign off that you're terminally ill, it's not considered suicide in the eyes of insurance companies? They make a distinction between medically assisted deaths and regular suicide."

I didn't know this, but nodded my head like I did, unconvincingly, before Anand went on.

"Adults with enduring and intolerable suffering, in cases where death was reasonably foreseeable, can also end their life without it impacting their life insurance. As long as two doctors sign off on it, and perform a regulated assisted suicide, their families can *still* collect the life insurance money, and believe me, never before has the subjective *reasonably foreseeable* been more coerced out of practitioners."

"Are you sure?" was all I could spit out.

"Listen to me, you're not getting it! Both of these points are covered in Bill C-14, and the United States has done the same with their laws. Time Dream not only lobbied for this to happen, but when the life insurance companies went bananas over this change, they were given billions of dollars in payouts to shut up about it. And all of this happened in advance of Time Dream's one-year coma jump suicide deal being announced. You hear what I'm saying?"

I feigned ignorance to hide what I was thinking, because from the moment I heard the announcement by Eric Byrne, I was considering Time Dream's offer for myself.

"I know, I know," I said, feeling a little defensive, and naive, "but didn't you say some lower level Time Dream employees told you the company was originally funded by the US Government? To research innovative solutions for population control and global over-crowding? Well, that's starting to sound a lot more concrete now, *isn't it*? They've basically created a system to kill off the poor, the sick, the unhappy, the disadvant--"

"No Sean! No! They've created a system where those people will kill *themselves*. Don't you see? Philosophers have been pontificating about this one for thousands of years: The illusion of choice can compel people to do anything. Christ man, this is at the core of nearly every theological discussion in history. Every religion, faith, cult, whatever, usually centres around *God* bestowing the great gift of choice on us all. And do you know what else? I *am* leaking that fucking interview!"

"What!?" I was getting scared now—there was a wild look in Anand's eyes. "Man, that's not a good idea. Tell me why yo--"

"I'll tell you why. This moment has happened a hundred times before in history, and the politicians and the bureaucrats, and the scribes like me, and fucking everybody, don't do a God damn thing! And before you know it we have a totalitarian state again, or genocide, or the holocaust! Shit man, you're a Star Wars fan, evil empires are formed when decisions like this go unchecked."

"Ahh, I'm not sure you wanna make a comparison between Luke Skywalker's rebellion and the holocaust if you

wanna sway anyone in your next article. A comparison between *Thelma and Louise* and the holocaust, maybe." Anand
didn't even crack a smile.

"Shut up, you're missing the point, I'm––"

"No, I fuckin get it man," I interrupted, "but what I'm saying is you better not leak that interview. I just don't think that's
a good idea. It's not safe."

"*Safe*? What happened to you Sean? I used to be the one
talking *you* out of doing something like this. You used to brag
about how you'd do all these things if you had nothing left to
lose. Well?"

"It's not me I'm talking about here—you have a family!" I
pleaded. "I'm saying I don't think it's safe for *you* if that interview is leaked."

"Well, I thought about that, and I thought of an idea you
can help me with: What if Rocky Mountain News was hacked,
and it went public, so everyone knew about the hack, and the
interview was one of many things leaked online?"

"No," I said.

"No, *what*?" Anand asked.

"No as in it's a shitty idea."

"Why? You're always telling me about this stuff. Leaks,
ransomware, hackers demanding money from companies or
they will release the information onto the Internet," Anand
said, his logic shrinking in inverse proportion to his increasing
cloudy judgment.

"That's not the problem with the idea." I explained. "As
you suggested earlier, Time Dream is into the hundreds of trillions in profits. Do you know what kind of power *empires* like
this have? Not only can they hire and compel anyone to trace
the legitimacy and origins of the hack, including the NSA probably, but they could very well have this room bugged right now.
This isn't even the place to be talking about this."

"I don't think the room is bugged," Anand said, annoyed
and shaking his head.

"Really? You think my smartphone, your smartphone

and the impenetrable, aforementioned, soon to be hacked RMN computer network can't have a well-paid threat actor combing through them right now? I'd consider it a miracle if you, me and RMN weren't being monitored already. Just like it'll be a miracle if you don't get Lee Harvey Ozwald-ed and have your family watching you on the six o'clock news with two bullets in your head. Come to think of it, *that* would get Wanda the headline she wanted, so go for it, save your company from layoffs!"

"I'm fucking releasing it!" Anand yelled. He was standing now. So was I. I don't remember when I stood up.

"Don't do it."

"If you're not gonna help, then just leave. You think I'm tryin' to get a *fuckin headline* here? You're a fuckin idiot. Some things are more important than your own well-being."

"Like breast implants?"

"Everything's a joke."

"Anand, calm down, this is crazy, I'm just—"

"Just get out!"

We both paused after he said this. I've been kicked out of offices, meetings, classrooms, churches, even hospitals, and it never bothers me, but when your best friend says something like this it penetrates into your soul, like when a parent commits the cardinal sin of telling their young child they are stupid, and the child, not so young, knows they meant it. When we were younger, Anand himself described this feeling much more eloquently, after a then girlfriend asked what he'd do if I hit him, to which he replied, "I wouldn't do anything, I'd probably be sad and wonder why someone I love just hurt me." I left his office.

CHAPTER 12 – IF YOU BUILD IT, THEY WILL COME

I woke up Friday morning—my last *suspended with pay* day off because I was due to check in with my boss, Staff Sergeant Brian Forbes, on Monday—to nearly every TV channel reporting on the massive lineups at Time Dream. Suicide lineups. Or were they just people who thought reliving the best year of their life in a coma jump, with no laws, suffering, or accountability, was worth dying for? I thought it was worth dying for. For my one-year coma jump I would pick a year when my sons and parents were still alive, quit my job, convince my wife to quit her job, and go on vacations all over the place: Moose Jaw to Montreal to Moscow—well, maybe not Moscow, I grew up in a time filled with anti-Russian propaganda, so all I see at the end of that journey is a rabid ten foot Ivan Drago flipping over our *Lada* built tour bus on the way to the Kremlin.

We would take breaks from the vacationing—like George Costanza going for lunch after sleeping under his desk all morning—to go to the movies, play catch, buy the pet I never did get for my sons when they were alive, or do whatever came into our heads.

I would've kept planning and daydreaming about my one-year coma jump, fueled and inspired by the droves of people on my television set already in line, but an annoying feeling of guilt had my conscience in a headlock: Anand—I should help him. I should be offering up suggestions on how to pull off his idea of leaking the Davey Sandhu interview onto the Internet. Not because I agreed with his plan, but because with my background, he might actually get it online without leaving a digital footprint so obvious a *Seniors Learn to Surf the Internet Club* could follow it.

Why? Well, I have two talents in life I've been good at from day one, with no practice. 1. Children trust me. 2. Breaking into computers, networks, hacking, and moving around or through online obstacles without leaving a trail, is like breathing to me. I have *some* technical skills sure, but nothing like they falsely portray in movies where people crack networks in mere seconds: It's more like ~~Turned~~ GONE *in Sixty Seconds*—the story of Nic Cage and Angelina Jolie trying to teach Vin Diesel how to turn a laptop on in under a minute.

No, what made me good at weaselling into networks when I was young and defending them as a cybersecurity analyst for the RCMP now, was a talent for social engineering. Most popular descriptions of social engineering, as it relates to cybersecurity, define it as the psychological manipulation of people into performing actions or divulging confidential information. Put simply, it's a way to get you to do something you didn't want to do on your computer, smartphone, iPad, tablet, wireless solar-powered dildo cam, whatever.

But here's what it really is: an inherent understanding of how different technologies are perceived by various groups of people. It is to exploit how people think. It doesn't have to be a technological hack, in fact, the best scams are often effective because of their simplicity. For example, different versions of the following story have been told for decades:

A man lives in a border town between the US and Canada. He lives on the Canadian side but works in construction on the US side. Every morning, he walks over to the American side, and every evening, he comes back over to the Canadian side with a wheelbarrow full of sand. And, every day without fail, the Canadian Customs officers check him for any contraband he might be trying to smuggle in. For twenty years, the man works nearly every day for the construction company, and every day customs checks the sand in the wheelbarrow, trying to find hidden goods. They sift through the sand, dig in around it, but find nothing. As the years go on, they try to be more clever. They x-ray the wheelbarrow, run tests on the sand, check inside the wheels and axles—whatever they can possibly think of. In desperation, they even strip search the man a few times and run cavity checks. Year after year, they find nothing. Finally, twenty years later, the man is old and set to retire. On the day of his retirement, he once again pushes a wheelbarrow full of sand across the border. The customs officers stop him and ask point-blank, "Look, we know you've been smuggling something across the border all these years. You have to be. But we've searched through your sand every day for twenty years, and we've found absolutely nothing. It's killing us— please, we'll give you a free pass, wipe away any past crimes, if you just tell us what it is you've been smuggling all these years!"

In my version of this story, the old man politely tells them to go fuck themselves and walks off into retirement good and wealthy from all the profits he's made smuggling wheelbarrows for two decades. Moving right along, my talent is to combine a little bit of technical knowledge with an understanding of human behaviour.

When I was twenty-three, and working in the private sector, we had a pretty good and relatively unheard of little racket going on at an IT firm I ran with three other guys. These days, this racket is referred to as a *vulnerability assessment*, or, and this is my favourite name for it in the cybersecurity vernacular, a *penetration test*—which brings on visions of Casey Kasem shouting out the Sodomy Top Forty list, with music from the gimp scene in *Pulp Fiction* playing in the background.

We would offer to break into a company's network, then break in with their approval, which amounted to placing a computer document in a so called secure area of their network, and finally, sell them a security solution afterwards with the assurance it would prevent anyone else in the universe from doing the same thing to their network—which was right up there with other non-binding business fables, such as encouraging folks to drink a Diet Coke with their Mc-Heart-Attack combo to lose weight. This usually worked quite well, but every now and then we would run into a company whose security was almost impossible to break through—be it physically, by picking a lock, or digitally, in trying to find a way in through their computer systems. We hit such a company back then, and after two weeks, we were about to throw in the towel and give this pharmaceutical distribution company—let's call them *Florez Distribution*—a pat on the back. Then, I had an idea. We knew from our research that Florez Distribution outsourced all its IT support to a huge international organization. Let's call them *Mantis Computer Systems*. Like most big companies, Mantis could cover all hours of support 24/7, but weren't great on the *personal* side of customer care—you'd be lucky to see a real person once every five years instead of the usual remote support across the telephone.

So, we made up thirty-two copies of a fake letter to mail to Florez Distribution, which would appear to be from Mantis Computer Systems. We put in a lot of effort to make the letter look like all the other communications Mantis sent, and by effort I mean we crawled through the garbage of Florez Distribution, and other companies supported by Mantis. We had the company logo and letterhead looking perfect, the style of print was a dead match, even the paper was the same. Then, we did the same thing with a specially crafted email message, making sure it looked exactly like what Mantis sent on a daily, hourly, and minutely basis to all its customers. How did we do that? We became a customer of Mantis ourselves, temporarily, to see what their emails looked like.

With that, we were ready. We couriered the special letter to all thirty-two different sections of Florez Distribution's three buildings. Couriering the letter was key, because it let us track when the letters arrived. What was in the letter? A notification of a new IT Helpdesk phone number—

which was really just a number pointing to us—that all Mantis Computer System customers should phone going forward, with a grace period where both old and new phone numbers would be dually accessible for a month, of course! We even got our own 1-800 number and answering system, making sure to have all the familiar Mantis Computer System options and slogans on the prerecorded message, but no matter what button the caller pressed, it would forward to a cell phone I carried.

Then, we waited, but not for long—I got a call the same day we couriered the letter. A nice woman named Sapphire, who worked in the reception area of Human Resources at Florez Distribution, and was probably the lucky soul who picked up the mail for HR every day, called about a computer printing problem. Now here's the beauty of this attack: Sapphire phoned me, not the other way around. Case in point, most people out there are pretty clever in common scenarios, where if you phone them at home or at work and try to fool them, they're ready, and have their guard up. But imagine if *you* were doing the phoning in contacting your company's IT helpdesk. Would you be ready? No, you wouldn't expect anything suspicious to happen at all, and like I said above, Sapphire not only phoned me, she phoned with an aggravating printing problem that was ruining her day.

> Me—answering as Mantis Computer Systems on their new helpdesk phone number: "Good afternoon, Mantis Systems, my name is Ernie Coombs."
>
> Sapphire: "Yes, hi Ernie, this is Sapphire White, I can't print, and I have about fifteen things open, so I DON'T want to reboot."
>
> Me: "Hi Sapphire, I understand, sorry to hear that, where are you calling from?"
>
> Sapphire: "Florez Distribution, Human Resources."
>
> Me: "Thank you, OK, no worries, we should be able to fix you up. Before we get started, can you tell me if other folks in HR are printing OK?"
>
> Sapphire: "Yes, everyone else is fine, I'm the only one hav-

ing trouble—because God hates me apparently."

Me: "Haha, I bet my wife hates me more than God hates you!"

Sapphire: "Heehee, oh you're bad, that's too funny."

Me: "Haha, thanks, I try, but I'm also pretty good at getting printers going. So is this a shared printer, or is it just you who uses it? Like, is it connected to your computer with one of those USB cables?"

Sapphire: "Yes, it's my printer only, it connects with USB."

Me: "OK thanks, so what happens when you hit print each time? Does anything happen at all, or no?"

Sapphire: "Well, like I said, it looks like it's going to print, and kind of starts to do its thing, and then nothing happens." *At this point I already have a pretty good idea how to fix the problem—restart the printer spooler on her computer—but I don't just want to fix the problem, I want to break into Florez Distribution's network, so we can sell them a ridiculously over-priced security solution!*

Me: "Hmm, that's odd, I think it might be best if I shadow your desktop and see what's happening. Is that OK?"

Sapphire: "Oh yah, that's fine."

Me: "OK, good good, I'm going to email you a link. All you have to do is click it, login with your Windows username and password, and then I can join the screen with you. I have you at sapphire.white@florezdistri-bution.com, is that still correct?"

Sapphire: "You got it."

Me: "Right on, I sent the link. Let me know when you reciev––"

Sapphire: "I've got it, and I already clicked the link and logged in."

Me: "I see that, excellent, and I'm now on your desktop with you. That's your wallpaper with the picture of a black dog in a red Santa hat right?"

Sapphire: "Yes, that's my dog *Blacky*! He's so cute." *Nice, you couldn't make that one up, Sapphire WHITE with a dog named BLACKY—she could fit in at the local KKK affiliate on multiple levels. But, funny coincidences aside, due to Sapphire's clicking of my link, and entering her password, I not only could see her screen, but had loaded some malware in the background allowing me to control her computer across the Internet. And I had her username and password as well. But the job was not finished—I needed to actually fix her printer problem for two reasons: 1. Sapphire wouldn't think anything was wrong if I fixed her up, and 2. If anyone asked, she would say the new Mantis Systems helpdesk number worked just fine.*

Me: "That's awesome, OK, I guess just try and print again and I will watch what happens."

Sapphire: "OK, boom, did you see that?"

Me: "Yes, and good news, I know exactly what that is. You just need to restart your print spooler."

Sapphire: "Oh God, how do I do that?"

Me: "Haha, no worries, I can do it from here. I'll drive for a second." *I went into 'Services' on the screen, with Sapphire watching on her end, and then restarted the 'print spooler' service.* "OK, try printing again now Sapphire."

Sapphire: "Well, I doubt that's gonna work but—OH MY GOD it worked—it's printing! You're a genius!"

Me: "That's great, can I help you with anything else today?"

Sapphire: "No, thank you! Have a great day. Goodbye."

Me: "You too Sapphire! Goodbye."

At this point, I had enough to say we'd broken into Florez's networks, and to notify Florez we had completed the penetration test, but we decided to see what else we could pick up before someone discovered our scam.

The thing is, after two more weeks, *nobody* ever caught on! We did over fifty fake support calls which garnered us nearly every corner of the Florez computer network. It was just silly. Even after we did the debrief with their executive and security teams, and hocked a useless piece of security software over to

Florez, my phone still got calls from their employees asking for IT support.

When I explained this, Florez went so far as to send out communications to their employees describing what happened and told them the number they received was a fake. However, Florez Distribution was so efficient, they had posted new signs with the fake 1-800 number all over the company, and even though they quickly took them down, the number got in people's heads and contact lists. A year went by and that phone was *still* ringing every now and then.

"*WEE-OOOO, WEE-OOOOOOOO,*" I was snapped out of my past cyber exploits daydream by an insanely loud alert on the television. "*WEE-OOOO, WEE-OOOOOOOO, This is an Alberta Emergency Alert,*" the creepy male robot voice said, which always put an idea into everyone's head of what a bionic child molester might sound like, instead of making us focus on whatever the damn AMBER alert was about. Actually, this was only an *emergency* alert. AMBER alerts are supposed to be used for abducted children or—as it evolved in some jurisdictions—an adult with a proven mental or physical disability, but it makes you wonder what might happen to the emergency broadcast system if the PETA people keep up their radically successful lobbying for animal rights—we'll all be hearing AMBER alerts for somebody's lost parakeet before you know it.

"*WEE-OOOO, WEE-OOOOOOOO,*" the TV shrieked again, effectively bringing my attention back to it, "*This alert is in effect for the province of Alberta but is being broadcast in regional areas across Canada and the United States. All Time Dream locations are full. The crowds outside Time Dream storefronts have made many areas surrounding Time Dream locations unsafe due to line-ups and protests. Effective immediately, no one will be able to attend a Time Dream location in Canada or the United States without booking a reservation in advance via TimeDream.com or the Time Dream app. Proof of reservation must be presented to gain admittance. Please see TimeDream.com for more information.*

"*WEE-OOOO, WEE-OOOOOOOO,*" the alert ended and the

local TV station came back on with a reporter practically yelling to be heard outside of what looked like one of the New York Time Dream locations, so I muted the TV.

I sat there unmoving in a state of disbelief for a bit, and then turned the volume back up and flipped around the channels. Most TV stations had changed their tone from excitement to more of a cautionary broadcast, following the alert, and because government officials, law enforcement and other first responders were beginning to use more alarming words like *riot* and *outbreak* versus *large groups* and *disturbances*.

My immediate thought was a selfish one, not proportionate to the gravity and seriousness of what was going on: *When would I get to do another coma jump with all this bullshit going on?* When would I get to start *my* one-year suicide coma jump? 365 days to be with my family again, to be with my sons every day, to be happy, and not alone. I wondered how Worf from Star Trek, with his, "*Today is a good day to die*," creed, would view my plan, but as I thought more about it, I didn't just think it was a good *time* to die, it was *how* I wanted to die—with that much time in a coma jump it could become my reality before things ended. Perhaps I was wrong, and my feelings actually were proportionate to the situation, because this might be how millions of people were feeling, albeit for different reasons. I was comforted by this self-awareness, and by seeing all the people on TV lining up to die, because it seemed to justify what *I* wanted. I wasn't giving up, I just wanted things to go back to the way they were.

I stayed inside for the rest of the weekend. I couldn't do a coma jump because of the massive lineups, and I knew Anand didn't want to speak with me unless I was willing to help him leak the Sandhu interview. Also, based on the chaos the television was reporting, staying in my suburban neighborhood, far from any Time Dream location, was a good move. After a whole week off with pay because of my suspension, both Saturday *and* Sunday felt like a Sunday night, with the dread of going back to work hanging over me. I had enough *I don't give a fuck* in me to last the rest of my life—literally, in this case—so I was impervious to any back to work jitters, but I was unsure what would come from my Sky Train platform incident. Once again, my real concern if anyone ever leaked my name to go along with the video, was not for myself, but for any disrepute I might bring Anand. I had a feeling Anand's incensed state of mind was going to bring him enough trouble, but no one could've predicted just how bad it was about to get.

CHAPTER 13 –
THE LEAK

I groggily woke up Monday morning to my good and faithful General Electric radio clock playing CBC 99.1 FM at 7:30am, in place of my alarm, which was an impressive option for the thirty-five-year-old device. Apparently one of us aged better than the other.

"*An Interview between Rocky Mountain News and former head of Time Dream, Davey Sandhu, has surfaced on the Internet.*"

I sat up immediately in bed, my heart pounding like I'd been injected with the same stuff they pump into horses at the Kentucky Derby."

The broadcast continued: "*The audio recording has gone viral, and Time Dream has already stated its release was unsanctioned, and that the interview was done without their permission. In the interview, an unknown reporter from RMN, known only as Sean, banters back and forth with Sandhu like they were the best of friends. Sandhu explains concepts, appears to accurately predict the Time Dream suicide announcement in advance, and is even more open and revealing of their technology than he was before Time Dream demoted him a few years ago. Here is an excerpt from the interview.*"

I sat there in my *Miami Vice* pajamas—Don Johnson's face sprawled across my shirt the same way it did when my mom bought it for me at age fourteen—paralyzed with shock and listened to my own voice come across the radio. My heart sunk when I realized Anand had leaked everything, even the part where Davey replied to one of my questions with, "Sean, listen to what I just told you, and this part *is* off the record," making me seem like a scumbag that set Davey up. I kept listening with interest, unable to move, each word ping ponging me back and forth between panic and anger.

"RMN has claimed responsibility for the interview, but has so far only admitted to making the interview, explaining it was the victim of a cyberattack where hackers released the interview onto the Internet unbeknownst to RMN."

Jesus, Anand executed his plan exactly like he said he would, word for word. I wondered if he'd written the RMN press release before I was even in his office the other day.

Before getting out of bed, I listened to a few more frantic takes on the interview by the media, and then my heart sunk further after hearing several messages on my smartphone starting with, "Hey man, is that you?" However, with me going back to work today to hear my fate, it was the short text message from Staff Sergeant Brian Forbes that caught my eye:

"See me as soon as you get in. Re: Davey Sandhu interview."

As stated earlier, I didn't give a fuck if I was suspended, fired, or if the RCMP shoved a pink slip up my ass—although I've watched too many episodes of *Oz* to be able to enjoy anything pink in that region of my body—I just wanted to have a way to support myself long enough to get my one-year suicide coma jump under way. But with what appeared to be a coma jump waiting list growing like a virus, I had a new found yearning to continue being gainfully employed by Canada's national police force—for now.

It was with this in mind that I bounded out of bed, got ready, and drove to work like a tornado was swirling behind me. Not that a tornado could do anything to my '70 LeSabre —armored tanks were more at risk. If Dorothy had been in my car at the beginning of *The Wizard of Oz*—the 1939 film, not the anally charged, high rated, HBO drama Oz I referred to earlier—

it would've been a much shorter film.

When I got to the McNeil building I walked in focused on what I was going to say to Brian. I was rehearsing different responses as I walked, not really paying attention to my surroundings, when a large hand went in front of me.

"Hey Sean! What-a-ya got in the bag!?" John the head security guard asked loudly, startling me more than I wanted to show. "Awww, did I interrupt you Riley?"

"You know what John," I admit I considered giving John a *go fuck yourself*, but figured he deserved something worse because I was in a bad bordering neurotic mood. "I think I saw something suspicious in the parking lot."

"No you didn't," John said, shaking his head like a parent who knew from experience their child was lying.

"What did you see?" Derrick, another guard who reported to John, asked.

"Leave it," John said, "He didn't see anything."

"No no, I did. I saw a bunch of guys unloading boxes from an old, rusting, over-filled Toyota minivan. It was red or maroon I think, and there was like five or six Middle Eastern looking guys, and I think the writing on the boxes was in Persian." I threw in the Persian part to spike their racially motivated terrorist training spider-senses. "It could be nothing, but it worried me a bit so I thought I should tell someone."

"Aww for fuck sakes!" John said.

"The writing was in *Persian*?" Derrick asked, innocently, with a worried look. He and some of the other guards moved towards the door.

"Or maybe it was English—it's hard to say with the two being so similar," I said, making sure not to smile. "Oh shit, I just realized the time, I'm late for work. Look gents, don't worry about it, I'm sure those guys are just the new janitorial crew." Which I knew was true. I had a friend in the Facilities department who recently mentioned the RCMP just negotiated a new contract for a cleaning company to handle custodial services in the McNeil building. "See ya fellas!" I smiled and walked away.

I didn't even bother stopping at my office and went straight to Brian's office knowing he would have a note on my door to come and see him. I was moving quickly and thought I heard Linda yell out some kind of warning. No time, I went straight in.

"Good morning Staff Sergeant!" I said with a smile that could rival Garfield on his most mischievous of days.

"Close the door and sit down," he said, not the least bit startled, even though he was looking down when I came in.

Despite being lord of the dicks, he was cool under pressure—a gunshot in the middle of the night wouldn't make this guy flinch.

I closed the door.

"OK, right to the point, and don't fuck around, is that you talking to Davey Sandhu on the leaked interview?"

"What interview?" I asked, displaying a confused look so believable I could've been a contestant on Celebrity Jeopardy—where stars answer questions so poorly one might think they're suffering from the very disability they are trying to raise money for. If Tiny Tim's survival was hinging on Lindsay Lohan's knowledge of national capitals, then *A Christmas Carol* would've ended very differently. Thank God, Alex Trebek and Pat Sajak for airing Wheel of Fortune right after Jeopardy every night, so we can all feel like an idiot and a genius in the same hour.

"You know what interview I mean. The one all over the news today," Brian said.

"I'm not sure I know what you mean, Sir."

"It's on every TV station in the world. You know what I'm talking about Sean."

"I don't watch TV in the mornings. My mother was an elementary school teacher, and never let me watch anything before school because she thought it made children tired. I guess the habit kind of stuck with me."

"It's all over the radio, the Internet, TV, everything. You're honestly telling me you don't know what I'm talking about?" Brian asked, without raising his voice, but his eyes were wide, and I saw his hands shaking.

"I'm not really sure Boss," I said, while scratching my chin and looking upwards, "Can you please pull it up and play it for me?"

"Fine." Brian turned around, looking more flustered now, and attempted to login to Windows on his computer. He inserted his login token, for two-factor authentication, and entered his password, but it didn't work. Twice, still no luck. After five bad attempts his account locked out automatically, and Brian lost his shit: "Dammit Riley!"

"Hey boss," I said, smiling more and more, "I think you locked your account out—" Stating the obvious was a sure fire way to make Brian go even more apeshit. "—by entering it in wrong five time--"

"I know what happened!" Brian screamed—he actually yelled, but it amuses me more to say he screamed.

"Hey, maybe pull it up on your smartphone," I suggested, knowing Brian still had one of the last BlackBerries in existence, and also knowing he was as adept at using it as he was a ballerina.

"Yes, yes, OK I got it," Brian interjected, feverishly hitting each button on the BlackBerry with enough force to crack a walnut, "NBC has it right here on their website." Brian hit play, but the video just kept spinning like the connection was bad. About a minute went by and nothing was playing yet. "God dammit!"

"Hey boss, do you wanna use my phone? Here ya go," I handed it to him and voila, the video was queued up and ready to play after he did a quick search. He handed my phone back to me as the NBC news bulletin started to play:

"RMN is still claiming they were the victims of a cyberattack, and had nothing to do with its releas--"

I stopped the video from playing, before my voice was even heard, looked up quickly, and said, "Ohhhhh, that interview, yah that's me!"

"Ahhhh!" He lunged at me across his desk, sliding half onto it, and shaking the whole room. A few pictures fell off the wall, and I moved before he could grab me. I should've been scared, but it was funny to me because he had reacted this way a few times before—once, after he lunged at me on a public sidewalk, I fell down and pretended to be hurt because he was in uniform, and people crowded around thinking I had been the recipient of police brutality.

He stumbled trying to grab me again, when the door swung open.

"What's going on in here!?" Linda yelled.

"He tried to touch my penis," I said in a fake, emotional, crying and whimpering voice, while holding my crotch with both hands in a horseshoe stance. Brian was pulling himself to his feet, calming down a bit, but still with a face redder than Ted Kennedy's after twelve *Chivas Regal* whiskies.

Linda laughed. "You boys behave in here," she said, and then closed the door.

"Christ sake. Was that necessary?" Brian asked, straightening his chair and sitting down. I sat back down as well before he continued. "OK, so what the hell are you doing in that interview?"

"I've been exploring my artistic side," I answered, simply.

"Not while you're working here you're not. We didn't spend half a million dollars training you over the last fifteen years for you to end up on the national news twice in one week."

"Well, *am I* still working here?" I asked, getting to the point myself.

Brian sighed before answering. "If it was up to me I would fire your ass, but the Inspector and Chief Superintendent both indicated you're to stay, so long as your identity and involvement in the public incidents stays hidden. You've been through a lot over the years," he paused—Jesus, even this fucking guy felt sorry for me, "but if your name, and involvement with the RCMP, does surface—it's just not defendable."

"OK, so do I go back to work?" I asked.

"No, we've decided you're still suspended with pay until this interview bullshit blows over."

169

Once again, I tried to force a solemn look onto my face, but like a junior poker player sitting on a pair of aces, I knew I looked happy at some level. I stared at the ground to mask my excitement—getting suspended with pay was like collecting a pension before you were retired!

"And I have some more questions for you, like how in the hell did *you* end up talking to the most powerful man in the world?"

"You mean Hulk Hogan?" I asked. I should've said *He-Man* in this situation, but that would've been inappropriate and inaccurate, since He-Man is the most powerful man in the *universe*, not just the *world*.

"Get out!" Brian pointed to the door, already looking away from me, and back down at his BlackBerry, shaking his head slowly.

CHAPTER 14 – ANOTHER LEAK

I walked to my car in the RCMP parking lot without encountering any Persian terrorist janitors, tickled pink with the news of my suspension being extended, and decided to phone Myah in the hope she could pull some strings to move me to the front of the list for a one-year suicide coma jump. Despite my fears of Myah trying to talk me out of this plan, she was somewhat businesslike and hastily accommodating on the phone, like I was just another number amongst Time Dream's trillions of dollars —perhaps I was, and Myah was simply being worked off her feet with the added storms of people all showing up for their coma jump of death.

Unfortunately, she wasn't able to meet with me to work out the details until four o'clock. With this in mind, and knowing I wouldn't be able to squeeze in an impromptu coma jump —I had three free ones left—at any of the busy Time Dream locations, let alone the Lougheed location, I decided to head over to Forest Lawn and see if Quan had my fake credit cards and driver's licenses ready.

"Sean, you sneaky criminal fuck," Quan said, as I strolled into the pawnshop, "Why you take so long to come pick up your stupid IDs? And why pick stupid names? They don't fool anyone. You unda-stand? They not beweevable."

Upon hearing this, I confess to thinking of Cher's song *Believe* yet again, and picturing Quan in the shower, rubber ducky in hand, happily singing *"Do you beweeeeeeve in wife after wuv?"* while scrubbing his back with a loofa, shower cap and all.

"Well old buddy," I answered, "I'm not going for believable this time round."

"We not buddy, you pay me fake money once, member?" he said, eyeing me with suspicion.

"Speaking of pay, how much do I owe you Quan?"

"A thousand bucks, buckaroo: one hundred dollah for each pair credit card and driver's license."

"Sounds fair to me," I said, despite Quan's logic defying cost markup. "You want cash as usual Sir?"

Quan almost looked disappointed I didn't haggle with him over price like we used to, but an extra couple hundred dollars spent on illegal identification wouldn't matter to me in the very near future. I thanked him, shook his hand, exited the pawnshop, and ran quickly back to my car to avoid being stabbed, shot, robbed, raped, sniffed, or spoken to in the Forest Lawn parking lot.

Then, just as I finished locking the doors, CBC Radio crackled out another breaking story, one that would irreparably change a lot of lives—including mine.

"CBC has just learned about a video circulating on the Internet. Famed Rocky Mountain News reporter and writer, Anand Dhami, is shown having sex with several women on multiple occasions. In the video, there are a number of political, racially charged and misogynistic statements made by Mr. Dhami. However, it's what Dhami said to the mother of a five-year-old girl, right before the two engaged in intercourse, that has people calling for him to be investigated and fired from RMN. The woman and mother known only as Jasmine, in the video, is taken aback when Dhami suggests she bring her daughter into the room so they can have sex in front of the child. After the mother vehemently scolds Dhami, this was his response, which is a clip taken from the video: 'Well, she has to learn about sex sooner or later.'

The two are shown arguing for a few minutes after this exchange, and then have intercourse. Within a few hours of the video going viral across the web, social media sites started to see someone going by the name of TamaraRockszz1985 make posts where she claimed to be the mother in the video, and said she reported what happened to police when the incident occurred two years ago. To help us navigate through this, I'm joined now by retired Inspector John McCusker—who is the former head of the Toronto Police Service Sex Crimes unit, Detective Jill Whitehead—a member of the Behavioural Sciences Unit from the Ottawa Police Service, and Dr. Anne Cohen—a child psychologist in the Calgary area. Welcome. John McCusker, let's start with you. You said one of the details being overlooked in all of this, is that it appears Dhami was secretly recording all these women without their consent, and apart from the trouble he's in regarding the statements made about the five-year-old girl, he could also be facing voyeurism charges..."

I turned off the radio, after missing the nob twice and reeling from what I heard. I called Anand immediately—it went straight to voicemail, indicating his phone was off. I phoned his work desk number—no answer. I called his home phone and got voicemail there too, this time hearing the answering machine play a cheerful family greeting where Anand, and his wife and kids, all spout out in between gleeful laughs, "Dammit, the damn Dhami's aren't here, please leave the Dhami's a message dammit." I didn't leave a message, nor did I on the first two calls, completely unprepared on what to say. I wasn't thinking clearly, I was confused, and my decisions on what to do next were rapidly changing by the second, so I called Anand's wife, Karima.

"Hel—Hello?" She answered, shocking me first by picking up, and then again with the bewildered frailty in her voice—she sounded so scared.

I took too long to answer, so Karima spoke again, "Sean? Are you there?" I must have entered the unblock code when I created contact entries for Anand and his family, because all RCMP phones, like mine, defaulted to block number, so our calls *usually* showed up as *private caller* on caller id.

"Hi Karima, yes, it's me."

"I don't know where Anand is, I don't know what to do—" she trailed off, crying.

In between my fears and speculation, I was heartened by Karima not having any anger in her voice, only love and concern for her husband's well-being. "Do you know where he is?"

"No, I was hoping you did," I said, and felt especially useless and helpless talking to her. "His phone is turned off."

"His phone is here," Karima said, pumping more dread into my mind.

"Listen Karima, what they're saying about him is bullshit, that video is not true."

"I know he's seen other women over the years—"

"I don't mean that part," I said, thinking this might not be the most productive use of time right now, with Anand apparently missing, "I mean the part about the little girl. I haven't even seen the video. I just heard part of it on the radio a few minutes ago. I know it sounds like Anand talking, but he would never say or do anything like that."

"OK," Karima said softly, sounding a little more confident, but not as convinced as I hoped, so I went on.

"And the woman he was with: *Jasmine* I think it said—no mother in the world, other than Courtney Love, would proceed to have sex with a guy after hearing something like that. It doesn't add up."

Karima sniffled out a laugh, in between cries. "Um, he got a phone call," she said, in a disclosing tone.

"What? When?" I asked.

"Someone phoned Anand earlier before the video went all over the Internet. I think the man told him he wouldn't release the video if Anand admitted to collaborating with Davey Sandhu over the last year," she said.

I felt lightheaded. "*Was he* working with Davey Sandhu all this time?" I heard nothing on the other end of the line, and then a few whimpers. "Karima, you gotta tell me or I won't be able to help Anand." I hoped no one was eavesdropping or secretly spying on the conversation, but my gut told me none of this information was news to Time Dream at this point anyway.

"Yes!" Karima was sobbing. "Davey has been over to our house several times. He reached out to Anand about eighteen months ago." She gasped for air in between sentences. "Davey originally contacted Anand about pairing up with him to write Davey's autobiography. He said Anand was his favourite writer."

"Davey said the same thing to me—that Anand was his favourite writer," I said, my mind nothing more than a chaotic storm of nerves by this point. "What else? Is there anything else you can tell me?"

"They wanted to stop things," she said.

"Stop what?!" I asked, and realized I was interrogating her with this tone. I softened my voice. "I'm sorry Karima, I know this is hard. What do you mean?"

"Davey didn't agree with where Time Dream, umm, I mean, he didn't agree with where Eric Byrne wanted to take the company, or the government involvement. Anand said Davey didn't want to be part of engineering the world's first voluntary mass extermination—he wanted to stop it."

"Anything else?" was all I could spit out.

"Yes," Karima was all out bawling now, each shriek making me flinch as I listened. "Anand wrote you a note a few days ago, sealed it in an envelope, and told me to give it to you if anything happened to him. We were keeping it in our safe upstairs. After he left this morning, I found the envelope lying on the kitchen counter. There is a sticky note attached to it that says, *Give to Sean*."

My heart sank, knowing what the envelope could mean. I put every bit of effort into sounding confident in what I said next. "I'll find him. He'll be fine. He's too stubborn to give up, you know this, it's what makes him a great writer. It's why everybody loves him." In truth, I really did believe what I was saying, because Anand's impervious epidermis not only made him good at what he did, but also made me think he could survive being a politician if he ever fulfilled his childhood dream of serving in public office—in short, he had the thickest skin of anyone I'd ever come across. In spite of this, and in being convinced of Anand's resolve, I had a horrible, foreboding sense of dread, lingering after every thought. "Do you have any idea where he might have gone Karima?"

"Maybe—to the school. Maybe to the school to see the kids," Karima whimpered before continuing, "one last time." Karima was cut off by her crying, and I could tell she was trembling, but her intuition proved she was still as smart as they come—she achieved a 4.0 in university—even in a situation like this. The school was a good thought on where Anand might go if he was as low as we both suspected.

"OK, are the girls still going to that French immersion school?" I asked, trying to sound calm.

"Yes, *École Sylvain*, by the house," Karima explained.

"OK," I said, "Can you phone them and—"

"I'll ask them If Anand was there."

"Yes—well—no, don't just ask the front desk of the school, make sure you talk to one of the girls and verify if Anand came by," I said, wagering the receptionist at École Sylvain was as happy in her job as Rhonda the receptionist was at Alex and Owen's school. When the boys were still alive, Rhonda wouldn't bother to phone a parent even if a kid was eaten by wolves—she was too busy mellowing, like an old chainsaw.

"I'll call Alana on her smartphone!" Karima said. This new direction on Anand's whereabouts seemed to give her life.

"OK, phone me right back after you talk to her please. I'm going to call RMN and see if they have any ideas, OK?"

"OK, bye Sean."

"Bye."

After hanging up with Karima, I phoned the main line at Rocky Mountain News. The receptionist answered on the first ring, in fact, it barely made it to half a ring before she picked up.

"Rocky Mountain News, Sheila speaking, how may I direct your call?"

"Hi Sheila, how are you?" I asked, knowing that spending the extra seconds to banter with her, despite being in a worrisome hurry, would actually save time and garner me more information.

"I'm good, how are you?"

"Not great Sheila, I bit myself shaving," I said. She giggled, and I went on, "So, I'm good for a Monday I guess!"

"Well that sounds painful!" Sheila said and giggled some more.

"Painful?" I switched my voice to a high-pitched female voice, "This one time, at band camp, I stuck a tuba in my," I paused then switched back to my voice, "Are you an *American Pie* fan by any chance Sheila?"

"YES, oh my God you're so funny, she said *flute* in the movie. A tuba would definitely be painful. So who is this? What can I do for you?"

"It's Sean Riley, I'm a friend of Anand Dhami's, well, he's my only friend actually. That's a lie, I'm overstating with the word friend—I owe him money."

"Really?" Sheila asked.

"No, not really," I said, and then laughed affably. "I'm just a friend, but I can't get a hold of 'em. Is he around?"

"Oh," Sheila said, with absolutely no giggle this time, her laughter gone with the wind, unintentionally exposing she knew something more, or at the very least, had heard about or seen Anand's video careening across the Internet.

"Uh oh, that sounded ominous Sheila, and I'm not talking the largest instrument in the brass family meets genitalia ominous. What's up?"

"Well, I shouldn't say, but I'm sure it will be on the news any minute now anyway: Mr. Dhami was fired today. Sorry, I—"

"What?!" I belched out reflexively, although I shouldn't have been surprised. Even if RMN believed Anand was innocent of the more serious pedophile insinuation, the rest of the implications behind the video probably made the decision to terminate him an easy one. "OK, thanks for telling me that Sheila, I really appreciate it. Look, I'll level with you, I'm worried about him and I need to find him. Is he still in the building by any chance, and if not, do you know when he left?"

"He never even came in today, but I know Wanda and some of the bosses instructed all of us girls at the front that he'd been fired."

"Wanda *Poole*?" I asked, knowing the answer, but hoped my name recognition—from meeting Wanda in Anand's office last week—might imply I knew Wanda better than I did.

"Yes, do you know Wanda?" Sheila asked, a little surprised.

"Yah, we're friends," I lied, which was more of a double lie considering how much Wanda enjoyed meeting me the other day. "Do you think you could patch me through please?"

"Well, I think she's in a meeting, but I can transfer you directly to her cellphone."

"Thank you Sheila, I really appreciate it."

"You're welcome! I always liked Anand, good luck. OK, I'm going to transfer you now." The line went quiet, played elevator music, then it started to ring.

"Hello, Wanda speaking," came a crisp, cold and caustic voice.

"Hi Wanda, it's Sean Riley."

"What the fuck do you want?"

"I'm trying to track down Anand, do you—"

"Well you won't find that sick fuck here!" Wanda cut in. "He's been terminated, his swipe card is deactivated, and our people have been instructed not to let him in."

"Be that as it may, he's my friend, I jus—"

"Some friend."

"I just want to track him down Wanda, did he come in today? Do you have any idea where he is?"

"He didn't come in today, and he didn't pick up the phone, but we made it clear to him on voicemail, email and text that he's done here. Anything else, I'm busy."

"Yah, do you have a number for Davey Sandhu at Time Dream?" I asked, or rather, begged, grasping at straws and not wanting to report back to Karima that I'd come up with nothing.

"Yes, but it won't do you any good. He was let go by Time Dream this morning. Don't you listen to the news?"

"Apparently not enough, what do you mean *let go*?" I asked.

"Idiot," Wanda said under her breath. "He was fired. He's no longer with Time Dream. Not that it matters—there are rumours he'd disappeared already anyway."

"What?" I was flabbergasted. It was like hearing they fired Ronald McDonald from McDonald's, or Wendy from Wendy's, or Vin Diesel from a shitty movie.

"Goodbye," Wanda said, and hung up.

I immediately called Karima back, encouraged that if Anand never showed his face at RMN, he must've gone to visit his girls at their school. The line picked up.

"Sean! Sean he's gone!" Karima screamed into the phone, still crying.

"What do you mean?" I asked, feeling my chest tighten. "He's not at the school? He left town?"

"He's dead Sean!" Karima screamed, and then all I could hear were gasps and sobs. My chest tightened so much I could feel it in my rib cage.

"What do you mean Karima, how do you know this?" No answer came, just more sobbing. "Karima!"

"He hung himself! I found him in the garage!" Karima screamed again, sobbing wildly, "He never left today, he was here all along. AHHHH," Karima whimpered, gasping for air, and made a harrowing sound.

I knew this sound—it was the same haunting, unforgettable noise my wife Angela made when the RCMP told us that both of our sons had died. "I have to—go, the police are here." The phone line went dead, like my friend.

CHAPTER 15 – KICKED WHILE DOWN

Four days went by until Anand's funeral on Friday morning. Larry and I were the only people at the funeral not related to Anand. One uncorroborated story released, and the whole world turned their back on him and his family.

No one from Rocky Mountain News showed up. No fellow journalists. Not even one person from his beer league hockey team came by.

I thought back to when I warned Anand about the power of an organization like Time Dream: "They can do worse than kill you. They'll leak ten stories for every one story you write. Weird stories, character damaging stories..."

I was close—Time Dream leaked a video that made Anand kill himself. The video was bullshit. I knew he was sleeping with other women, and the hidden camera was news to me, but there was no way he was a pedophile, and no fucking way he propositioned a woman to have sex in front of her five-year-old daughter.

I spoke with only two people at the reception after the funeral.

First, I talked with Larry, who, knowing his oldest friend all too well, explained he was ready anytime for when I wanted to deliver some payback, and that he had my back. Lawrence Reinhart: The friend you rode your bike with when you were six, the friend who convinced you silk shirts would get both of you laid when you were fifteen, the friend you could talk to after not seeing each other for years, the friend you weren't going to let get involved in any kind of revenge on Time Dream because he might be all you had left.

Then I talked to Angela, my ex-wife, who surprised me by showing up to the reception. Her late presence making a total of three people at the funeral not related to Anand. Angela and Anand had a falling out many years ago when she and I were still together, and like most stupid squabbles between friends in this world, I couldn't remember what the hell their fight was even about. I was moved by seeing a familiar face, and although we didn't talk long, Angela said something before she left the funeral that put some piss and vinegar back into me.

"Sean."

"Yah."

"You know how I used to ride your ass about lettings things go?"

"Don't say *ride* and *ass* in the same sentence, it makes me horny, even at a funeral. It's like saying *bomb* at the airport."

"Horny as in Horneya Slutsova eh? The girl you should've married." Angela smiled, still classy, and still able to cut through my bullshit.

"Good memory," I said, and smiled back.

"Anyway, you know how I was always ragging on you to let things go?"

"Vaguely," I said, and gave her a wink.

"Well," Angela put her hands on each side of my head and moved to within two inches of my face. I could feel her breath, and her smell sent heavenly tingles throughout my body. "don't let it go this time. Go after them." She smiled and kissed me on the lips.

"Time Dream?"

"Yes, as your attorney, I advise you to go put a foot up their ass." Then, fresh off paraphrasing Hunter S. Thompson— who she knew was one of my favourite writers—and still holding my head, Angela kissed me once more, and left.

181

Later that day, long after the funeral, I thought about what Angela said as I stared at the envelope on my kitchen counter. It was the sealed envelope Anand left for me. Karima slipped it into my hands at the funeral, and I just couldn't open it. I don't know why, since I have a long established pattern of behaviour where I look at the things I'm not supposed to be looking at: Christmas presents in November as a kid, the high school computer system to change everyone's grade ten math marks as a teenager, and my former boss Greg's Internet history as an adult—nothing says leverage come raise time like pointing out your RCMP superior's proclivity for weird sexual subgenres of porn like *cumming-on-figurines*.

When I pointed out Greg's amiibo friendly *click* habits on the covert Internet computer—a PC not on the main RCMP network—assigned to him, he immediately offered to give me my own vehicle—a luxury usually reserved for employees much higher up than me—to which I, in true Robin Hood fashion, declined, asking instead that he permanently supply free soda and bottled water for our entire unit—the *Intelligence Unit,* believe it or not.

Amiibos are plastic figurines of Nintendo's most popular characters, like Mario and Toad. Needless to say, Princess Zelda and Princess Peach tend to get a lot of attention, and Staff Sergeant Greg Laird's gigabytes upon gigabytes of browser cache surfing history is the unsettling proof of this—behold, a further subgenre *cummingonamiibos* was born. Later that year, at the Intelligence Unit Christmas party, hosted at Greg's house, Angela couldn't understand why I wouldn't let Alex and Owen play the Nintendo Wii-U with all the other kids. I'm pretty sure I made them wash their hands three times that night. Ewww.

"BVVV-MMMM-RRRR, BVVV-MMMM-RRRR!" The loud vibrate setting of my smartphone, buzzing like a blind guy playing a game of *Operation,* rattled me out of my daydream, and took my focus away from Anand's envelope to see the call display indicating my current boss, S.Sgt. Brian Forbes, was phoning me.

"Hello?" I answered, as if I didn't know who it was.

"Hi Sean, it's Brian. How are you?"

"Peachy, no, Princess Peachy," I said, filthy figurines still dominating my thoughts, "How are you Sir?"

"Look—ahh—I'm sorry to hear about your friend."

"Thank you," I said, wanting the day to be over, or more broadly, my life to be over. I was six seconds away from cracking open a new bottle of vodka before Brian phoned. That said, I was curious why he was calling and offering his condolences, knowing him and I didn't exactly have the kind of boss to subordinate relationship that would encourage this behaviour.

"Anyway, this is hard to say, and HR wanted me to say this to you in person, but I wanted to let you know right away: We're going to have to let you go."

"What?" I asked.

"You are terminated effective immediately. We can arrange a time for you to come in next week and get your stuff, and sit down with HR."

"Why now? You said the Superintendent had my back." When the two things you love most in the world—my children —are taken from you, you're instantly endowed with enough *I don't give a fuck* to make you immune to any negative event, but after fifteen years with the RCMP, and Brian's assurances the bosses wanted to keep me around as of a few days ago, I was a little perplexed at this sudden change. Worse, I still needed to make money to keep myself afloat until I could sign up for Time Dream's one-year suicide coma jump, and spend the last year of my life being happy with my sons, my wife, my family.

"No, I told you Monday that the Inspector and Chief Superintendent both indicated you are to stay, so long as your identity and involvement in the public incidents stays hidden."

Like a bad poker hand about to unfold, where you know what your opponent is holding before they even show you the cards, I knew what Brian was going to say next.

"Your identity has been revealed on the Internet."

This was news to me.

"About an hour ago, Rocky Mountain News aired a story indicating you were the one on the sky train platform. They have also revealed that you were the mystery man in the Davey Sandhu interview.

"Your picture, full name and employment with the RCMP were outlined. Additionally, following this story, RMN released a statement indicating you and Anand Dhami acted alone, without RMN's permission, in releasing the Davey Sandhu interview onto the Internet. And that you, Sean Riley, concocted the lie to falsely state RMN was hacked, before you intentionally leaked the Sandhu interview onto the Internet.

"These events, supported by our belief in the accuracy of RMN's account on what has happened, have brought disrepute to the RCMP. Your actions are not defensible, so to maintain the public trust in our organization, we must end your employment."

"Any other good news?" I asked.

"No good news, but I'll give you a nickel's worth of free advice: Get a lawyer. However, and I think you know this, the actions that have landed you in trouble did not occur while you were on the job, or in the execution of your duties, so no legal representation will be provided by the RCMP. Your computer access and all physical swipe card access to any RCMP building have been revoked. You no longer work here."

"Yah I got that Brian." Some bosses have your back and would fight upper management to keep you around in this situation, but I could pretty much guarantee Brian supplied the nails for my coffin. I'm sure it's of no surprise to learn many of my bosses in the past were forced to defend my frequent and illegal jaunts outside the rule book to achieve *organizational goals* —aka catch bad guys.

I admit this freely, and when I worked in that area of law enforcement, in the Intelligence Unit, our targets were usually organized crime members or their affiliates, so you didn't feel too bad about it. What really made me go unhinged though, were the pedophile child abduction cases, where I cut every corner, broke a shitload of really good laws, and ignored any rule of evidence and disclosure in the hopes we could find someone's son or daughter before it was too late.

In these situations, it was tough, because although moving this quickly was better for the sake of the abducted child, it also reduced the chances of getting a conviction, because the dirtbag pedophile's lawyer was able to get evidence thrown out due to the corners we cut. There would even be information collected we didn't even bother to try and admit as evidence, because we obtained it unlawfully—I had an old boss who affectionately referred to this inadmissible evidence as *intelligence*. It was with this in mind I considered what Brian just dumped in my lap.

There was enough inadmissible evidence to fire me, but not enough to actually charge me with anything, for now, but it was pretty clear Time Dream was flexing its muscle and gave RMN an ultimatum. It was also possible Time Dream leaned on the RCMP via some kind of high-level political maneuvering. Or maybe not so high level—Time Dream puppeteering a few people into firing me was nothing more than a bug hitting their windshield.

"Hey Brian, on that note, do you wanna hear a joke?"

"No."

"Aww come on Brian, why kick a guy when he's down?"

"Fine, go ahead."

"Knock Knock!"

"Who's there?"

"Go Fuck Yourself!" I hung up the phone. It was obvious Brian wasn't behind this, but it was Brian for Pete's sake, I had to insult him on general principal.

Next, I decided to phone RMN.

"Rocky Mountain News, Sheila speaking, how may I direct your call?"

It was time to put a whole lotta bugs on Time Dream's windshield.

"Hi Sheila, how are you? May I please speak with Wanda

Poole?"

"May I ask who's calling?"

"Lucius Green, Time Dream Legal," I said.

"Right away Mr. Green, I'm putting you through now."

After a ten second pause the line rang a few times, and then Wanda picked up and started speaking right away, as I hoped she would.

"What is it now Lucius?" Wanda snapped, "I have you on speaker phone and Paul Lambert from *our* legal team is here with me. We've done everything Time Dream has asked—what do you want now?"

I hung up the phone, having confirmed everything I needed to know.

CHAPTER 16
– REVENGE IS
RESEARCH

I woke up Saturday morning in a trance. I wouldn't say I was determined, focused or any of the other bullshit *after school special* feelings you might expect, but rather, possessed—much like I described earlier, when the Inspector used to walk in and tell us a child had been taken: You don't think, you don't calculate, you just act, and despite the tunnel vision created by this state of mind, everything you had to do was clear.

I drove to the Lougheed Time Dream location in my ozone piercing '70 LeSabre in just under ten minutes. There were still lineups around the block, like every Time Dream location, because of Eric Byrne's one-year suicide deal, so parking was impossible. Even the wheelchair accessible parking spaces were taken, probably because some folks were happy to trade in their remaining body parts—as per Eric's, *"We are pleased to announce the only cost for this free assisted suicide, preceded by a free one-year coma jump, is that one agrees to be an organ donor..."*—for a year of happiness like everyone else. A year without disease or with limbs they may have lost twenty years ago, depending on the scenario. Or, more likely, some asshole just took the accessible parking space.

So, despite the heavy police presence patrolling this and all Time Dream locations for safety and traffic control, I rolled my car up onto the sidewalk and parked two metres from the front door. Three out of four wheels on the curb to boot. Picture how Britney Spears might've parked during her driving test, err, tests.

I got out, and before my second foot hit the ground, two cops were in front of me. Thankfully, unlike the rest of the world, filled with people who get nervous when they see police, my confidence level actually goes up around them—despite a life of cybercrime from age twelve to twenty-five—because police are like family to me.

"Sir, what are ya doin'? You can't park here," said Officer #1: Constable Smail of the Calgary Police Service—according to his name tag.

"Sorry about that," I said, and pulled out my Police ID and showed it to them. You see, the trouble with guys like S.Sgt. Brian Forbes jumping the gun on employee terminations with an early phone call, because they're so excited to let you know you're fired, is that you still have your police ID.

"Ahh come on man, we still can't let you park here," said Officer #2: Constable Bullard, in acknowledgement of my ID, "there's a million people watching. Besides, *Sean*," he got my name from the ID, "that's a Mounty ID, I should give you a ticket for that reason alone."

To explain, Constable Bullard didn't mean he should give me a bigger ticket because I should've known better, he meant he should give me a ticket because municipal police generally hated feds. *I* even hated the feds and I worked for them. But it's a love hate, and blue loyalty is very strong—sometimes disastrously so. That's why in rare occasions when a cop rats another cop out, you will see a flood of media show up to write the story.

"Yah, and ya just scared about fifty people jumping the curb like that," Constable Smail said.

"Well, on the bright side, if I scared 'em off I probably just saved ten lives!" I joked, sort of.

"Nice," Bullard chuckled.

"You guys gonna to take the suicide deal?" I asked, still

smiling because I knew the answer already based on an approximation of their ages.

"Fuck that, I got three years to go," Smail said.

"I got two and I'm done. No fucking way," Bullard said.

They meant their pensions. A cop with only a few years to go towards full pension wouldn't part with that goal even if you offered them super powers—a good super power even, like the ability to go a week without peeing.

"Well, I just got fired at the fifteen-year mark yesterday, and I'm pretty sure Time Dream had something to do with it. I also think they're responsible for the death of my friend, so I'm gonna mess with them," I said, almost too plainly, revealing more malice than one should let on while indirectly threatening the world's most powerful company in front of law enforcement. But, after fifteen years of working with the police, I knew my audience: They would dive in front of a bullet to save an ordinary citizen without thinking twice, but like me, feeling a wee bit disenfranchised from time to time, they wouldn't shed a tear over a big bank, a big insurance company, or in this case, Time Dream, getting roughed up a bit. "Can you cut me some slack?" I asked.

"Yikes," Bullard said, and then after a pause asked, "So what did you do for the Mounties?"

"I worked in cybersecurity—among other things. I actually worked in a JFO," that's *joint force operation*, "with the Intelligence Unit when I was younger. We had some Mounties, Canada Border Services, CSIS and a bunch of you CPS guys too," I said.

"Haa, I bet *that* team was efficient," Smail joked. "I bet they couldn't agree on a stapler colour. So you were in cybersecurity *eh*? That field is exploding these days. My brother works in cyber for the Mounties out of Edmonton."

"Holy shit," I said, recognizing the name, "is your brother *Rod* Smail?"

"Yah!" he said, looking relieved that I probably was who I said I was, "you know 'em?"

"Well, you know, I don't wanna make you uncomfortable, but I cheated on my wife with him a few years back. I was on course in Edmonton, and I was lonely, and I really felt like he listened to me. Like what I was saying was the only thing that mattered."

I kept a straight face, while Bullard started laughing and pointing at Smail. Then I laughed. Then Smail started laughing too as he shook his head.

"So how long are you gonna be in there?" Smail asked, glancing towards the Lougheed Time Dream front entrance.

"Fifteen minutes, twenty tops," I said.

"Fuck it, just leave it where it is but give us the keys brother. If anyone says anything, I'll tell 'em your car is an un-marked police vehicle and park it behind 1411 for you." Smail said, as he pointed to a police car just around the corner.

"Unmarked my ass!" Bullard jabbed, "Look at all the rust on that thing. You need to give it some lotion, or a hug or some-thing."

"I think your car has the same skin disease Michael Jack-son had," Smail said, keeping a straight face, while Bullard started laughing and pointing at me.

Then Smail laughed. Then I started laughing too as I shook my head. I gave the keys to Smail.

"Jesus, I can't thank you enough," I said, and meant it.

"Don't worry about it. If helping you fucks up Time Dream a little bit, that's fine by me, it's all pensionable time," Smail said.

"That thing looks more bullet proof than a tank," Bullard said, still eyeing my car the same way you'd look at a recent win-ner of a Strongman competition.

"Hey, what did ya get fired for anyway?" Smail asked?

"I was dealing crystal meth," I said, and both of their smiles vanished. "Ha, just kidding, I suppose you could say I was tossed for being a shit disturber."

"Fuckin guy, I believe it. Get outta here! See ya in twenty minutes—*tops*," Smail said, shaking my hand. "And don't kill anybody."

I said goodbye and ran in the front entrance. There were already about another 200 sets of eyes on me when I walked in—Time Dream employees *and* customers—which made what happened next even more enjoyable. Quan is my hero.

"*Werewolf Seamen, welcome to Time Dream!*"

"*Joo C. Tuatt, welcome to Time Dream!*"

"*Pat York Hunt, welcome to Time Dream!*"

"*Mel Ester, welcome to Time Dream!*"

"*Jenny Taylia, welcome to Time Dream!*"

"*Jenny Tulwort, welcome to Time Dream!*"

"*Lube McCock, welcome to Time Dream!*"

"*Willy B. Hardigan, welcome to Time Dream!*"

"*Sean Riley, welcome to Time Dream!*"

"*HO LEE FUK, welcome to Time Dream!*" On a personal note, Time Dream's automatic greeting system reading this one off made me laugh the most, because I could visualize Quan cursing while he created the IDs for it.

"*Horneya Slutsova, welcome to Time Dream!*"

As the last name in my wallet was read off I saw Myah hurrying towards me from the back room. She looked angry.

"What are you doing here?" She asked. "I told you to make an appointment first!"

"Myah! How are you?"

"I TOLD YOU TO MAKE AN APPOINTMENT!" My acute powers of observation told me Myah really was angry.

"How do you know I didn't?"

"Did you?"

"No," I said.

"Well then you're wasting my time."

"Well, if I'm a waste of your time, then why did you come all the way out to greet me? And why did you arrange for me to see your brother? And why did you courier me over that package with an Elvis calendar and a four-litre bottle of *Regular Strength Triple Action Relief Gold Bond* moisturizing lotion?" I looked at Myah and smiled, ignoring the urge to point out she

didn't spring for the extra-strength—*ultra-puissante* in French—
Gold Bond moisturizing lotion, then spoke softly, "Hey, kidding
aside, thank you for getting me in to see your brother, it really
helped," I said, and meant it, for the second time that day—it
felt eerie being genuine with people.

"You're welcome, and I came running out because of the
filth that started playing over the intercom."

"Yah, what the hell was that?" I asked, not fooling anyone,
"And you can hear the intercom all the way in the back?"

"If I have my headset on, yes," Myah said, shattering my
dream of the whole building hearing the name *Werewolf Seaman*
broadcast with the voice of Moses.

"Anyway, look, I'm in no position to ask you for a favour,
but do you think you could—"

"Sean! I told you, the one-year suicide jump needs to be
booked in advance. We have backup bookings two months long
at this location. Even longer at other locations!"

"No no, sorry, um, I was just gonna ask if you could get me
in for a *one-hour* coma jump?" I tried to act pathetic and needy
as I said this. Sadly, it wasn't much of an act.

"Well," Myah said, before sighing hesitantly, and continuing, "regular coma jumps need to be booked in advance now too,
but since you still have three coma jumps left on the research
contract, I suppose we could fit you in with one of our decommissioned coma jump rooms."

"What-a-ya mean decommissioned?" I asked, not liking
the sound of that, but I was also relieved Time Dream hadn't
banned me from all their locations or cancelled my remaining free coma jumps. Why would they need to though? They
had legalized assisted suicide for adults in the USA and Canada,
reduced me to nothing, eliminated my friend, and fired Davey
Sandhu without breaking a sweat. Time Dream looking into
my use of their facilities would be like Wilt Chamberlain trying
to remember the name of every woman he'd slept with. I was
nothing more than the *Jenny Tulwort* on the bug on their windshield. However, those of us among the *great unwashed* can be-

come quite the fuckin thing when we have nothing to lose.

"Decommissioned as in old and not in our booking pool, and happens to be the only place you're gonna get to do a coma jump *today*, mister. Take it or leave it."

"Right right, sorry, I just meant, is it safe for my brain?"

"What brain?" Myah asked.

I suppose I deserved that one.

"Well, if you were saying, 'Hey Sean, you can borrow my old *shovel*', I might not make any inquiries, but when you say, 'we can fit you in with one of our old *coma jump rooms*', in reference to the greatest and most complicated invention the world has ever known, that makes a sandbox out of people's brains, I generally like to ask some follow-up questions. Like: Is the decommissioned room prone to errors where otherwise semi sane humans can wake up from a coma jump thinking they're a character in *Goldilocks and the Three Bears*."

"Goldilocks?" Myah rolled her eyes.

"Yah, or Jack from *Jack and the Beanstalk*, or the Giant in Jack and the Beanstalk. Or the Giant's beanstalk." I said the last part while looking down at my belt buckle twice, and then smirking.

"The decommissioned room has the exact same coma jump equipment as any other room. The *furniture* is just old, and the walls are a little drab, so we need to renovate the room for aesthetic purposes only."

"Got it. If you can fit me in, that would be great."

Myah smiled. "OK, follow me."

I followed her to a part of the building I hadn't seen yet. It seemed like we walked the entire circumference of a hockey arena when we finally turned into a hallway with a red doorway at the end. We entered a room that looked exactly like the room where I did all my previous coma jumps. The kitchen chairs and fancy apparatus in the ceiling of the *screening room* were still there. The dentist looking seat behind the glass wall was also there. Everything in this *decommissioned* room looked the same. Then, one of my senses came through for me:

As previously stated, just like a German auto maker dealership showroom, every part of the Lougheed Time Dream location *smelled* expensive, except for this room. It smelled like the deep underground cellar my Grandmother used to store canned vegetables at her home in rural Saskatchewan. As a child I was convinced there were dead bodies or zombies in there—I *still* think there are dead bodies and zombies in there. A few more minutes passed and before I knew it I was strapped in and ready to go for my eighteenth free coma jump.

"Sean," Myah said over the intercom, the glass wall already closed and separating the two of us, "if you don't mind me asking, and I know this isn't my business, but why are you choosing a date from last week for your coma jump? I know how much you miss your sons. Um, are you sure you don't want to use this coma jump to see them?"

"I'm positive," I answered, "and I really appreciate you asking. And it *is* your business considering you've seen me pee my pants and sob like a guy who was just forced to watch a rerun of *Gilmore Girls*. I really appreciate everything you've done for me. Anyway, the reason I'm choosing the Wednesday before last at 8am, is so I can relive meeting Davey Sandhu. From what I've heard in the news, I'll probably never get to see him again, and possibly find myself incarcerated. I mean, it was like meeting Gandhi or something, or the Dalai Lama, or Garth Brooks."

"OK!" Myah said and giggled. "That makes sense, sort of! Do you remember your coma jump exit phrase *Lorelai*? I'm gonna let your Gilmore Girls comment slide handsome. I love that show."

I was on top of the world after hearing the word *handsome*, which was another indication Myah might actually have those kinds of feelings for me. I let this wishful thinking percolate in my head a tad too long, because she asked me the same question again with some doubt in her voice.

"*Sean*? Do you remember your exit phrase?"

"By the power of Greyskull?"

"No, what is it Sean—I need to hear you say it."

"Unrelenting, unrelenting, unrelenting rescue."

"Thank you Mr. Riley," Myah said sarcastically in a fake, higher than usual voice, and began the count as per usual, "3....2....1....Good luck Sea—"

Myah was cut off from saying my name once again, and there was a brief silence of pure quiet, again. Time Dream should sell a side product called *quiet jump* where you just get stuck in this spot between reality and your coma jump—peace and quiet is worth something. For a brief moment I felt like I was doing somersaults in midair. Then, I was back inside Time Dream's Calgary Headquarters for the Wednesday meeting.

But I lied to Myah—well, it was more like I omitted some of the truth. I trusted her, but she'd already previously explained they could pick up a lot of your thoughts in the screening room. I really did enjoy meeting Davey Sandhu, and I wouldn't mind reliving that experience, but the main reason for this coma jump was something else entirely: I needed to get the direct phone numbers—desk number, but more importantly, cellphone number—of Time Dream president, Eric Byrne, and Time Dream's head of legal for Canada, Lucius Green. I wasn't even sure I would be able to, because if my brain hadn't encountered the phone numbers in real life, then they wouldn't be there in this coma jump, but with lady luck on my side, I had my answer in less than ten minutes.

In the first part of the meeting, during the introductions when things were still cordial in Time Dream's fancy boardroom, right before everyone started teasing Anand about his giant tape recorder, I saw both Eric and Lucius giving their business cards to Anand. This was fortunate, because I still can't figure out why people feel compelled to hand these things out with all the other electronic alternatives available—to support pulp and paper mills and eradicate a few more trees from our earth I guess. I carefully observed Anand putting the two cards in his wallet. This was as good as having the phone numbers, so I quickly uttered my exit phrase.

"Unrelenting, unrelenting, unrelenting, rescue."

"Sean, what are you sayin—" Anand asked, and although it was good to see my friend again, he was cut off by the end of my coma jump. Three minutes later I was hurrying out of the screening room with Myah asking what was wrong as I walked away.

"Sorry Myah, nothing's wrong at all," I said, moving past her and towards the door. "It's just that I remembered today is my buddy's birthday, and I'm supposed to be having breakfast with him right now."

Myah frowned. "Is that true?" she asked, while glancing at the tablet with her earpiece in, like she was trying to get a read on what was going on in my deranged brain.

"Not even remotely. See you later." I walked out of the room and left the building as quick as I could. After getting my keys back from Constable Smail, and thanking him again, I phoned Karima from my car with a couple hundred people still staring at me, parked on the curb. I asked if I could come over and she said yes, so I did a 180 to turn around, squealing my tires so loud I'm sure dogs three miles away were going into heat from the sound, and headed over to the Dhami house.

CHAPTER 17 –
THE ENVELOPE

"Hi Sean, come on in," Karima said politely as she opened the door, which was more than I deserved and more than she owed anyone after what she'd been through. Jesus, no, what she was *going* through: Karima looked like she hadn't slept for days, and I immediately had second thoughts about visiting her one day after her husband's funeral to ask if I could rummage through his wallet. I walked in and closed the door behind me.

"Hi Karima, do you think I could—" I was thrown off for a bit, nearly all of the relatives from Anand's funeral were still at the Dhami house—there *were* a lot of cars on the street come to think of it—and they became quiet upon seeing me. "Hi," I said sheepishly, doing a half wave while looking at everyone in the living room, and then the people in the kitchen farther away as I surveyed the main floor. "Anyway Karima, this is gonna sound a little odd, but, ahh," I lowered my voice because the room stayed quiet, and nobody's gaze left my Peter Parker frame, making me feel smaller and more awkward by the second. "I was wondering if you have Anand's wallet handy?"

"What?" Then she giggled with a gasp, like her vocal cords hadn't been permitted to laugh for a while—the audible equivalent of a dry lip splitting when you yawn or talk for the first time after waking up. It was safe to say she hadn't predicted me asking this, so with some wide-eyed faces all around the room, I decided to try and accomplish my goal while lightening the mood at the same time.

"Well, I'm a little low on cash, so I thought I'd stop in and see if Anand had any bills left." Now there were jaws dropping to go with the wide-eyed faces throughout the room. "I figured it would be easier than trying to park at that bloody 7-11 just to use their cash machine. Those idiots have been renovating the place for two years! I mean seriously, how long does it take to re-tile a wall? I think Tom Hanks' character did the same work in three hours for a chocolate bar and a coupon to the airport Baskin-Robbins in *The Terminal*."

Karima started laughing, then laughed some more with heavy breaths, before tears streamed down her face as she reached out and hugged me.

"Thank you Sean, we needed some laughter around here," Karima said, wiping her cheek as she let go of me. As she did, I saw someone I didn't get to talk to at the funeral coming towards us: Anand's brother, Jaz—*Jaswinder*—who I remembered well despite only meeting him once before, because Anand told me his brother's namesake was a famous singer, Jaswinder Singh Dhami, and Anand teased Jaz every five minutes about it.

"Hi Sean," Jaz said, smiling, and shaking his head about my wallet comment.

I said hi back and we shook hands, and then Jaz pulled me in for a hug as well. He reminded me so much of Anand that I felt *my* eyes tear up a little.

"Come on in man," Jaz said, since the three of us were still standing just past the doorway.

The room became louder now as people went back to talking and snacking on the delicious smelling food that was laid out. If the best part about funerals is the reuniting of family, then the food has to be a close second—I briefly remembered my Mom's cooking during similar times back home. I followed Jaz and Karima to a familiar, smaller room on the back side of the main floor.

"Karima says Anand used to spend a lot of time in here," Jaz said, looking all about the mini office, and then motioning for me to sit down as he and Karima did the same.

Jesus, I realized Jaz had probably never been in their home before Anand died, because he lived in Australia.

"Yup," I said, "this is the spot where Anand conjured up all those great columns for RMN that made him famous. Almost as famous as his superstar brother: Folkhop singing legend, Jazzzzzzzz Dhamiiiiii!"

"Come on man, now you're gonna start with that shit?" Jaz complained, while all three of us smiled.

"Anyway, about that wallet," I said.

"Oh, you were serious about the wallet?" Karima asked with a smirk and her eyebrows high.

"Yes yes, I really could use the money," I joked, "no, ahh, seriously, I'm looking for something I think Anand put into his wallet."

Karima reached into the drawer at the front of the desk where Anand spent over two decades perfecting his literary craft. She pulled out his wallet.

"What's up?" Jaz asked, looking at me with one of his eyebrows in the air.

"I'm looking for two business cards that were given to Anand by the head of Time Dream, Eric Byrne, and the head of legal for Time Dream Canada, Lucius Green. They should be in there."

Karima thumbed through Anand's absurdly thick, scoliosis inducing, George Costanza-like wallet. After some fiddling she produced two business cards.

"These?" she asked and handed them to me.

"Yes!" I said and felt even more revved up when I saw the cards had everything I needed on them: desk line phone number, mobile line, email addresses. There was even a field on both men's business card that said *Mobile (Private)* to go along with the usual *Mobile* field—as in their unpublished *direct lines,* ideally. Clearly, whatever Anand was into with Davey Sandhu, was not apparent to Eric and Lucius at the beginning of the interview when they handed the business cards to Anand. At that point, the cocky sons of bitches still had it in their heads Anand was going to write them a storybook article—fable!— about how nice, divine and magnanimous Time Dream was.

"You can have them," Karima said.

"Thanks, but I just need to take a picture of them." I took a few photos of the front and back of the cards with my phone, and then handed them back to Karima.

"Why do you need those?" Jaz asked.

"Ask me again sometime," I said.

"Are the stories Anand used to tell me about you, true?" Jaz dug further, turning his head to the side, and squinting like he was sizing me up. His face reminded me of my son Owen doing the same when he used to playfully interrogate me.

"You mean the laminated Wynona Ryder photos?" I asked, smiling. "In my defense, I don't how those ended up taped to the ceiling of my bedroom, and under my pillow, and in my underwear drawer, when I was in university. Someone played a ghastly prank on me."

"No, but I know that story too. I meant the hacking and breaking into company's networks and all that. He told me one story where you almost got *The Northwest Territories* renamed to *Bob* back in 1996—when political leaders asked folks to propose new names for the region in an online poll. There was another one where you rigged some kind of national beauty contest voting system for a girl."

I was thankful I only told Anand about *some* of the goofy shit I did when I was younger, and hadn't revealed any of the stuff my former employers—RCMP *and* the private sector— swore me to secrecy on.

"I have no idea what you're talking about Jaz," I said, winking, and then standing up. "Thanks so much for this Karima, I'm gonna run for now." They walked with me to the door.

"You're going after them, aren't you?" Jaz asked, just in front of the door.

"I'm not sure I know what you mean," I said, smiling like

Vanna White after turning over another letter.

"Good luck," he said, shaking my hand.

I went to hug Karima goodbye, but she put a hand on my back to gently direct me outside onto the porch. The door shut behind us.

"Sean," she said, looking at me seriously with bloodshot eyes, "the story RMN aired, saying you and Anand released the Davey Sandhu interview onto the Internet without RMN's per- mission. And that you," Karima pointed at me, "came up with the idea to falsely state RMN was hacked, before you intention- ally leaked the Sandhu interview onto the Internet."

"Yah," I said, flinching in my mind and bracing for Karima to hit me, or attack me, or unleash a barrage of hate on me for causing her husband's death.

"I know that wasn't your idea."

I didn't move or make any facial expression whatsoever.

"I know it was Anand's idea, and that he acted alone."

I remained quiet, unsure of how to respond or how Karima knew this.

"I know you tried to talk him out of it, and you were wor- ried about all of us, and he was mad at you. He told me about it when he came home that day. You were one of the few people who could make him think twice. He respected you. I tried to talk him out of it too, but we both know how he is."

Karima smiled at me, and then frowned while looking at the ground.

"How he *was*." She paused, and now I was staring at the ground too. "Thank you Sean," her gaze back on my face, "I can't imagine what you've been through. Anand was always worried about you, every day, after you lost your beautiful sons. And now, you've lost your friend."

She smiled warmly.

This last statement made me feel sickeningly guilty in too many ways. Karima was one of those people who truly loved everyone, unconditionally. She had a kindness that un- settled the rest of the world—I couldn't even swear in front of her. She was so good and decent to everybody, including people like me who didn't deserve it, that you wanted to do better in her presence, almost like you would under the watchful eye of your own mother as a child. *How could she be worrying about me at a time like this?*

"Karima." I paused, looking and feeling like I couldn't have let her down more. "Thank you," I said, stumbling to convey how I felt. "I should've helped him. I could've—"

"There is nothing you could've done to stop him," she said, trying to console me again, my guilt spreading through me like a virus.

"No, I mean I should've helped him instead of telling him it was unsafe and then hoping he would back down. Pretending he would back down—I knew he wouldn't. I could've made the leak and hack look like they came from a lighthouse in the Philippines when someone tried to trace it. It's what I was trained to do for God's sake. It's the only thing I've ever been good at. He was asking for my help and I didn't help him Karima. We could've come up with a better plan *together*. I just—" I wanted to confess I didn't help Anand, my friend, her husband, because it got in the way of my plan to spend an entire year with my sons in a coma jump, before ending my life, in taking Time Dream's suicide deal. But I didn't say this, I was a coward. Even at that moment, being with Alex and Owen again was the only thing that really mattered to me.

Karima shook her head. "Time Dream was going to figure out what Anand and Davey were doing either way."

On this part, we could agree.

"Sean?"

"Yes."

"Did you read the note in the envelope that Anand left for you."

"I haven't opened it yet," I confessed. Pathetic.

"Oh," Karima said sadly, obviously wanting to hear what it said and feel a part of Anand in the note's words.

"I'll go read it now," I said, feeling monumentally stupid

and wishing I could press a button to be in front of the letter right away. I hugged Karima and drove straight home.

I opened the door, entered the alarm code—a system guarding things I didn't care about anymore—and went to the counter where I'd left the 8.5 by 11 envelope. It had white and red stripes that had the Rocky Mountain News letterhead on the back with big default words saying *Sensitive* in red. It always amazed me when companies, including my former employer, used special envelopes to protect secret information, when in reality, it's like emblazing a bullseye on them that says, "Make sure to steal this envelope first."

I opened it up and slid out the letter inside.

To: Sean.

You have a small penis.

From: Anand

Although funny, my heart skipped a beat—there had to be more. I built Anand's note up so much in my head I was convinced there would be some kind of answer for me from the smartest person I had ever known. I reached into the envelope and was relieved to see another letter inside.

To: Sean

Hey buddy, if you're reading this, it means something has happened to me—likely because of Time Dream.

I paused, remembering Anand wrote the letter a few days before Time Dream released the videos that likely caused him to take his own life. In spite of this, Anand's opening words still gave me a chill. I continued reading:

I know you don't agree with what I have done, but the following will make you understand.

When Davey Sandhu learned about Time Dream's new suicide direction a few years ago, he outright refused to participate in moving the company towards this goal. Davey didn't want to be part of engineering the world's first voluntary mass extermination—he wanted to STOP it. This is what got Davey removed from the board of directors, and also why they voted to bring in a new president, Eric Byrne, to replace Davey. There wasn't a whole lot he could do about it. A few years went by and Time Dream moved closer and closer to getting the suicide laws changed—all while it secretly worked to be ready for when the laws did pass. And by ready, I mean the one-year free coma jump suicide deal Eric Byrne has announced and offered to the world. Somewhere in that time range, Davey decided he'd had enough and reached out to me. Davey and I have been working together for a year and a half. Our plan was simple: Write a scathing article that would make the public, our governments, and the world, realize what was going to happen. Davey used what little influence he had left at Time Dream to plant the idea (a few hops and bodies removed from the board of course) of me writing the article. Eventually it worked, the idea found its way up to the board, and I was assigned to do the interview and article on Time Dream. Unfortunately, we didn't realize the US government, the Canadian government, and possibly a few other G7 nations, were not only supporters of Time Dream's plan, but were actively participating in the world's first sure fire answer to population control. And when Eric Byrne and the board realized no complimentary article was coming, they put a gag order on everything. In short, I leaked the interview as a last resort.

You already knew all of this though, didn't you? What you didn't know, was how close you were to unraveling what was going on. You said something to me when we were talking on the day of Eric Byrne's big suicide announcement. You remember don't you? It was right after Wanda and Paul left my office, and right before you told me not to leak the interview, not to mess with Time Dream, not to STAND up. You said: "Yah, there's just one thing I can't figure out. How the hell do they make money out of this?" I berated you for saying it at the time, because I didn't think money was the chief issue with so many lives in Time Dream's suicide crosshairs, but it started to eat away at me, because you were right—why the fuck does the most profitable, money hungry company of all time, take on a money losing initiative? Well, they didn't, and there is much more to it than money. Hopefully, the person who revealed the following to me has gone into hiding, or they may be dead already.

Eric Byrne said: *"We are pleased to announce the only cost for this free assisted suicide, preceded by a free one-year coma jump, is that one agrees to be an organ donor—lives will be saved, with lives being ended."*

Davey Sandhu said, to you, in the helicopter: *"Sean, listen to what I just told you, and this part is off the record only because it hasn't been achieved yet, but we could very well have the cure for everything—indirectly—or, at least every brain disease. Right now, coma jumps still ultimately occur inside each person's brain, but when the time comes where we figure out how to have multiple people enjoying a coma jump together, the possibilities are endless. What that achievement could mean for medicine, healing the brain, the body, and even psychoanalysis —where a counselor could walk through your memories with you—is beyond what any of us can even fathom at this point. We don't know where it could go."*

"The cure for everything" is what this is all about. That line, that one sentence, is what scared the Time Dream board so much about that interview being released. Time Dream, and some very powerful long term thinkers within our governments, realized THEY HAVE TO KILL PEOPLE OFF WITH THE SUICIDE DEAL BECAUSE OF THE GAINS AND CURES DAVEY ALLUDED TO. Medicine and a cure-all for every disease scared the shit out of them. Global overcrowding and climate change estimates are already looking grim in the future due to massive population growth—

but tack on a species changing millennial jump in preserving human life the way Davey and Time Dream's scientists are predicting? Something like that will wipe the planet out. *"We don't know where it could go."* Well, I believe Time Dream did see where this breakthrough would go, as did the US government, and they have acted. But the *money*, what about the *money*? Here is the money: During all of this, the US Government made another deal with Time Dream (as an incentive to the company) to offset the losses Time Dream incurred while transforming itself for the suicide deal. *"The only cost for this free assisted suicide, preceded by a free one-year coma jump, is that one agrees to be an organ donor."* TIME DREAM IS GOING TO SELL THESE DONATED ORGANS TO THE RICH AND WEALTHY FOR BILLIONS. These organs won't be going to any fair and equitable organ donor waiting list, they're going to the highest bidder. On average, twenty people die each day while waiting for a transplant in the United States (which supports the goal of population control), but soon, Time Dream will control and own the rights to an almost infinite supply of organ donor bodies. It's like Time Dream is betting on both sides of a situation they created (massive suicides) to ensure profit and control regardless of the outcome—they are hedging their bets in a game where the poker chips are human lives.

Oh yah, after reading this, I'm sure you now realize the helicopter ride you took with Davey Sandhu was not a coincidence. I brought you along to be my technical advisor because I knew you wouldn't last fifteen minutes in that boardroom without antagonizing somebody and getting yourself chucked! True to form, you got kicked out in even less time than that, with Davey onsite and waiting patiently for you.

Sean, I know you wanted to take the one-year coma jump

deal the second it was announced, and I don't blame you, but I think this is the real reason why you didn't want me to leak the Sandhu interview: You didn't want to risk screwing up a chance to spend a year with your boys. I also know what you are capable of, and what you could do with the information I have given to you in this letter. So, my friend, you have a decision to make, but before you make it, there's a line from your favourite movie, *The Shawshank Redemption*, where the character Red, played by Morgan Freeman, says something that applies to you now: *"Get busy living or get busy dying. That's God damn right."* I'm hoping you didn't die when your two sons were killed in that car crash Sean...because you weren't in the car.

    Take care,

    Anand

    Like I said, he was the smartest person *I* ever knew.

CHAPTER 18 – THE CRYSTAL BALL

After reading Anand's letter part of me wanted to go right back to the Dhami house and share it with Karima. Well, the guilty conscience part of me wanted that to happen, but for good or for bad, my guilty conscience didn't usually win too many arguments in my head. I mean, I don't want to sound like a lunatic, but the second best compliment I ever received was from an RCMP senior crime analyst with a PhD in something I can't spell, who said, "Sean, I think you might be the only pure sociopath I have ever met who isn't a criminal, but your ability to read people lets you fit into society." As entertaining and contradictory as it was to hear this, and she *was* smiling—probably fucking with me a wee bit—while saying it, she got it backwards: I'm *not* a sociopath, but I *am* a criminal, I just chose not to be one. And it was with this self-realization that I decided not to head back to the Dhami house.

I'd already made up my mind to go after Eric Byrne and Lucius Green the second I found out Anand took his own life. That was another lie. I was thinking of messing with them the second I heard the fabricated video they produced to make Anand sound like a pedophile, and my plan was only to try and get them to admit to this video fabrication using an old trick, however, in light of Anand's letter—oozing with so much content bent on changing my mind it could be something from the movie *Inception*—I was faced with the temptation of getting them to admit a whole lot more.

The old trick I had in mind was something I'd come up with when I was younger, which my colleagues in the RCMP Intelligence Unit later named: *The Crystal Ball.*

Let me rewind back to when I was ten or eleven years old. At that age, and even when I was a lot younger, my mother would occasionally allow me to walk over to my Dad's office by myself after school. Dad was a guidance counselor for the high school at the time. He was an airplane mechanic many years before, and then realized how much he: 1. Loved teaching, and 2. Loved the two-month summer holiday teachers enjoyed yearly.

Walking through this huge building unsupervised was like walking through a spaceship when I was younger—I loved it. L-O-V-E-D I-T. I mean the school seemed so damn big and mysterious the first time I walked through it at age five, full of adults and big kids—*monsters* to my over active imagination— it might as well have been a spaceship. I purposely would try to take a different route from the school's front door to my Dad's office, each time I visited. When I got really familiar with the place, I could unexplainably—to my Dad—and repeatedly get *lost* and find my way to the gymnasium to shoot hoops, or get lost and end up in the computer lab.

When I did get to my Dad's office, it was even more fun, with my Dad giving me his master set of keys to open any door, and a new mission each time I visited to acquire—steal—a specific item from other teachers he wanted to provoke for being assholes to students. By the time I was ten I could get in and out of a classroom, to liberate a stapler or hole-punch or even a TV my Dad wanted moved to another room against another teacher's wishes, without leaving a fingerprint. But, as fun as this was, I started to get a little bored with the routine and moved onto more sinister ways to entertain myself at the high school.

One day, when my Dad left me alone in his office for about the hundredth time, so he could attend an after-school staff meeting in another part of the building, I decreed *tele-*

phones would be my next adventure. Dad had two phones on his desk, one for him, and one for troubled students to use so they wouldn't interrupt his calls. To paint a picture for anyone born after the year 2000, they were land lines with curly phone cords from the receiver to the main unit, and phone line wires going into the wall from the main unit. Each one had the usual early eighties office phone features like on-hold music, transfer call, multiple lines accessible by a button press, and even a speaker phone option—not to mention the intercom which was also a source of unending fun. These phones were the ultimate toys for me at that age.

Naturally, I started making prank calls, crank calls, fake calls, pretend telemarketing calls, pizza deliveries to unsuspecting friends, I even made complaints to local businesses with my best grownup voice, culminating with me getting my favourite lunch snack's—a hoagie, and if you don't know what a hoagie is, you're probably one of those assholes born after 2000 I referred to earlier—price reduced back down to a dollar at the local convenience store. And, after never getting caught performing any of these *civic duties*, I escalated to phoning the parents of kids I didn't like, and pretended to be one of their teachers in spouting out lie after lie on their child's wrongdoings. Shit, this scam even started to work better when call display came out in the early nineties, because the phone I was dialing from showed up on their home caller id as the local high school!

These shenanigans went on for a year before I discovered the ultimate trick in phone pranking: *use two phone lines at the same time.* More specifically, use two lines on speaker phone and dial two people who know each other, or even people who don't know each other, or people who hate each other—it's up to your imagination really. If you time this right, and these two people answer your call at roughly the same time, they start talking to each other because they can clearly hear one another's voice via the speaker phones—*my Dad's* speaker phones with me listening to be exact. When the ploy works, both victims of the prank are unaware that neither of them dialed the other. It usually went something like this:

"Hello?"

"Hello."

"Bob?"

"Yah, is that you Gary?"

"Yah, how the fuck are ya? What can I do ya for Bob?"

And then...they would have a full conversation covering any number of subjects with the comfort two people speak with having no idea they are being recorded. I SHIT YOU NOT. My body temperature instantly went up ten degrees and my heart rate must have exceeded 200 beats per minute the first time I did this.

Remember, I was only about eleven. I also remember my brain pumping itself with about forty doubts per second as the call went on, my mind flying through every scenario of why I should hang up because I would get caught, but as the call continued, and my addiction to this private world sunk its hooks into me, I couldn't think of a single logical scenario of *how* I would get caught. It was nearly impossible to get caught. Even if someone suspected something—never happened, not once, worst case folks hung up—what could they come up with? There was no caller id back then, and as mentioned, when caller id was created, the call would show up as being from the high school main line.

As time went on, I came up with ideas to reduce the risk in situations where only one of the parties answered the phone: I would usually use my Dad's office computer to play a sound file of a recent telemarketing message—that I recorded in advance —floating around at the time. If only one person answered when I executed this little spy operation, I hung up the other speaker phone line and simply played the telemarketing message sound file, so I wouldn't raise suspicion. Upon hearing the telemarketing message, most people hung up, or I just hung up —no worries. This wasn't enough for me though. Listening to adult conversations was great, incredible actually—picture me listening to a call between a husband and wife in a town so small everybody knew everybody—but after a while I started to use my invention to spy on friends, kids I knew, and best of all: girls I liked or girls who I *thought* might like me.

I would often phone after school, because as mentioned I was in my Dad's office after school, and most times parents were not home because they were still at work around 3:30 pm, so the two girls, or worst case other kids in the family, would answer their home phone. I would listen to girls talk for over an hour sometimes, only hanging up when I heard my Dad coming back from a staff meeting.

To put a label on all this at that point in my life, I had discovered a magic key into people's private lives. Aside from hearing the occasional unvarnished truth about myself, my family, or people I loved, there was really no downside. As time went on, and technology evolved, I started running things with the two phone lines my parents had at our house—back then households would have a line for voice and another line for fax or modem—using common Telco features like block caller id. Years later, when the world wide web took off, I used websites and online tools that would let me anonymously call people using the computer microphone and speaker, and display whatever I wanted for caller ID: *Walmart, Office of the Prime Minister, Ford Motor Company, Horatio's Pest Control, Source Adult Video, anything*!

Now, let's fast forward to my first days and weeks on the job in the Intelligence Unit. I wasn't supposed to end up there, but something in my opening interviews and entrance exams, to get hired on with the RCMP, led some decision makers to believe *I* belonged in the Intelligence Unit. I mean, if they had assigned me to the *Employees Who Illegally Download and Pirate Movies Off The Internet Unit*, or the *Prolific Masturbation Unit*, it would've made sense to me. My personal theory was they wanted *one* geek running around in this highly secure, multi-agency area (RCMP, Canada Border Services, CSIS, Calgary Police Service), instead of having to bring up a *different* tech or engineer every day, and risk compromising sensitive information.

Anyway, even though every interaction I had with police up to that point in my life had been bad, or involved Mounties chasing my friends and me around on our snowmobiles when I was back home in the Northwest Territories—they never caught us, snowmobiles have better traction on snow and ice than Ford Crown Vics—I fit into this unit perfectly. It was weird, I was warned by people that the unit was hardcore and to watch out, but each and every one of these folks treated me like family.

In fact, speaking of family, the way the members of this unit treated me, when my then infant son Alex was in critical condition at the hospital for six months, was the first time I felt like I had a community around me since I left my small town many years earlier. If I had to put my finger on the one thing we all had in common that made me fit in so well, it was sports. All these guys were ex-athletes like me, so the Intelligence Unit just felt like another locker room. And within this new locker room, we began to trust each other, and my colleagues soon learned of my ability and eagerness to circumvent a lot of computer, network, and Internet security, as well as my thirst for social engineering people.

As previously mentioned, social engineering is the psychological manipulation of people into performing actions or divulging confidential information. Put simply, it's a way to get you to do something you didn't want to do on your computer, smartphone, IPAD, tablet, whatever—often without realizing you were taken advantage of.

One day, I heard a few detectives from one agency in the Intelligence Unit fighting with a detective from another agency. In this heated *discussion*, the two detectives were railing on the other copper so bad I kept thinking of a young Mike Tyson's multiple knockouts in less than a minute in the first round of a heavy weight fight—sometimes dropping a guy so quickly the ring announcer hadn't even found his seat. The verbal bashing went on, and the outnumbered copper had tears in his eyes because he dropped the ball at the end of some kind of important and expensive two-year operation, but just as they were finishing their Spanish Inquisition, I heard the following:

Pissed Off Detective 1: "There's nothing left to be said, we're fucked. There's no way we're gonna get a Part VI now." To explain, a Part VI refers to the section of the Canadian Criminal Code that governs wiretaps. In this case, the enraged detective is referring to a *general* wiretap which requires judicial authorization. Also, by this time in North America, wiretaps didn't involve breaking into someone's house and planting a device on their phone. These days, a law enforcement agency simply has the phone company (AT&T, Sprint, Telus, Bell) simultaneously duplicate everything on the bad guy's phone line to another line housed by the police, so the police can record everything with their system of choice—with judicial authorization of course. Pissed Off Detective 1 is complaining that the judicial authorization will never happen because Dejected Detective 1 screwed something up.

Dejected Detective 1: "I'm sorry, what-a-ya want me to do?"

Pissed Off Detective 2: "There isn't anything else we *can* do now, you fucked us, and here's the kicker: We didn't necessarily need to use this in court later on, but we needed to hear these two dirtbags talking," he is referring to two organized crime higher ups, "to find out who their movers were, and where these people were gonna be when the deal went down, or at least *who* they were so we could tail the fuckers. Now it's just a dead end, we've got nothing."

After a few more sheepish apologies from Dejected Detective 1, I couldn't stand it anymore. "Hey guys, I don't mean to interrupt, but I have an idea. It's not legal, it's probably criminal, but you'll never get caught, and I have a way to do it that's untraceable." After a lengthy discussion where I explained, you guessed it, my little trick for eavesdropping on folks via two phone lines, and after doing a live demonstration of the concept by *dual speaker phoning* the two heads of the Intelligence Unit, while the four of us listened, these guys started to take me seriously. Then I told them the next step was to purchase two burner cell phones via cash in disguise. This was option one.

Option two was to use a computer on a website that allowed you to make false caller ID phone calls, while masking where our IP address location came from in case the website logged this Internet traffic somehow—something that was more difficult back then, whereas these days, you can fire up the TOR browser, otherwise known as *The Onion Router*, and nobody can trace where you accessed the fake caller id website from. Once again, I showed the detectives the steps as we practiced calls on friends and colleagues for a proof of concept. It worked, and I also introduced the team to the pre-recorded telemarketing sound file risk mitigation approach I used as a kid, where you play a current solicitation message, or some political party's bullshit wannabe Gallup poll survey automated message, in situations where one of the targets—a bad guy—didn't pick up the phone and you needed to hang up without raising suspicion. A new technique was born—one that couldn't be disclosed in court, and one that was very illegal, but also one that was very effective in dealing with the worst pieces of criminal shit on the planet, not to mention untraceable. It's still untraceable to this day if done correctly. After a number of successful executions of this technique, and about two years later, the good people of the Intelligence Unit crafted a name for their new super-secret eavesdropping procedure: *The Crystal Ball*. We even incorporated a variation of an old primer tactic, where we would leak a fake story about our targets to the media that would compel the bad guys to be more loose lipped prior to us listening to them.

Getting back to the present, where I just acquired the phone numbers of my two targets thanks to Karima, and Anand's overstuffed wallet of business cards, my path was clear: I wasn't heading back to the Dhami household anytime soon. I was going to run a Crystal Ball play on Eric Byrne and Lucius Green, and I would need some help.

CHAPTER 19 –
PHONE A FRIEND

"Hello?"

"Hey buddy, it's me," I said across the phone to my oldest friend, Larry Reinhart. I didn't want to involve him, but sometimes, like when your pee starts to burn, you just gotta ask for help. "You're still alive?"

"Fuck you," Larry said, but I could tell he was happy to hear from me by the amusement in his voice.

"Look, I'm about to do something fantastically illegal, ill advised, and stupid, but at the very least, it will make life difficult on the guys responsible for Anand's death. Will you—"

"I'm in," Larry said, in a reflexively loyal *I don't give a shit about the consequences* way that only a guy you've known since you were in kindergarten could. "You're still gunning for that penile enlargement surgery eh?"

This brought me back to when we were around twelve where Larry had imparted sage survival advice beyond his years: "*Sean, don't ever admit to any guy that his dick is bigger than yours. Even if you and Kareem Abdul-Jabbar are standing naked next to each other in the locker room, you still keep talkin' shit.*"

"Awesome," I said, "how soon can you get here?"

"Why don't *you* come *here*?" Larry complained, no different than when we were kids, flip-flopping back and forth on whose house to play at. When you grow up in -50 weather, this is a thing.

"Because when I went to your place last week it could've been an episode of Fear Factor where you were dared to walk through a haunted house filled with expired food—and the same mold they used to invent penicillin."

We argued for five more minutes, and then Larry agreed to come over. About a half hour later he was at my house and I showed him Anand's letter. Then I began to methodically walk him through all the details from start to finish: what really happened, what was true in the media, and what I wanted to do. I even explained some of the Crystal Ball operations I did when I was with the RCMP despite an oath to never talk about any of it.

This made Larry chuckle, because he was the one person I revealed this little prank to when we were kids, and now he found it amusing to hear it had been successful in entrapping bad guys. I did leave out one part of my plan, where at the end of all this, I still intended to sign up for the one-year suicide coma jump, if at all possible. Hearing this would compel Larry to try and talk me out of it, taking time away from the job at hand.

I went on for an hour explaining things, and through it all Larry remained calm and undazzled and only asked a few short clarifying questions in the moments I paused. I should point out that Larry was a bit of a *Columbo*, where, working in construction for a living, he often appeared disheveled and came across as a low IQ ex-jock, causing people to let their guard down, but in reality, the man breezed through two books a day —something he'd done since he was a child to combat a lifelong fight with insomnia—making him one hell of a well read and unassuming human being.

"All right, I got it," Larry said, when I finally finished, "but I don't understand, what-a-ya need me for?"

"These two guys," I was referring to Eric Byrne and Lucius Green, "are gonna be a little harder to nail with the Crystal Ball attac—"

"Stop calling it Crystal Ball ya fuckin nerd," Larry interrupted. "You're not a sorcerer in Harry Potter."

"Do you mean a sorcerer *in* Harry Potter as in sodomy, or

in the *universe* of Harry Potter?"

Larry looked calmly annoyed, like he was expecting that, so I got back on track. "Anyway, these guys are gonna be a little harder to fool than your average criminal, or a couple kids I was spyin' on in junior high. The setup before I phone them is the most important piece. We need to catch them when they're panicked and not paying attention, and not ready, and I need *you* to help me with the *not ready* part."

"How?" he asked.

"Well, it's going be pretty impossible to know where Eric Byrne is at any given moment—he's the head of the most powerful company in the world. We'd have an easier time trying to track the Pope or the president of the United States."

"Or Val Kilmer," Larry said, and then smiled.

"Right, but Lucius Green, head of legal for Time Dream Canada, is less important, and hence, will be less difficult to track in person. *And*, he's based out of the Time Dream Calgary headquarters at *The Bow*."

"Man, they got a good cafeteria at The Bow," he said, continuing to mess with me just like old times, "but it's expensive. I paid more for a stick of celery than you'd put down for a massage."

"I don't know what's more impressive in that statement: how big a lie it is that you ever ate a stick of celery, much less paid for one, or that you're the first person in the history of the world to use the words *celery* and *massage* in the same sentence —at least, I hope you are anyway."

"Nahhh, maybe the first in North America—vegetables and massages go together like Bert and Ernie over in Japan. You've seen the game shows," Larry said, smiling again. "So you want me to follow this Lucius Green guy? To what end?"

"Well, like I was saying, I need to fire the Crystal Ball," Larry rolled his eyes, "at them at the right moment. Ideally, I'm gonna need you to tell me when Lucius is driving home from work, or at least when he's in his car and leaving work."

"How the fuck do I know what he drives? How do ya

know he's not an Uber lover or something?"

"Well, normally, we'd have to sit outside The Bow and its parkade until we eyeballed what car Lucius is driving, but I may or may not have asked an ex-colleague at the RCMP to run him on CPIC (the central federal police database hosted by the RCMP), so I happen to know he drives a white Lexus LC 500 Hybrid with license plate: *LOOSH72*. That should narrow it down for you," I explained. "Also, how many rich lawyers do you know who take Ubers man?"

"OK, that's easy. So I just watch for him and then phone you when he comes out?" Larry asked.

"Yes, but I need you to follow him for a bit too," I went on.

"Also easy," Larry bragged, "I once followed Christina Applegate all the way from the Calgary International Airport to Banff. Shit, I was skiing beside her half the damn week when—"

"I don't wanna know," I jumped in, "actually, I do wanna know, but not now. So—" I hesitated, "there's just one more thing."

"What's that?" Larry asked, one eyebrow going up like he was in a Jeff Goldblum imitation contest.

"I need you to crash into his Lexus with *Old Yeller*," I said, wincing in anticipation of his reaction. Old Yeller was an ancient, yellow, unregistered truck sitting in Larry's backyard. The corrosion on it was so bad the rust marks looked like bullet holes—or maybe they *were* bullet holes, I never knew with Larry.

"I need you to rear end Lucius hard enough that you guys get out to exchange information. Only, you don't tell 'em shit, you just make up some fake name. I even have one of the old Northwest Territories license plates we used to collect at the dump back home." Northwest Territories plates are shaped like polar bears—one day, the rest of the world will start doing this, and we'll see a Thailand license plate shaped like a man molesting a boy. "We're gonna put that plate on your truck temporarily."

"Great," Larry said sarcastically, and then shook his head.

"Anything else?"

I zigzagged through the rest of my plan for a while, sparing no details, with Larry's eyes bulging out like a caveman seeing fire for the first time.

"Jesus Christ! *Is that all*?" Larry asked with even more sarcasm.

"It'll work," I said.

"OK," he said and then exhaled a long sigh. "So when are you planning on doing all this?" He was smiling again, but this time with a grin you have when you know your friend is going into a hornet's nest, but you go with him anyway because you knew him when he couldn't tie his own shoes. Larry actually *was* the first kid to tie his shoes in our kindergarten class, and to count to a hundred. I was the first one to pee my pants—a prophecy, perhaps.

"Monday afternoon," I said.

We spent the rest of the afternoon chatting about the plan and catching up with each other. Larry was still unemployed—which helped in terms of his availability for my scheming—but had turned things around a little bit since we last met. His family was still gone, but his wife allowed him to take his kids out for ice cream a couple times—unsupervised without her there the second go around. I enjoyed hanging out with my oldest friend so much that my enjoyment was tainted by the fact we had wasted all these years. We lived in the same city and it felt like we only saw each other in person every decade, and now, if my plan worked out, I would never see Larry again—encounters in my one-year suicide coma jump aside. With this in mind, despite wanting to see my kids again more than I can describe, a small part of me thought it might be nice to see Larry more in the future if I didn't get to take Eric Byrne's indelible deal.

Like any two friends reunited, talking and firing jokes at each other at a pace fit to erase years of being apart, and catch up on everything under the sun, the day went by in the blink of an eye.

Being Saturday night, we could order just about anything,

and since Larry had set the *recently single guy* world record for ordering pizza over the past couple weeks, we opted for takeout from *Bagolac*, which is the best Vietnamese restaurant in Calgary, or maybe even the world—*although one would hope Vietnam might have a few that could beat it*. With his belly full, and after having some time to digest not only his food, but the plan I had hatched, Larry put on his *consigliere* hat—fortunately, or unfortunately in terms of the devil's advocate viewpoint he was about to lay on me.

"Look buddy, I'm with you on this no matter what, but did you ever wonder if you should be doing this?"

"What-a-ya mean?" I asked.

"Well, I know you wanna fuck this Eric Byrne guy up a bit, and after what happened to Anand, we *gotta* go after him, but, did you ever think Time Dream might be right?"

"How so?"

"Well, think about it, maybe their suicide deal *is* the only way to save the world. Maybe the only way to stop global overcrowding and climate change *is* to combat the massive population growth by letting people who are suffering die. Not only die, but die after a year of happiness, and from a certain point of view, a bottomless supply of organs for people who *do* want to live sounds pretty good. I—"

"Rich people," I interrupted.

"What?" Larry asked.

"You mean rich people. It'll be the *poor* dying and giving their kidneys to the *rich* because it's their best option," I said.

Larry looked puzzled. With him being a man of the Spock *the needs of the many outweigh the needs of the few* logic variety, I knew his opinion would be vastly different than Anand's.

"Anand explained it. He said, 'Time Dream hasn't created a system to kill off the poor, the sick, the unhappy, and the disadvantaged. Time Dream has created a system where those people will kill *themselves*.'"

"I know, I got that," Larry said, "and all I'm saying is that might not be a bad thing in terms of where the world is headed.

It might be the best option, and maybe we shouldn't get in their way. I mean, it's not as if they're out there feeding the ducks?" He made a peculiar face.

"*What*?" I asked, chuckling.

"Ducks," Larry said. "The wildlife people say you can't feed the ducks, because if you do, you might irrevocably affect the food chain causing the complete and utter destruction of the surrounding ecosystems. In fact, I'm just waiting for when the terrorists stop strapping on the vest, and start feeding bread to the geese instead."

"Fuckin guy—what are you getting at?" I asked.

"Well, do you remember when your little guy—Owen I think it was—got out of bed, came to the living room, and said loudly to everyone at the party you and Angela were hosting, that 'broccoli cures AIDS'?" Larry asked, chuckling himself now.

"Yah," I said, happily remembering the occasion, but dropping right back to feeling sadness as I always did when I thought of my sons.

"You'd told him how good broccoli was for combatting cancer for so long, that he came up with the AIDS thing on his own. Anyway, the only thing funnier was half the adults at your party took it seriously when Owen said he heard it in school."

"Where ya going with this man?" I asked, feeling more and more like Larry was still smarter than me, just like when he counted to a hundred in kindergarten, as mentioned earlier, and I only made it to thirteen.

"The cure all pal. In Anand's letter he said the *cure for everything* is what this is all about. And that Davey Sandhu had forecasted a cure for nearly everything based on what Time Dream had discovered. They're all freaking out because they think they've discovered the *broccoli* Owen was talking about!"

My confused look prompted Larry to go on.

"OK, let me break it down: A few years ago Davey Sandhu predicted they were moving towards a cure for everything, and the Time Dream board of directors, *and* the US Government, were scared shitless because of the future global overcrowding implications—other governments too according to Anand's speculation. They all believed Davey because he's the smartest guy to ever live. My point is that people will believe anything if the scenario is right. Did it ever occur to you that he could be wrong?"

Larry had my mind spinning. "No," was all I could say in reply.

"Fuck it, what the hell do I know," Larry said, and then sighed. "No matter how they stumbled onto this direction, or what the genesis of it was, I'm just saying it might be the right direction."

Larry paused for a bit, and I could see he was itching to say more.

"What's up? Spit it out," I said.

"Well, there's one more thing. Not everyone in this world has a happy memory or a time in their past where everything was great, or even *OK*," Larry said.

"What?" I asked.

"This whole one-year free coma jump deal."

"Yah," I said, briefly turning my palms up in mild bewilderment.

"It's based on the idea someone is willing to trade their life in to go back to a time when things were good. That is a totally western and privileged perspective. Some people, in third world countries, even here in North America, have had it bad their whole life, and there *is no* happy time from their past. Shit, I bet ninety percent of Africa hasn't even done a coma jump."

"Yah, and now they will, because it's free," I said, "and in a coma jump they can control the outcome of their shitty past a lot differently than they did in the real world—piss on a dictator's face, whatever. You know this man, you got addicted to coma jumps like everyone else. If anything, when Time Dream gets the suicide laws changed in poor countries as well, there will be an even higher percentage of people lining up for the one-year coma jump deal than there is here in the west. That's what Anand was afraid of."

We went back and forth on this topic for another hour, debated which Golden Girl would win in a UFC fight—Dorothy, obviously, but Larry said some shit about Betty White being on uppers her whole life so she would have the strength of *The Hulk* —and then turned in for the night. Larry stayed in the guest room downstairs.

I lay awake for hours thinking about everything Larry said, and about Monday's plan, but mostly, I just thought about getting to spend a year with Alex and Owen. Sunday went fast with Larry and I strategizing the whole day, and getting a few things setup. We were ready. What Larry didn't know, was that I finally convinced Myah to book my one-year suicide coma jump, and I had booked it for Monday evening.

CHAPTER 20 –
MONDAY

"You ready?" I asked Larry over the phone.

I was ready. In addition to my home phone that I was talking to Larry on, I had a prepaid cell phone bought with cash, two laptops logged on and ready to go with microphones and speakers, and my favourite caller id spoofing website fired up and accessed from an anonymous Virtual Private Network —*PrivateInternetAccess.com*—paid for through paygarden.com with a gift card I bought with cash, to make me untraceable, and via the TOR browser to further cover my trail. I also had another computer running in the background with a *Blue* brand *Snowball* microphone recording everything just in case.

"Yah I'm fuckin ready," Larry said, "I've been sitting here since one o'clock."

It was just after 4:30 pm on Monday afternoon.

"I should've crashed my truck into this Lucius fuck when I saw 'em driving back from lunch—it would be Miller Time already if I had."

"Nah, this is good, one way or another, we know he's gonna roll outta there at some point to drive home," I explained.

"OK genius, what if he doesn't leave till nine pm?"

"Hey, that's why I told ya to pack a snack man. Does your tummy hurt pal?"

"Fuck you."

"Cause if ya need a tummy rub I know a place downtown just a few blocks from your location. They usually get paid for rubbing other things, but I'm sure they'll make an exception when they see you roll up in that fine luxury automobile you're in."

"Don't make fun of Old Yeller man," Larry said. "You wanted distracted? When I hit his Lexus with Old Yeller he's gonna forget his own name."

"I don't wanna concuss the bastard, I just need you to fender bender him," I said. "Anyway, back to your nine o'clock worry, that's never gonna happen. I googled and profiled the shit outta Lucius online, and his wife looks like Pam Anderson. He won't be going home late."

"*Is it* Pam Anderson?" Larry asked, like a six-year-old asking his parents if they will take him to McDonalds.

"No," I said.

"Well that don't mean shit anyway: no matter how good looking a woman is, no matter how sexy, some guy, somewhere, is tired of fucking her. It's the same with women and us."
More *Larry Logic*, how could this plan ever fail?

"Whatever, like I said, he's gotta come home eventual—"

"Sean!" Larry interrupted, "I see him pulling out right now!"

"Fucking rights, the traffic is nice and busy this time of day, so he won't be able to pull away. You know what to do buddy. I just hit send on the email with the link to the YouTube video. Subject: *Eric Byrne's plan to kill the poor and sell them off piece by piece*. I made that the *title* of the video too. Media, half of Time Dream, and Eric Byrne were all recipients of the message, and will be worrying about this shortly. Just run into him now —"

"Yah yah, stop talking!" Larry cut in. "Fuck, this fucking guy drives like a maniac."

I heard the brakes lock up on Larry's truck in the background.

"I can barely keep up to him in this traffic, it's gonna be

hard to get close enough to hit 'em. Fuck! Fucking little Jap driver fuck, get the fuck outta the way!"

I decided it wasn't the best time to council Larry on racial slurs or Asian stereotypes—as in all Asians are bad drivers, not Sony versus JVC stereos—or his abundant use of the F word.

"Just jump the curb to get to him if you have to!" I yelled into the phone.

"It's fucking 4:35 in the afternoon on a weekday in downtown Calgary—they'll think I'm with ISIS if I plow through fifty pedestrians on the sidewalk. FUCK, FUCKING FUCK!"

"Stay with him!" I yelled again.

"I am, fuck sakes, we're stopped at a red light now."

"OK, we're good," I said calmly, trying to settle Larry down, "when you catch up and hit his ass, leave your phone on. Just leave it on speaker and throw it in your pocket before you get out to talk."

"You want me to take a selfie with 'em too after I crash into him?" Larry asked sarcastically.

After what felt like five minutes, the light changed.

"We're moving again, I'm two cars back now. We're changing to the right lane."

"Nice," was all I could say, my heart starting to pound a little faster. I glanced at one of the laptops to see where Larry was with the GPS tracking software.

"OK, I'm behind him now. I'm on this guy like a shit-fly on shit!" Larry yelled. "He's signaling to turn right. I'm gonna ram into him like I don't see 'em slowing town to turn. Here goes—"

"*CRUNCH!*" I heard the impact.

After another few seconds of me holding my breath, Larry spoke. "OK, OK, here we go Sean, he's getting out. I'm getting out too, I can't talk for a bit."

I heard Old Yeller's door creak open and then I heard Lucius say, "What the fuck? Are you blind?" There was another creaking sound as Larry closed the door.

"Oh," I heard Lucius say timidly, no doubt seeing Larry's 6'5 300Lb frame covered with old, dirty clothing, and realizing he'd better be nice. So far so good.

"Heyyyyy, that's a great car duuuuude," Larry said, acting as high and as unstable as he could. "Is that a Mercedes!?"

"It's a Lexus," Lucius said.

"Ahhhh duuuuude, I'm soooo sorry! Peace brother."

"Ah, yes, anyway, I'm going to need your information—*please*," Lucius said, sounding uncomfortably deferential.

"What's that brother?" Larry asked, playing the part perfectly.

"Your information Sir—I need to get your name, address, and insurance information," Lucius explained.

"Ahhh duuuude, I don't have insurance," Larry said.

"Fine, well, ahh, then if you can just give me your name and number, I'll take a picture of your license plate," Lucius explained.

"Sure duuuude, no problem at all."

I could hear Larry rustling like they were walking.

"What the? Ahhh—is that a *Northwest Territories* license plate?" Lucius asked, sounding nervous.

"Yahhhhh duuuuude, this is my buddy's truck!"

"Your buddy's?"

"Yahhhhh duuuuude!" Larry yelled, and I hit mute on the phone because Larry's *dude upon dudes* were cracking me up. We planned for him to act like he was on drugs, but he sounded like some kind of redneck surfer from the Rockies.

"Well, anyway, can I please have your name and number and I will be on my way?" Lucius asked, obviously just wanting to get back in his car and get the hell out of there at this point.

"Sayyyyy duuuuuude, what does *LOOSH72* mean on your license plate?" Larry asked, stalling a bit more.

While listening, I quickly looked at the hit counter on the *Eric Byrne's plan to kill the poor and sell them off piece by piece* YouTube video, and saw it growing like a virus already. Beauty.

"Ahh, well my name is Lucius, look, I have to get going—can I please have your name and number?"

"Sure duuuude, my name is Sheldon Wood," Larry said, ignoring my advice to use the name Sheldon Johnson.

"*And your number?*" Lucius followed up.

"Right right, sorrrrey duuuuuuude," Larry said, and then gave the phone number of a random business we looked up the day before.

"OK, thank you," Lucius said, sounding farther away like he was walking to his car.

"Wait duuuuude, aren't ya gonna write that down?" Larry asked.

"I'll remember it, you fucking drug addict slob!" Lucius yelled, and then I heard a distant car door close, and tires peel out. Hmm: *Redneck Surfer from the Rockies* or *Fucking Drug Addict Slob*—tomAYto, tomATo.

"Did you get all that?" Larry asked, completely audible again.

"Yes, nice work. I'll talk to you in a bit. It's my turn now. Later."

"Later, good luck."

I hung up, took a deep breath, and then made my first call to Lucius with my pre-paid cell phone set to speaker phone—the caller id on this pre-paid phone was just some random number. I dialed the number listed on Lucius' business card as: *Mobile (Private)*.

"Ahhhhhh fuck, hello?! *Hello?*" Lucius answered, sounding wildly impatient.

I hit play on the recording I made, just for this occasion. It made the sound of an airplane taking off and then said: "Congratulations! You've won a free getaway vacation with WestJet Travel—"

"Fuck," Lucius said.

Before he'd even started swearing the second time though, and halfway through the first sentence of the recording above, I set my caller id to Eric Byrne's number and phoned Lucius at his same *Mobile (Private)* number again, this time via the caller id spoofing website. Simultaneously, I called Eric Byrne via the spoofing website, with my other laptop, but set the caller id on this call to Lucius' number. Then I hung up the pre-paid cell phone, and crossed my fingers. Both phones started to ring—once, twice...

"Hello?" I heard Lucius answer, but Eric hadn't picked up yet. FUCK! Then, when I was just about to hang up both calls, Eric answered.

"Mr. Green!" Eric bellowed, "You're watching the video no doubt."

"What?" Lucius asked.

"The video. It's bad, but we can handle it—it's manage-able. This fucking reporter is still causing problems though. Even from the grave."

"*What* video?" Lucius asked desperately.

"You haven't watched it yet?" Eric asked, doubtfully.

"No, ahhh, I'm driving home, and some idiot just caved in the back of my Lexus. What reporter?!" Lucius asked, sounding more and more exasperated.

"Anand Dhami. Look, just listen, I'll play some of the video for you across the phone while you drive. I've got Sandy in here with me, so I'll put us on speaker phone. The guy in the video reads off a letter in a skeleton costume, with plastic body parts lying on a table in front of him. Like the kind you would see in a grade ten biology lab. There's a little heart, kidney's, a liver, everything. He's also using some kind of device to make a fake voice. I'll hit play now."

The fake voice was actually my own—another hobby of mine—because they might eventually suspect it was me based on the video's contents anyway. Also, I was wearing a skeleton suit in the video just like Johnny wore in *The Karate Kid* when he and his buddies were beating Daniel Larusso's ass—there was no reason this couldn't be fun.

"Fine," Lucius said, still flustered.

"*Hello World, it's time to hear about the REAL Time Dream.*" This was my video all right. "*Thinking of getting in line to take the one-year suicide coma jump deal? If you are, you should know how your government is involved with Time Dream, and that Eric Byrne is planning on selling your body off, piece by piece, to the highest bidder. Please listen to the following letter. The information in this letter came from inside Time Dream."* At this point in the video, I started to read Anand's letter off word for word—minus a few edits to try and conceal my identity. Then, I finished off with the following:

"That letter was provided by former Rocky Mountain News reporter, Anand Dhami. The video leaked about Anand Dhami was not completely true. He WAS with a lot of women in his time, yes, but the part of the video portraying him as a pedophile was false, made up, and fabricated by the president of Time Dream, Eric Byrne, and Lucius Green, head of legal for Time Dream Canada, to discredit Mr. Dhami. Anand Dhami gave his life to get the information in this video to you all—PLEASE hear it."

Lucius, still in his car no doubt, spoke first after hearing the video: "Son of a bitch! How the fuck is that *manageable* Eric?"

"Easy, easy Loosh," Eric counseled, "it's not great I know, but the public was probably going to find all that out anyway—"

"A few years from now, maybe," Lucius said, and I heard him grinding his teeth and grunting, "but the agreement with our supporters, including three countries I might add, was that we keep the organ bidding model under wraps in the beginning."

"So? The public knows about it ahead of time now," a confident female voice I hadn't heard before said.

I figured it was the *Sandy* mentioned by Eric earlier.

"Worst case, we have smaller lineups and better parking at all of our American and Canadian locations for the next few months." There was laughter after this statement on Eric's phone line. "Don't worry Looshy, there will *still* be plenty of worthless people standing in line to kill themselves tomorrow honey, trust me." Bingo, Sandy's *worthless* comment was my *first* gem in the Crystal Ball attack.

"Yah, ha ha very funny. Do you think Anand Dhami and the fucking skeleton in the video pointing out we have *engineered the world's first voluntary mass extermination* will be ignored as well?!" Lucius roared. "Jesus! I mean the video is say-ing, in simple terms, that our business plan is to kill off millions of people because of the medical gains *we* are about to make!"

"That *is* our business plan, and the government's too, but the public doesn't know this. We'll simply dismiss it as an inter-pretation made by the video maker in our *own* media release, and remind the public we are offering the free one-year coma jump suicide deal to stop people from suffering, to help people —we already have two teams working on it. The public will be-lieve what *we* tell them to believe, not what some nerd in a pair of skeleton pajamas is telling them," Sandy said—*gem number two* acquired from a person who obviously worked in media re-lations for Time Dream.

"I agree," Eric said. "Look, we were never worried about the public finding out *what* we were doing, but rather, *why* we were doing it—so as long as we control *that* message, and no one finds out about the brain experimentation, or that we're taking people's organs before their one-year coma jump is over, public trust and our bottom line won't be affected by any of this in a significant way." *Gem number three acquired,* although it left me wondering what Eric meant exactly.

"Maybe," Lucius said, "but I just pulled over and the video's hits are going up on YouTube by the thousands every time I refresh."

"Relaaaax, this time next week, after the public has ab-sorbed our own rebuttal to the claims in the video, this will have all been forgotten," Sandy said, confidently again.

"Yep," Eric said in agreement, "OK Loosh, let's talk tomor-row, Sandy and I gotta run down to media—they want us to take a look at the statement I'm gonna read. Don't worry about this big guy, and try not to bang into any more cars on your way home."

"Fine," Lucius said, "and I didn't bang into anyone, the other guy banged into me."

"HAHA, OK Loosh, thanks for phoning, actually, come to think of it, why *did you* phone if it wasn't about the video?" Eric asked.

"I *didn't* phone you. You guys phoned *me*," Lucius explained, assertively.

"Ahhh nooo, you phoned us Loosh, maybe you bumped your head when you were busy *not* banging into the other guy!" There was laughter once again on Eric's line, as him and Sandy yukked it up.

"I DIDN'T PHONE YOU," Lucius said emphatically.

"Well whoever phoned who, I gotta run," Eric said. "Easy buddy, you just head home. Gotta go, take care—"

"Wait!" I heard Lucius yell, in irritation, but Eric's line went dead. "Idiot," Lucius mumbled. I disconnected both calls on my end—Crystal Ball attack complete. It was time for part B of the plan.

I immediately played back the recording of the whole conversation. My Blue brand Snowball microphone hadn't missed or distorted a single syllable in recording my *friends* at Time Dream—perfect. I googled 'Time Dream Public Affairs Sandy' to learn Sandy was Sandra Lee, director of public affairs for Time Dream. Then I put my skeleton costume back on and quickly setup my camera to create another video, which went like this:

"*Hello again world, the millionaires and billionaires at Time Dream are busy trying to come up with a plan to make you believe our first video is a lie. Well, luckily, we here at 'Skeleton Lycra and Spandex', are good at discovering the Pinocchio in even the largest and most powerful of organizations. Please listen to the following recording of Eric Byrne, president of Time Dream, Sandra Lee, director of public affairs at Time Dream, and Lucius Green, head of legal for Time Dream Canada. This was taped only a few minutes ago.*" I hit play on my recording of the conversation and only stopped it near the end, with Eric saying, "*Don't worry about this big guy.*" I finished with the following: "*You were right Sandra, or should I say Sandy? 'The public will believe what Time Dream tells them to believe, not what some nerd in a pair of skeleton pajamas is telling them.' The world has heard you.*"

I hit stop on the video camera and uploaded the newly recorded video without even playing it back once to see how it turned out. I put the video onto the same YouTube channel as my first video, and labelled it *Time Dream's re-BUTT-ill, absorbed.*

Lastly, I sent out an email, with a link to the new video, to multiple execs at Time Dream, every major newspaper and news outlet in Canada and the United States, including Rocky Mountain News, and, of course, to Eric Byrne and Lucius Green's email addresses once again. I swear to God, Jehovah, Fred Penner, and the Tooth Fairy I was tempted to wait a few minutes, and then run another quick Crystal Ball play on Eric and Lucius, just so I could enjoy hearing them flip out, but I heard a knock at my door.

"Did it work?" Larry asked after I opened the door, bumping me as he flew past like there was a fire *outside* and he was running *inside* to safety. He continued running down the hallway to the bathroom.

"Jesus, what the fuck, man?" I asked.

"You try holding your piss for six hours and see how you feel!" Larry yelled, with the sound of his urine hitting the toilet water echoing throughout the house like he'd ingested the same drug they give horses to increase their urine flow—*Stallion Stimulators*, or something like that. Although a drug with that name would probably be for something...*else.*

"Well, I told you to bring a bucket to pee in man. Or you could've worn one of my Tranquility brand adult diapers. Just like that astronaut who put on a pair of diapers so she could drive fourteen hours without stopping to murder another woman dating a guy she liked. They should teach that story instead of Romeo and Juliet in high schools."

"That's a myth, some reporter made the diaper thing up to sell the craziness of the love triangle more!" Larry yelled from the bathroom.

I heard a toilet flush and saw Larry appear way too soon to have washed his hands—some things never change.

"Also, why the fuck do you have all those adult diapers

again? Actually, never mind, I don't wanna know. How we doin'?"

"Better than I could ever have imagined," I said, "They had a whole conversation—a damaging one. Their public affairs director was on the line too—"

"Lemme hear it man!" Larry jumped in. "Play the whole thing."

"You can watch it on YouTube. I already uploaded a new video and its hits are going through the roof," I said, while glancing at the video's hit counter on my smartphone.

As the video played for Larry it was entertaining to see his facial expressions at various points in the video. Despite the gravity of what he had heard, I still think he was most satisfied about Lucius being pissed off about his car—replaying that part of the video over and over.

"What did he mean by *brain experimentation* and *taking people's organs before their one-year coma jump is over*?" Larry asked, zeroing in on the most important part of the video, after he finally finished watching.

"I'm not sure, but we're gonna find out. We can head over to the Lougheed Time Dream location and I'll ask Dr. Wade."

"What-a-ya mean *we*?" Larry asked, and smiled. "I'm not going anywhere near a Time Dream location, or even outta this house after what *we* just pulled—and I think you said her name was *Myah*," he said, and smiled even more, obviously having figured out there might be something between Myah and me, or that I wanted there to be.

"I need you there," I said, withholding my intentions, what was going to happen, and why I needed him there.

"Fuck it, let's go," he said in a reflexively loyal *I don't give a shit about the consequences* way once again. "Does she know we're coming?"

"I have an appointment for 7pm."

CHAPTER 21 –
SALVATION IS
ON A HILL

I turned sharply onto the street of the Lougheed Time Dream location and slammed on the brakes to avoid hitting the wall of people in front of me. The entire road for as far I could see was filled with picketers holding signs and howling, "Murderers! Murderers! Murderers!" Immediately filled with a sort of ignorant, post incident guilt one gets after realizing the effect of something was much bigger than anticipated, I looked over at Larry.

"Well, did your *crystal ball* predict this one *Igor*?" Larry asked, but didn't smile this time.

I was speechless, and a little thrown off, so I said nothing.

"Great, greeaaaaaat, not a good time to go from clairvoyant to speechless pal. Back it up, let's get outta here," he instructed, looking worryingly behind us to see if it was clear in that direction.

"Wait," I said, pulling over onto the curb, "let's just park here, no one's gonna mess with a '70 LeSabre when they have perfectly good cars from this century to vandalize."

"Fuck the car, I'm worried about *us*. We're not going into that crowd!" Larry ordered.

"Well I am,'" I said, and opened the car door on my side.

Larry swore under his breath but opened his door and got

out at the same time.

I pushed through the crowd and most people didn't give way until I nudged them a little. Larry stayed close behind me and every now and then I could feel his hand on my back, pushing me forward. It felt like an hour before we got to the Lougheed Time Dream front entrance, only to see a long row of cops had formed a human wall, blocking the way in. Luckily, I saw a familiar face among them.

"Mr. Riley!" Constable Smail yelled, so he could be heard over the noisy protestors.

I grinned and moved closer to him.

"Where did you park this time," he said, looking left and right in jest, "on the roof?" He glanced over at Larry. "Who's this, your bodyguard?"

"This is my friend, Lawrence Reinhart," I said.

"Call me Larry."

"*Larry,* holds the Time Dream record for the most non-human sexual partners during a coma jump."

Smail and I laughed. Larry did not laugh and was still obviously unhappy about being there.

"Can we go in?" I asked.

"Sorry fellas," Smail said, and shook his head, "we've been instructed by Time Dream not to let anyone in unless they have an appointment made prior to today."

"We do."

"Oh really?" Smail said, turning his head to the side and smiling at me like a teacher not buying some student's lie about losing their homework.

"No no, it's RILEY," I said, "it comes from O'*Riley*, not O'*Really*."

He shook his head and said, "OK," and motioned a man over who was holding an umbrella—it was raining pretty good outside again, which was the norm for Calgary in May. He was obviously not a cop and pulled out a tablet to show Smail the screen. Smail scrolled for a bit and then pointed with his finger touching the tablet twice. "Right there, I'll be damned, seven o'clock appointment for Sean Riley. Go on in fellas!" Smail yelled, so all the other officers could hear him.

They made a small opening in their perimeter of bodies to let us squeeze through. We walked in the front entrance and the now brotherly familiar male computerized voice immediately came over the intercom:

"Werewolf Seamen, welcome to Time Dream!"

"Joo C. Tuatt, welcome to Time Dream!"

"Pat York Hunt, welcome to Time Dream!"

"Mel Ester, welcome to Time Dream!"

"Jenny Taylia, welcome to Time Dream!"

"Jenny Tulwort, welcome to Time Dream!"

"Lube McCock, welcome to Time Dream!"

"Willy B. Hardigan, welcome to Time Dream!"

"HO LEE FUK, welcome to Time Dream!"

"Horneya Slutsova, welcome to Time Dream!"

"Lawrence Reinhart, welcome to Time Dream!"

"Sean Riley, welcome to Time Dream!"

Larry looked at me, then looked around the room, shaking his head, "Fuckin guy—well, everyone knows we're here now dummy."

I didn't care—it was worth seeing all the employees looking around like something had malfunctioned again. The few remaining customers—my videos having turned all the other ones into protestors—just looked confused. Then, well beyond the long and wide Lougheed Time Dream front counter, I saw a woman with her hands on her hips, scowling at me. Her expression was not unfamiliar to me, having set the record for pissing off the most nuns in Catholic school. Myah started walking towards us and then met us at the counter.

"Come on back, but we need to talk first," she said, which was what I wanted to do first anyway.

"This is my friend Larr—"

"Just come on."

After a walk upstairs, somewhere I had never been yet, Myah led us both into a boardroom.

"Nice boardroo—"

"Sit down," Myah said, cutting me off again. Before our buts hit the seats, she started in on me. "Why are you doing this?"

"I'm not sure I know what you mean Myah," I said, playing dumb, but with no real certainty of what she was referring to since I had *done* a whole lot of shit in the past twenty-four hours. I decided to launch into my own questions, with the clock ticking before 7pm. "You've seen the skeleton videos on YouTube then?" I asked.

"Me and half the world. I'm not really sure how I'm going to drive home tonight at this point. It's a zoo out there."

I ignored her, feeling momentarily guilty, but focused on what was ahead. "I need your help Myah." I paused before continuing. "Can you tell me what Eric Byrne meant by *brain experimentation* and *taking people's organs before their one-year coma jump is over*? Is Time Dream screwing people? Are people *really* getting a whole year in the suicide coma jump deal, or are you just killing them?"

"No," she answered, "in fact it's just the opposite in some cases."

"Opposite," my forehead wrinkled, "what-a-ya mean?"

"Why? Do you actually care Sean? Do you actually care at all about what might be happening to these people? About what is *already* happening to them? Or are you just asking because you want to make sure everything is OK for *you*, and your one-year coma jump!"

"What!?" Larry said, looking at me with suspicion.

"He's scheduled to die at seven o'clock tonight!" Myah shrieked. There were tears in her eyes.

"No, I'm scheduled to see my kids again for a year, and *then* die—I *think*? If you'd give me some answers, I'd *know*."

"Do you even know *why* I'm crying?" Myah sobbed.

"I think I do," I said, looking at the ground, my stomach hurting all over, "but if you really feel that way, if you care about me, then you'll tell me *how* Time Dream is getting

MITCH MOHAN

people's organs before their one-year coma jump is over."

"But I'll be—fired—for, for telling you," Myah whimpered, and I could feel my own eyes getting red.

"Please Myah."

"No one can know I told you, but," she paused, then went on, "they found a way to do coma jumps with only your head left."

"Jesus Christ," Larry said.

"In the one-year suicide coma jump deal we're offering, all that's left of people is their head and brain—that's all that's needed. They even take your eyes, and tongue, and ears out—they're worth money. With just a head hooked up it saves space at all our locations, and they get all the organs right away to be sold." Larry and I exchanged disgusted glances, and on seeing this Myah continued. "There's more: The contract people are signing says Time Dream can do research on their brain, and not just dead ones—the brain can be kept living long after the one-year coma jump is up. Specifically, the contracts say a one-year coma jump will be given in exchange for a person's life—for their organs—but there's nothing saying Time Dream can't *extend* a person's coma jump for as long as they want."

"Thank you," I said, trying to appear calm, but in reality all I felt was guilt. No, I felt ashamed. Not because of what Myah just revealed, and that it was *different*, no, *worse* than I expected, but because I had been recording our whole conversation since we sat down, and knew what I was going to do with that recording without ever being around to face the consequences.

"Can you please take me to my appointment now?" I asked Myah, and then glanced over at Larry, his face instantly going from disturbed to shocked, and then to angry—even violent.

Myah gasped, but the look my oldest friend was giving me drowned her out for the moment.

"*What* did you say?" Larry demanded. "Did you not *hear* what she just said?"

"I heard her just fine."

"You're gonna go through with this after hearing *that*? She just said these fucks are Frankensteining people—"

"I know," I cut in.

"Fuck that! You're gonna live like a lab rat for the next thirty years?"

"I get to see my kids again for a year, it's as simple as that."

"You don't even know if she knows everythi—" Larry stopped abruptly, looking away from me to Myah, "Can you please leave for a second Myah, I need to talk to him."

"I'll be outside," Myah said, and then left the boardroom.

Larry rolled his chair closer to me, and leaned in to talk, staring down eight inches from my face. He looked like his father, who—when we were kids—often lectured the two of us as if we were brothers, rather than friends.

"What the fuck are you doing? You don't even know if there's more to this that she doesn't know about. You could be tortured."

I looked at the ground—

SMACK!—Larry's hand struck my cheek so fast I didn't see it coming, but felt the sting of the impact immediately.

"Are you listening to me Sean?! You might not even get to see your kids—it might not be like a regular coma jump. Do you understand? And after what you just put on the Internet, who knows what might happen."

"I'm willing to take the chance."

"Don't do it."

"Look," I said, shaking my head and smiling in a way that conveyed the impossibility of what Larry was asking me, "whether I end my life with Time Dream, or the old-fashioned way with scotch and a handgun, I'm gonna die. I can't shake it man. I don't wanna feel like this anymore."

The anger on Larry's face slipped away, and I saw the life and hope drain from him as if *he* had just died. He looked away from me.

There was a long pause—I'll never know how long—and then I continued, "But I need one more thing from you buddy. I need your help with something I won't be able to do."

"Anything," Larry said. His eyes were now red.

I played the recording of the conversation I just made while making sure the volume was low enough so Myah didn't hear it from the hallway. "I need you to upload this for me."

"*What*?" Larry asked, looking confused.

"I've already emailed you the audio file. It's in MP3 format," I said. "In the same email you'll also find a username and password for the YouTube channel. The *Skeleton Lycra and Spandex* YouTube channel." I smiled. "I need you to make a third video where you explain Myah is a doctor at Time Dream, and then play the audio file. Can you do that?"

Larry paused, smiled, and shook his head, and I could see the life coming back into his face, like my words had restored some kind of faith in him. "Fuckin guy, you gotta be provoking someone even when you're dead too, eh? Yah, I can do that. I'm not wearing any fucking spandex or skeleton costume though."

"What are ya gonna wear then?" I asked, wondering if this was the right subject for the last conversation I'd ever have with my friend—or possibly anyone.

"I was thinking I could be that guy from the *Slap Chop* infomercials. Or maybe what he'd look like if he let himself go after a couple decades of ShamWow-ing people out of their money for absorbent towels and food choppers."

"Fair enough," I said, as I stood up slowly, "just make sure you cover your face, I don't wanna scare off all our viewers."

"Yah yah, I know," Larry said, standing up at the same time, "and mask my voice and make sure nothing is in the background of the video to identify me or where I am. And I should use the TOR browser to upload it."

"Spoken like a true prodigy," I said.

"Hey Sean," Larry said, as we stood in front of each other.

"Yah man."

"Just level with me. Are you doing this tonight because you think Time Dream is gonna be shut down?"

"They're never gonna be shut down man," I said, "they

probably have more money than any country on earth *plus* whatever the Slap Chop guy made in profits combined. But it *is* possible the one-year coma jump suicide program will be *chopped* due to public outcry. If nothing else, Eric Byrne will likely be fired, but if they do cancel the suicides, no one will be able to stop the ones already in progress—especially with only a brain left behind, and I'm counting on that."

"Shit, you never had a brain to begin with. I'm surprised their equipment didn't seize the first time they hooked you up."

I grinned and put out my arm to shake Larry's hand. He grabbed it and pulled me in for a bear hug. "Hey buddy," I said.

"Yah?"

"I never really had sex with your mom in a coma jump."

"Really?"

"No, I lie, we did," I said, smiling and laughing, and then pulled away from Larry to stand at the door and call Myah back in.

"I'm ready to go," I said to her.

"Fine," she said.

"Take care buddy," Larry said.

"Take care."

Myah and I started to walk down the hallway—.

"Wait! Shit, I almost forgot! Thank God," Larry said.

"*What is it*?" I asked—a little worried.

"Can I have your *Sopranos* DVD collection?" he asked, smiling like Cheech from *Cheech and Chong*.

"You can have more than that," I said, flipping him the keys to my car and to my house, "I left everything in my will to you, Angela, and Anand's family, and you're my executor, as you'll read in the email I sent to you. I know you and Angela didn't get along, but check in on her from time to time, *OK*? She was never the same after Alex and Owen died—like me."

"Will do," Larry said, and we were not smiling or laughing anymore.

"Thanks. See ya."

"See ya."

I turned around and walked down the hallway with Myah, leaving Larry in the boardroom. We walked for what felt like two football fields, and then went down a glass elevator to the main floor. After another long straight away, all in silence, I once again started to realize how cruel it would be to have a lengthy walk from a death row inmate's cell to the electric chair —it gives you wayyyyy too much time to think, and I wondered if Myah had taken the route on purpose. Finally, we rounded one more corner and came to a set of double doors like you would see in a hospital to separate the emergency ward from the waiting area. The word *SALVATION* was written in huge red letters spanning across both yellow doors.

"Sean Riley to check in," Myah said coldly. She never once looked at me.

"*BZZZRRRRRRRAAAAMMM*"—a buzzer went off so loudly, while the doors started to slide open like they would in a correction facility, that I seriously started to feel like I *was* going to the electric chair. Anand's comment about *The Shawshank Redemption* careened around in my head like a pinball, and moved me onto thinking of *The Green Mile*. In a word, I was *scared*. The doors were now fully open and a guy behind a glass booth motioned me forward with his hand.

"Myah, I—"

"Do you think I'm stupid?" she said. "I heard every word between you and your friend back there."

I froze, feeling my face redden, and knew I looked guilty as sin. I briefly gazed over my shoulder down the hallway, giving away my consideration of running back down it to warn Larry. I hoped he was out of the building already.

"Oh gimme a break," she said, "if I wanted, you would both be in handcuffs already. How do you think you even got in the building the last two times? I cleared your name even though it was flagged in the system. And I knew you were recording me today, but I told you that information anyway because I believed you would do the right thing with it. I just didn't think you would destroy me in the process. Did you even think about what might happen to me when that recording is played in *my voice*, using *my name*, across the Internet?"

I hadn't, and although I felt even worse than before, it didn't matter—like a junky impossibly addicted and minutes away from his fix, the only thing I could hear were the memories of Alex and Owen's laughs. The sound of their happiness was my happiness, and I was so close.

"I know you're responsible for the first two skeleton videos," Myah said, desperate for me to react, but I didn't.

"Thank you for everything Myah," I said, turning forward, and then walking into *Salvation*. The doors started to close behind me. I looked back over my shoulder again to see Myah was crying. The doors closed...on my life.

Thirty minutes later I was strapped into the dentist looking chair once again, and about to go for my final coma jump. My final *anything*. I signed the contract authorizing Time Dream to take my body parts, and my life, in exchange for a one-year coma jump with my family. In exchange for happiness that didn't exist—that *couldn't* exist—for me in the real world. Picking the starting date and time for the coma jump was the easiest decision of my life: I chose the day my boys were killed in the car crash, only, I chose a time seven hours *before* they were taken from me. My dreams were filled with doing that day over again before I'd even heard of Time Dream. *"Alex and Owen are going to sleep over at Grandma and Grandpa's."* *"The fuck they are, they're staying right here, with me."* That's all I would have to say. That's what I should've said the night I lost them.

"Mr. Riley," I heard a voice, but I didn't acknowledge it. "Mr. Riley. *Mr. Riley*?" asked the man in a white lab coat over the intercom—the glass wall separating us already closed. There was also a second doctor beside him, because suicide coma jumps required two doctor's fingerprints at the same time to initiate the jump. I didn't remember either of their names.

"Yah," I said, feeling a little dizzy, and looking around the room and through the glass wall. Everything was basically the same as the regular coma jump rooms, but seemed to have more stuff you would see in a hospital room or a doctor's office. No surprise there—Myah's revelation meant they would be prying parts out of me quicker than a pit crew at Daytona once I went under.

"Mr. Riley," Time Dream suicide Doctor 1 said, "I'm going to ask you one more time: Are you *sure* you want to go through with this?"

"Yes."

"Thank you," Time Dream suicide Doctor 2 said. "Sean, I need you to repeat after me. Starting now: *I Sean*."

"Starting now: I Sean," I said.

"No, no, just repeat everything I say *after* starting now, OK Mr. Riley?"

"OK Mr. Riley," I said, I mean really, they were making it too easy for me.

"MR. RILEY, I'm sure this seems humorous to *you*," Doctor 1 said, "but if we can't establish and record your consent, we will not be proceeding."

"OK Kevorkian, my bad."

"*Excuse* me?" Doctor 1 said.

"You know, Dr. Kevorkian," I said, "the obdurate, lime-light seeking, handsome, Colonel Sanders without facial hair looking suicide doctor? Sometimes called *Dr. Death*. Don't tell me you guys don't know who *he* is? Jesus Christ, stop the press boys, I'm not gettin killed by suicide doctors that don't know who Kevorkian is! That's like getting your tooth pulled by someone who hasn't heard of the Tooth Fairy. Or raped by someone who's still a virgin—"

"STOP IT!" Doctor 1 said.

"Yah, you're right," I said, "a virgin going around trying to rape someone is rather *cause and effect* isn't it. Come to think of it, what percentage of the people who have already taken this one-year suicide coma jump deal were virgins?"

"That's it, start repeating after me or your appointment will be cancelled with no possibility of rescheduling for a year," Doctor 1 said. "*I Sean Riley*."

I swear to God, The Honourable Elijah Muhammad, Wonder Woman, and the ghost of Michael Jackson, I wanted to mess with him a bit more for the *appointment* comment, and point out the fact I already signed their contract, but I wanted to hold my sons in my arms again *more*, so I complied, "I Sean Riley."

"*Agree to allow Time Dream to perform a medically assisted suicide on me.*"

"Agree to allow Time Dream to perform a medically assisted suicide on me," I echoed.

"*In exchange for a one-year coma jump.*"

"In exchange for a one-year coma jump."

"Thank you Sean, are you ready?" Doctor 2 asked.

"Yes Sir."

I heard the familiar mechanical sound once again, and saw the helmet looking device come into view above me, and then lower down so it was around my head, but not on it. My heart was going even faster than it was in my first coma jump, pounding my whole body with each beat. I felt warm all over as Doctor 1's voice came over the intercom and instructed me to close my eyes. I did—terrified and anxious at the same time. Then, he started a count:

"3....2....1....—"

Doctor 1's voice ended abruptly and there was total silence and darkness—much longer than in any of my previous coma jump transitions. I felt like I was doing somersaults in midair, but they didn't stop after a couple seconds like they had in previous jumps—I kept spinning and spinning, and with each spin it was like someone was turning a dial on my anxiety. Was something wrong? Then...I stopped spinning.

"Daddy, why are your eyes closed?"

I opened my eyes to snow coming down and my son Owen looking at me with a forced squint, in anticipation of my answer. I started quivering and went into a primal, heaving, uncontrollable cry. I moved towards Owen before he could see my tears, and picked him up in a *squeeze hug*—a term he invented.

"Because Daddy's wish came true pal. Because Daddy's

wish came true." I looked around to see about twenty other kids—we were on the top of a sliding hill two blocks from our house. I scanned the whole hill, desperately looking for my oldest son.

"Dad!" came a voice from behind me, "Are you gonna push me or what?" I turned around to see Alex sitting on his toboggan. I reached down and grabbed him, while still holding his brother, and picked them both up.

"Three way hug Daddy!" Alex said. I held them both for two minutes in a death grip.

"Come on Dad! Will you push us now?" Owen asked, smiling. Alex was smiling too.

"Sure buddy!" I said, and then heaved both of them down the large hill. I was almost levitating in blissful happiness. I wasn't going to have to leave them before I knew it, like in the one-hour coma jumps. I could play with them all afternoon, eat with them that night, not let them get in the car with either of their grandparents, and then tuck them both in to their beds—safely. I watched them glide down the hill once, twice, thirty times. I even ran down after them each time, exhaustion meaning nothing when up against joy, and towed them to the top of the hill, like I used to, for a workout.

I told them I would be quitting my job—such was the freedom of life inside a coma jump—so we could play like this every day, and their happy squeals and faces made a few hours go by just as quickly as my years of sadness were erased in their presence. I was completely and utterly at peace for the first time since they died. I was also unaware of anything around me, so I didn't notice a larger figure, an adult, until he was at my side.

"Beautiful day, isn't it," the man said, not looking at me but down the hill.

"As good as it gets," I said, keeping my gaze on Alex and Owen. I wouldn't be letting them out of my sight for a month at least I figured. Coma jump or not!

"So you're sure this is what you want?" the man asked.

"What?" I said, quickly turning my gaze to see who was

beside me. "AHHH!" I half gasped, half yelled, and instantly knew what it was to see a ghost: Davey Sandhu was before me.

"Hello Sean," Davey said.

"NO!" I yelled, causing a few parents to look over. I instinctively considered attacking Davey, or even killing him, since his presence must have represented some kind of end to being with my sons—I was wrong.

"Calm down Sean, you'll cause a scene," Davey said, and then smiled.

"HOW? HOW ARE YOU HERE?"

"We did it, Sean."

"Did what?"

"We found a way to put two people into the same coma jump. They don't even need to be on the same continent in the real world. I'm actually in Brazil right now!"

I stood there in shock but remembered Davey's words: *"Coma jumps still ultimately occur inside each person's brain, but when the time comes where we figure out how to have multiple people enjoying a coma jump together, the possibilities are endless."*

"Fine. What are you doing in *my* coma jump? I just got here," I said, still suspicious.

"I know, I know, the two *Kevorkians* you were messing with a few hours ago are friends of mine—part of my inner circle, if you will, and for some reason you were really easy to connect with, because all of your previous coma jumps have been heavily monitored as a result of you repeatedly *pissing your pants*, or something?" Davey looked confused and amused for a moment, and then went on.

"Also, Eric Byrne, and the rest of the Time Dream executive, don't know we pulled this off. They don't even know if I'm alive. I just came to check on you, and to see if this was really what you wanted, and to say thank you. The Time Dream board and a number of government officials are already calling for Eric and a few others to resign, and for me to come back on as president and CEO—thanks to your videos."

"Thanks to Anand," I said.

"Yes, right," he said.

"Look Davey, I appreciate you checking in on me, but I'm fine right where I am. I'm home," I said, continuing to keep my eyes on Alex and Owen, who were now dragging their sleds back up the hill without me. "If you wanna thank me, then thank me by making sure my coma jump isn't interrupted before I die in a year—no matter what happens with your company. Oh, and can you tell if they're already removing parts of my body from where you are?"

"That's not gonna be happening anymore," Davey said.

"What's not?" I asked.

"The one-year coma jump deal in exchange for body parts and assisted suicides. All of it! It's *all* on the way to being cancelled. A lot has happened and been announced in the last three hours since you went under Sean—including a third video put up on your YouTube channel."

Nice work Larry.

"I don't have a YouTube channel," I said.

"Fair enough," Davey smiled. "Anyway, even if I don't step back in as president, the writing is already on the wall—the suicide program is over for now. Time Dream will be Time Dream again. In the meantime, until that's official, the two doctors you were provoking will make sure no one auctions off your adolescent sized penis to the Children's Hospital. Or any of your organs, for that matter."

"Thank you," I said, and laughed a little.

"No problem, take care," Davey said. "I'm gonna check in on you after about eleven months. If you change your mind, and you do want to get back to the real world, you'll have the opportunity. You don't have to die in one year anymore Sean."

"It won't feel like dying to me Davey, I'll be happy, but thanks for the offer."

"I thought you might say that," he said, turning his gaze to my sons, and then back to me with a sympathetic and wise grin.

"Hey Davey, there *is* one thing."

"Name it."

"Could you please make sure Dr. Wade is taken care of, no matter what? Dr. Myah Wade, the one—"

"From the third video," Davey said, finishing my sentence, "I know who she is Sean—consider it done. See you around, kid." And with that, he walked behind a tree to where only I could see him, winked, and then vanished into thin air.

"Dad, who was that guy you were talking to?" Alex asked.

"Yah, and where did he go Daddy?" Owen asked, squinting again like a detective.

"Forget about 'em boys! Let's go home and eat some hot dogs." I gave Owen a push down the hill, then jumped on the end of Alex's toboggan after getting him moving, and slid back into the life that was taken from me.

THE END

Acknowledgements

Having attended more retirement parties than I can remember, I have heard a lot of farewell speeches. In every one of them I hear some version of "And last but not least, I would like to thank my [wife / husband]." It bugs me when family is mentioned at the end—*last but not least* seems like an insult. So, let me change that order here:

First and foremost, I would like to thank my wife for not poisoning me in my sleep during the writing, editing, and publishing of this book. Thank you for being my first reader, first editor, and personal shrink for the last three years. I can never repay the sacrifices you have made for my career and our family. THANK YOU.

To my two sons: You are the inspiration for this book. My deepest regret is the time I spent away from you to write this story. You are allowed to read it now.

To my Mom & Dad: Nobody will ever have better parents. I miss you.

To my cousin Cindy: Famished.

To my editor, and former prof from many moons ago, the great Robert Hilles: THANK YOU Sir. As I said when you offered to edit my book, you working with me is like royalty taking out the trash. With a first draft that violated nearly every rule of writing and human decency in existence, you were more exorcist than editor. You took my Snakes & Ladders looking manuscript and turned it into the book it is now. The English definition of a gentleman is someone who can conduct a heated argument with his hands in his pockets—thank you for putting up with my tantrums.

To my friends, colleagues and people I coerced into taking a look at my manuscript: Thank you for reading Coma Jump. You didn't know it, but every one of you stopped me from quitting with your praise and encouragement.

Special thanks to human-memory.net for their wonderful explanations of *memory* and *flashbacks* that formed part of the

Davey Sandhu character's dialogue.

I wrote this book in the middle of the night on weekends because my day job demands sixty hours a week—*on a slow week*. All of the people above made this book possible despite my ridiculous schedule.

To everyone who has lived another day even when you didn't think you could: You are not alone. Talk to someone. And if you still think you are alone, give *me* a shout, I'll talk to you. MitchMohan@hotmail.com

Last but not least, I'd like to thank Vin Diesel. Read the book—you'll get it.

Special Thanks

I would like to thank Mr. Black Enterprises for the Elvis calendar with lotion, sage pre-paperback editing, and this car:

Made in the USA
Columbia, SC
08 October 2020